# The Machine

## by

## Edward S. Baker

*Bartholomew Jones Series*

**The Machine**

Cover Art by *The Wild Rose Press*

The Wild Rose Press, Inc.
PO Box 708
Adams Basin, NY 14410-0708
Visit us at www.thewildrosepress.com

Publishing History
First Edition, 2025
Trade Paperback ISBN
Digital ISBN

*Bartholomew Jones Series*
Published in the United States of America

# Dedication

This novel is dedicated to my children and grandchildren, who fill my life with laughter and my mind with possibilities.

Chapter 1

Although he was fifty years older than she was, Kuzma Bodnar felt an attraction to the young woman which had begun during his business trip to Turku, Finland. For some reason, she had taken an interest in him, the old gentleman who had bid successfully on several pieces of antique furniture from the golden age of Imperial Russia.

She was not like the other young women he had met at antique auctions across Europe, who smoked heavily and drank too much and spoke in vulgarities. Not like the so-called liberated women who flirted with the businessmen and slept with them and each other as though there were no consequences for their behaviors. No, Mariya seemed to live beyond the drunkenness and sinful idolatry of the other young capitalists, as though deep within her there lurked an unnatural maturity far beyond that expected of someone her age.

During the Turku auction's early morning viewing hours, Mariya walked beside him, often holding his arm as a loving grandchild would do. They wandered between the rows of antiques, sometimes stopping to examine a piece closely, especially a brass samovar set that Mariya would have loved to possess. "Bid no higher than 8,000 markkas for that," Kuzma wisely advised. "Import duties at the border will add another 1,000 markkas to your total cost." Later, during bidding, he caught her arm and shook his head when she almost raised her offer to 8,500 markkas.

When the auction broke for lunch, she sat with him and conversed about little things as they ate the meager repast the auction house had provided for international guests. And at night, as they chatted on a sofa in the hotel lobby, she shared a cordial or two of French brandy she had purchased at a shop nearby.

Now, a week after his return to Odessa, Kuzma's heart was blissful because Mariya was coming from Romania to visit him in Ukraine and to see the marvelous desk he had bragged about purchasing at auction earlier in the year. Though he was only in the middle of restoring the massive antique piece, its highly figured walnut finish, its eagle-claw feet, and its hand-carved swastika drawer pulls were certain to amaze her.

In the morning, he dusted and oiled the desk for a second time. He stood back and admired the antique. He wanted it to please her. He wanted her to covet it. He wanted the desk to possess some part of her, much like he wanted to be young again and to possess the heart of the young woman who so intrigued him.

At one o'clock, he heard a vehicle pull into his driveway. He danced to the front door and opened it. His heart fell. Mariya was not alone. A young man held her arm as she approached the door to Kuzma's modest home. Her escort was tall and blond and muscular. He wore tan slacks, a tan dress shirt, a black belt, and matching black riding boots. Mariya seemed enamored with him and pulled at his arm.

Mariya's chestnut brown hair cascaded in ringlets from beneath her black beret. "Come, Meinhardt," she said. "Papa Kuzma was expecting us half an hour ago.

It is not polite to leave the elderly waiting."

Her words struck Kuzma's heart like a dagger. Nonetheless, he melted when her sparkling blue eyes looked up at him. The black frames of her glasses were rectangular, unlike the oval frames she had worn in Finland.

"Welcome to my home, Mariya. Who is this strapping young man at your side?"

"This is my friend Meinhardt. He is an aficionado of fine antiques." She waved her hand in Kuzma's direction. "Meinhardt, permit me to introduce you to the most knowledgeable expert in the antique business, my new friend Kuzma."

Meinhardt thrust his hand in Kuzma's direction. "The pleasure is mine, Herr Bodnar. Mariya has told me much about you. If you were my age, I would be extremely jealous of you."

Kuzma chuckled at the compliment. He shook Meinhardt's hand. "Come in, you two. May I offer you a glass of brandy?"

"That would be wonderful," Mariya said.

They sat in his small drawing room and chatted about insignificant things while sipping their brandy. Then bored by it all after half an hour, Meinhardt struck at the reason for the visit. "Mariya tells me you have come into possession of the desk once owned by Maria Orsic."

"Yes, that's what the auctioneer told the buyers. You know, she was a favorite of der Fuhrer. I thought more people would have bid on the desk."

"Yes, my mother used to tell me stories about Maria and the Vril Society. They claimed to have developed an antigravity flying machine which would have enabled the Nazis to win the war."

"Such poppycock, Meinhardt," Mariya said. She looked at Kuzma. "His mother was raised by former Hitler Yugen, so you see where his mind always goes: The Nazis should have won the war." She turned back to Meinhardt. "If the stories about that fantastic flying machine were true, wouldn't such a machine have replaced the airplanes which fly overhead today?"

"Meinhardt is correct, Mariya," Kuzma said. "The Vril Society had the backing of the Thule Society and the support of Rudolph Hess and der Fuhrer. They did, indeed, have plans for an anti-gravity machine."

Meinhardt threw one hand into the air, almost a Nazi salute. "And Maria Orsic worked closely with private scientists and a team of extraterrestrials to develop the flying machine."

Mariya laughed in disbelief. "You know, Papa Kuzma, Meinhardt also tells me Maria Orsic received the plans for the machine while in a psychic trance. Can you imagine? And now he claims she worked with space aliens to perfect it." She laughed again.

Kuzma chuckled, but he had heard the same legends.

"My mother says it was so," Meinhardt said. "The plans came to Maria Orsic in several languages. One was ancient Sumerian, a language Maria herself did not understand."

"And what became of her, Meinhardt?" Mariya asked.

"Mother says when der Fuhrer demanded the plans so the device could be weaponized, Maria and the plans simply disappeared. Some believe she escaped to the Pleiades with the aliens."

Kuzma broke into a broad grin. "The legend seems to have taken on a life of its own, hasn't it? It's the stuff of science fiction and conspiracy theory." He set his empty snifter on a side table and rose to his feet. "Come, you two. Let's go see the desk which was once owned by this mysterious woman of legend."

Mariya and Meinhardt followed Kuzma through a door in his kitchen and into a workshop with dusty floors and walls which were covered with miscellaneous metal and woodworking tools. In the middle of the floor sat the walnut desk. Kuzma pulled a string and overhead lights brightened the room.

"This is it?" Mariya asked.

Kuzma stroked the desktop's polished surface. "Yes, this is the desk which supposedly belonged to Maria Orsic." He pointed to a framed black and white portrait hanging on the wall. "There she is in all her beauty."

Mariya studied the enlarged photo for a moment. "She is stunning. No wonder Hess and Hitler befriended her."

"She was a beautiful woman, indeed," Kuzma said. "Without your glasses and dark hair, you might even favor her a bit."

Mariya returned her attention to the desk. She tapped on the desk's side with her knuckles. "It is more massive than I thought it would be."

Meinhardt nodded and placed his palm upon the desk's surface. "I'm certain getting this beast into such a small room was a difficult task."

"It caused me no physical labor. The auction company delivered it for a minor fee. Four men carried it into this room for me."

Mariya tapped her forefinger against her lips. "How will you ever move it into another room?"

Kuzma laughed and waved his arms in circles. "I may just build a room around it. You know, convert this workshop into an office or study."

Meinhardt dropped to his knees and felt the underside of the desktop. Then he tried wiggling sections of the desk's raised trim.

"What are you doing, Meinhardt?" Mariya asked.

Meinhardt rose to his feet and dusted his knees. "Often these older desks have secret compartments where money, jewels, and other items of value can be hidden from thieves. I was hoping to discover such a hiding place."

Kuzma pulled open the center drawer. "Do you see anything unusual?"

Mariya and Meinhardt stepped toward him and inspected the drawer.

"It's very shallow," Mariya said.

Meinhardt pushed Kuzma aside.

Kuzma staggered to keep his balance. His eyes opened wide in surprise.

Then Meinhardt wrestled the entire drawer from the desk and tossed it aside. He bent down. "There's another space under here, a place where valuables can be hidden."

He disappeared under the desk for a moment, then reappeared. "It's empty. The plans are gone."

"What?" Mariya asked. "How could they be? Papa Kuzma said the man at the auction house knew of no such secret compartments."

"Perhaps he was lying..." He turned and glared at Kuzma. "...or perhaps your Papa Kuzma has found the plans and kept them for himself."

Meinhardt grabbed Kuzma by the shirt collar and pulled him forward. "Do you know where Maria Orsic's plans are, you old fool?"

"I...I know nothing of what may have been in that hiding place."

"But you knew where to find the secret compartment."

Mariya touched Meinhardt's arm. "Meinhardt, please release my friend. He has done you no harm."

Meinhardt pushed Kuzma onto the floor. "Where are the plans, old man?"

Mariya bent down and wiped sawdust from the leg of Kuzma's trousers. "Let me help you up, my friend."

She placed Kuzma's arm around her neck and struggled with him as he rose to his feet. Once erect, he lifted his arm from Mariya's neck, but the crook of his elbow caught her hair and pulled it from her head.

Kuzma froze when he saw Mariya without her wig. Her natural hair was blonde. He looked from her face to the portrait of Maria Orsic. "You...you...you are Maria Orsic!"

Mariya screamed and threw her glasses onto the floor. "Where are my plans, Papa Kuzma? I must have them."

Meinhardt brushed past Mariya and slapped Kuzma in the face with his open hand, again and again. "We want those plans, you old fool. Where are they?"

Kuzma fell to the floor. Blood ran from his nostrils and puddled in the dust on the wooden floor.

"We must search the entire house, Meinhardt," Mariya said. "Let him lie where he is. If we don't find the plans, we'll extract their location from him later."

The couple tore through the workshop, emptying boxes and drawers and searching possible hiding places, but they found nothing. Seeing Kuzma was still unconscious, they returned to the main house and began tearing through each room, emptying drawers, ripping into sofa and chair cushions, casting aside valuable collectibles, and searching behind pictures and mirrors for wall safes.

Once they had left the workshop to begin searching his home, Kuzma opened his eyes and quietly closed and locked the workshop's door to the kitchen. Then, moving his pointer finger beneath the desk's right rear claw foot, he pushed a small button. The vertical front of the leg opened. He removed the compartment's contents—a collection of rolled papers and photos. He placed them into a canvas tool bag.

Kuzma opened the door from his workshop to his side yard. With tool bag in hand, he hurried past the shiny red sedan which had carried Mariya and her ruffian boyfriend to his doorstep. At the end of his driveway, he turned right, walked two blocks, and then hailed a cab.

A green and yellow minivan pulled to the curb. Rust had turned its quarter panels into Swiss cheese. Kuzma climbed into the back seat and handed his credit card to the driver. "To the airport. Quickly."

Chapter 2

My name is Bartholomew Jones, but my friends call me Bart or Jonesy. I used to be a detective with the Willow Falls Police Department, but I aggravated the chief a few times, and then "Defund the Police" came along and, well, I'm no longer a cop.

To add to my misery, my wife divorced me last year, legally forcing me to find the money to cover her monthly mortgage payments and living expenses. Without a regular paycheck, I was up the creek until a local businessman offered me a job as his private detective. I've been on his payroll ever since. But I digress, and I have a story to tell you...

It was a Saturday afternoon in Upstate New York. I took advantage of the unseasonably warm spring weather to travel to the Kayaderosseras Creek, half an hour north of Willow Falls, where I thought I'd try a couple of new lures on recently stocked brown trout. I was walking along the rugged creekbank with fishing rod in hand when the unthinkable happened. I put my weight on a rotten log. When it collapsed, I was standing eight inches deep in a garter snake den. Within an instant, a cantaloupe-sized ball of those slithery vipers crawled over my feet, up the inside of my pants leg, and melted across the bank in every direction. I stumbled backward in surprise and found myself hip deep in the frigid creek water. At that moment, my cell phone rang. Dripping wet, I climbed back onto the bank, dropped my rod onto the ground, and pulled my phone out of my vest pocket. It was Caesar French, the new CEO of Cabrillo Construction, and my most important client.

"Hey," he said. "I hope I didn't catch you at a bad time. Can you come in today? I have a favor to ask of you."

I swatted an eighteen-inch-long snake away from my feet and sat down on the hardpacked mud. "Can you give me an hour and a half? I have to throw some clothes in the dryer."

"Sure. See you around three."

Caesar had a way of catching me at inconvenient times, but he signed my paycheck, so I was at his disposal, twenty-four/seven. By placing me on a weekly retainer, Caesar had been good to me financially, and we were almost friends. But my relationship with him came at a cost for a former police detective. Not only was he the CEO of both Cabrillo Construction and Scentless Waste Management, but I suspected he also was head of the northeast division of Los Equis Cartel. Based out of Mexico, Los Equis were into everything illegal: drugs, prostitution, guns, human trafficking, car theft, money laundering, and cock and canine fighting. And if my suspicions were correct, Caesar quietly did it all right here in the capital region of New York. Yeah, I could have fully investigated my suspicions, perhaps built a case against him and turned him in to the authorities, but then I'd have no paycheck.

****

I arrived at Cabrillo Construction at three fifteen. It was a weekend, so Laverne wasn't at her desk to buzz me in. I entered the adjoining hallway and found Caesar in his office. He was dressed in a golf shirt, so I assumed he had come in from his country club.

"Good afternoon, Jones. Want some coffee? It's a fresh pot of Kona, flown in from Honolulu yesterday."

"Sure."

He poured me a cup, and then we got down to business.

"How was your golf game?" I asked.

"Not so good today, but it's my first time out since November." He finished his coffee and set the mug down on his desk. "But golf is what prompted me call you today."

I nodded, waiting for the ball to drop.

"The man I played with today has a problem and could use your help. Do you mind taking on another client for a little while, just as a favor to me?"

"I'll work for anyone, as long as you don't mind my doing so. You know I always run extraneous jobs by you before I accept them."

Caesar's expression told me he was searching his memory banks. Actually, I had never launched any investigations except those he had assigned to me. I was a one-man birddog.

He refilled his coffee mug and then briefed me. "His name is Henry Hawkes. He lives up in the Helderbergs." Caesar handed me a slip of paper with a phone number on it. "He's expecting a call from you this afternoon."

"What can you tell me about Mr. Hawkes?"

"He's very rich...probably a billionaire. He has a son in college by his first wife and a young daughter by his second wife. On weekends and evenings at home, he developed a mini surge protector that saves electronic equipment from power surges as well as electromagnetic pulses. The company took possession of his invention, and it is now installed in almost every electronic device manufactured in the world. Hawkes sued the company for patent infringement and won his case."

"Really?"

"Yeah, he settled for an unbelievable amount of money. He now receives large checks every month as the company keeps including his invention in products it mass produces."

"Sounds like the American dream."

"Yes, we should all be so lucky."

"So, what's his problem?"

"It's his daughter's nanny. Her grandfather has been beaten and shot. He's nearly dead, but the doctors at Willow Falls Memorial think he will pull through. Can you find out who did it?"

I figured the Willow Falls cops were already on the case because any gunshot victims must be reported to local police by the hospital that receives them. "Has Mr. Hawkes contacted the police? What do they say?"

"He can't go to the police because the nanny is an undocumented immigrant. As far as he knows, the police don't have a clue about next-of-kin."

"Aha. That explains a lot. The victim probably isn't saying anything to the police."

"I think the victim is still unconscious." Caesar picked up a ballpoint pen and pointed it at me. "So, you're going call Hawkes this afternoon?"

"Yeah. Can I use your phone?"

"You'll need to use Laverne's. I've got some other

business to do. Shut the door on your way out."

I downed the rest of my coffee and took the slip of paper back to Laverne's desk in the reception area. Her desktop was neat as a pin, except for the cluster of little troll dolls she had lined across the back edge where they couldn't be seen by customers. Their multi-colored heads of hair—red, orange, yellow, blue, purple, green, white—turned the area beneath the counter into a rainbow.

I picked up the phone receiver. It smelled like Laverne's cheap perfume. I dialed Henry Hawkes. I must have reached his cell phone because he answered after only one ring.

"Mr. Hawkes?"

"Yeah. Who's this?"

"My name is Bart Jones. Caesar French told me you have a problem that needs a private investigator."

"Yeah, I do. My daughter's nanny has a grandfather in the hospital. He's sporting a gunshot wound. I think it was an attempted murder."

"Mr. French gave me those details, but I think I need to speak with your daughter's nanny…the sooner the better. If you're still interested in my services, can you set that up?"

"Yeah. When can you be here?"

"At your convenience."

"How about tomorrow morning…maybe ten o'clock?"

"Sure."

Mr. Hawkes seemed like a man of few words. Maybe even a little gruff. But then, he didn't know me from Adam and probably was hoping that French wouldn't send him someone who couldn't handle the job. He gave me his address and a final piece of advice. "If my dogs are out, don't get out of your car until I have them on their chains."

Chapter 3

Several months ago, the small cabin I rented on Mariaville Lake was burned down by Caesar French's biggest rival, Onondaga Waste Disposal during a period of time I call "the Garbage War." I had no place to live, but my ex-partner Helen Martin offered me a room in her home until I could find better accommodations. In less than a week, I had pissed her off during a stupid argument that began over my leaving the toilet seat up. Those who have lived with someone of the opposite sex will know what I'm talking about. Anyway, I slept at the Y for two days. Then, rather than pull into Helen's driveway at eleven thirty at night and wake a woman who was already upset with me, I decided to drive away. The odds wouldn't have been in my favor, anyway.

That night, I found my way down to the river and slowed down at Roxanne Windsor's home. Roxanne had been a suspect in a juvenile murder case, but she had been innocent of any crime and, in fact, she and her chapter of The Black Hat Society had helped me solve a couple of other murders. And, well, she and I had had a short fling.

Roxanne's lights were out, but I figured I'd find less trouble with Roxanne than with Helen. So, I pulled into her driveway and walked around back to her granite patio, thinking maybe I would find a lawn chair where I could catch a few hours of sleep.

Luck was in my favor. Roxanne was sitting in the dark on an outdoor recliner. Beside her, a fat red candle was burning on a circular wrought iron table. Beside it was a bottle of wine, and Roxanne was holding a half-full glass.

"It's about time you arrived, Barty. I was expecting you an hour ago."

She poured wine into another glass and held it out for me.

The glass felt cool when I took it from her. "How did you know, Roxanne?"

Her green eyes gleamed in the candlelight. "I could feel you thinking about me."

I had forgotten that she's some type of psychic sensitive. "Sorry it's so late."

"I just got off second shift at the hospital. You and this wine are just what I need to unwind. I've done seven days straight, so I have three days off. Work has been frantic."

I sat in the wrought iron chair beside her recliner. Its canvas seat cushion was thin, and the chair would have been more comfortable if it had had a second cushion to keep its ornamentation from digging into my back.

She took a long sip of wine and then set her glass on the table. "You've been away for a long time. What's it been? Three weeks? Perhaps a month?"

I tasted the wine. It was something red, but then it was always red with Roxanne. It was a smooth blend with a piece of cork that I removed from my tongue with my finger and flicked away. "About a month, I guess. But I think about you all the time."

Roxanne threw her head back. "I know you do. I'm adorable." Then she ran her fingers through her chestnut curls. "You don't have another girlfriend, do you? You know how I feel about that."

"There's been nobody in my life, except you, Roxanne."

I had lied. I had had a one-night stand with my ex-wife's sister two weeks before. I hooked up with her in her minivan outside a bar in Amsterdam. It was unplanned and unintentional. She was already drunk when I spotted her with a group of single women. I think it was a revenge thing, and I felt guilty about it. I hope she never confesses to Rachel. Maybe she was too drunk to remember.

Roxanne stood and removed her robe. She was naked. The light from the candle danced across her breasts.

A shiver of excitement ran through my body.

"Into the hot tub, first. The chlorine kills germs and removes all strange colognes."

I followed her to her hot tub and set my glass of wine on its wide royal blue handrail. Roxanne removed my clothes like it was a ritual, and we stepped into the warm water together. From the array of lights inside the hot tub, she could see I already was aroused.

"My goodness, our little man certainly is at attention."

When our lips met, Roxanne gently stroked my privates. "You aren't too tired, are you? I might try to keep you up all night."

I've been camping out at Roxanne's ever since.

Chapter 4

Sunday morning I drove to the Helderbergs, a cluster of cliffs that remind me of the "escarpment" in Johnny Weissmuller's Tarzan movies. Basically, they are old mountains that push upward from the flat lands south of Albany and vault eleven hundred feet above the Hudson River. On top of the plateau, New York State has developed parks and trails for public use. But not all the land is relegated to parks. Some is privately owned, and Henry Hawkes was among those wealthy enough to possess a large tract which allowed him to look down upon Albany and the common folks who live there.

I followed the directions given to me by the female voice of my SUV's GPS. Soon I found the entrance to the Hawkes' estate by the number painted on a simple rural route mailbox nailed to a post. Beside it, a gravel driveway curved out of sight through a forest of mixed hardwoods and evergreens. I turned onto the driveway and followed it uphill for a quarter of a mile before Hawkes' home came into view. It was a spectacular three-story stone home with two wings. The main structure bore floor to ceiling windows. Beside it sat a matching, but detached, five car garage. This guy had some money.

The estate was gated with heavy gauge chain-link fencing but had no human sentry. Instead, a camera and speaker were mounted inside a kiosk on a post near the driver's side of my car. I rolled down my window to speak into the apparatus, but before I could utter a word a robotic voice spoke to me. "Welcome to the estate of Henry and Elizabeth Hawkes. How can I help you?"

I announced myself. "Detective Bartholomew Jones, here to meet with Mr. Hawkes."

"You may proceed."

The gate slid open. I drove through and watched in my rearview mirror as the gate closed behind me. When I reached the front door, I saw a woman leading two mastiffs away on chain leashes. I assumed they were the guard dogs Hawkes had mentioned.

A gentleman in his mid-fifties approached my car. He was wearing blue jeans, a white shirt and a blue five-button spring-weight cardigan sweater. His greying hair was swept back over his ears. "Mr. Jones?" he asked through my open side window.

"Yes. Would you be Mr. Hawkes?"

"Yes. Please come in. My wife will join us once she's attended to our pups."

I exited my vehicle and shook Mr. Hawkes' hand. "It's a pleasure to meet you, sir. I hadn't expected so grand a home."

"I hadn't expected it in my life either, but fortune found its way to me." He opened a carved oak door. "Come in. Come in. Can I get you a cup of coffee or perhaps a soda?"

"I'm fine, sir. I'd really like to learn what I can about your problem and then be about the business of investigating who may have shot the elderly gentleman."

He escorted me into a small elevator and took me

to the second floor of his home. I was immediately struck by the beauty of the view across the valley below and all the way to Albany, where the towers of the Empire State Plaza stood like granite soldiers in the clean morning air.

"This is marvelous, Mr. Hawkes. You're indeed fortunate to enjoy this view every morning."

"Yes, I agree, especially on a morning such as this. But it's not always so nice a picture. Sometimes in the summer, the smog is so bad you can't see the towers, and winter's gloom diminishes the view as well."

A woman's voice broke into our conversation. "Don't listen to his negativity. He loves it here as much as I do."

"This is my wife, Elizabeth, Mr. Jones. She is always reminding me not to dwell on the negativity in life, but to relish the positivity that surrounds us."

I guessed that Mrs. Hawkes was maybe in her mid-forties, but because of hair coloring, excellent make-up options, and plastic surgery, it has been getting harder for me to judge the age of a woman, especially one who has the resources to take care of herself. You know how it is: the rich have access to special doctors, personal trainers, and the free time to lather up in luxury. Mrs. Hawkes may have benefited in that manner. She was trim and fit, her strawberry blonde hair was perfectly sculptured, and her face bore no wrinkles or blemishes.

She shook my hand. "Just call me Elizabeth and call this old windbag Henry. There's no need to adhere to business protocols, even if you are working for us. We're beyond all that, and we like to cultivate friends rather than business associates."

"Thank you, Elizabeth." I looked around the great

room. "Where shall we sit to discuss this investigation?"

Elizabeth suggested we sit close to the picture windows, so we moved to a small cluster of white leather comfy chairs. "Did Henry offer you refreshments?"

"Yes, thank you, but I've already had my morning coffee."

We sat.

"Why don't you start, Henry," Elizabeth said. "Tell him about how we came to hire our nanny."

"Let me begin by saying that she's from Ukraine, but you'd never know she isn't an American citizen because she's fluent in English and her accent is flawless. She's well-educated, probably more so than most Americans."

I jotted a few notes. "How did you meet her?"

"I have a passion for breakfast biscuits, especially those with eggs and sausage. One day last December, I stopped at Happy Jack's in downtown Albany. You know, the one near the bus station."

I nodded. A small brown bird flew into the picture window behind Henry and fell to the ground. Elizabeth saw it happen, too, but didn't seem concerned for the tiny creature.

"When I parked, I noticed a woman begging for change from customers so she could buy something to eat. I felt compassion for her, so I invited her inside to have a meal with me."

Elizabeth cleared her throat. "Henry is always inviting the homeless into restaurants and buying them meals. I think he's on a guilt trip since we've come into money."

Henry crossed his arms. "Over our breakfast, I learned that Nadiya...that's her name: Nadiya Bodnar...Nadiya had come to Albany by bus from Eagle Pass, Texas. Her possessions had been stolen by the coyote who led her and a small band of refugees across our southern border."

"Refugees?"

"Yes, from the war with Russia. Nadiya and her mother were in the first wave of people who fled from eastern Ukraine."

Elizabeth couldn't control herself. "So, like he always does, Henry offers her a job watching our ten-year-old daughter without asking me first. No credentials, no vetting, no background check—"

"That's because I knew you'd say, 'No,'" Henry blurted. "You always do."

Elizabeth pointed her finger at her husband. "Illegal immigrants always bring trouble, Henry." She looked at me. "Don't you agree, Mr. Jones?" She turned back to Henry. "I've asked you numerous times not to hire them, but you seem to have a passion for it."

Henry raised his hand like a crossing guard. "You'd leave them to our social services system, sweetheart? Hrmmpff. Fat chance they'd get anything more than a menial job and two crappy meals a day. They'd be in poverty the rest of their lives." He lowered his hand.

"This has been informative," I said. "Is there a chance I could speak with Nadiya?"

Elizabeth excused herself and walked out of the room.

"She'll be back in a moment with our house guest and nanny, Mr. Jones. I think you'll be pleasantly surprised."

Elizabeth returned in less than a minute, followed by a young woman who was taller than she was. "Mr. Jones, permit me to introduce my husband's newest acquisition, Nadiya Bodnar."

The young woman's dark cocoa hair had been pulled into a ponytail and then piled on top of her head like a loose cinnamon bun, the way my cousin Beatrix used to wear her hair before she lost it all to cancer. Her eyes were puffy, probably from crying. She was dressed comfortably in stone-washed blue jeans and a Great Danes sweatshirt. Maybe she had found the sweatshirt at a discount store or gotten it second-hand from someone who had attended the University at Albany.

"Nadiya," Elizabeth said, "This is Detective Jones. We've hired him to help get to bottom of the attack on your grandfather."

Nadiya greeted me. Elizabeth motioned for her to sit on the ottoman nearest my chair.

"Tell me about your grandfather," I said.

Nadiya wiped her nose with a crumpled tissue she had balled in her hand. "His name is Kuzma Bodnar. He is a dealer in antiquities. He manages some repairs when necessary, but usually he buys high-end furniture and interesting collectables at auctions, and then he resells them at his small shop in Odessa."

"Would that be near Kiev?"

"No, it is in the southwestern part of our country, near the borders of Moldova and Romania."

I was going to need to consult a map because I had never heard of Moldova. Was it a city? I was a complete ignoramus when it came to any geography east of Italy. I wrote the word "Moldova" in my notebook. "Are you from Odessa, too?"

"No, when my mother married my father, she moved with him to Mariupol. I was born there and lived there all my life until we had to evacuate because the Russian army was coming."

"I'm sorry you were forced to leave. How is the rest of your family?"

"My brother and father were conscripted into the Ukrainian army. As the war began, my mother and I took the train to Lviv and then a bus to Krakow, Poland. When we arrived, my mother took ill with COVID. She died quickly."

"I'm sorry to learn of her death. What brought you to the USA?"

"Before she passed, my mother made me promise to take all our money and flee to the USA. I couldn't get a visa to your country, but I learned your southern border was open, so I bought a plane ticket to Mexico City. From there, I paid a man to drive me to Piedras Negras, where his friend guided me across the border near Eagle Pass in the early morning."

"From there, I assume you flew to New York City?"

"No, my journey took a bad turn at Piedras Negras. The man who guided me across the border took all my possessions at gunpoint...my clothes, my money, my passport. I was a lone female with no money and no identification. Fortunately, an old woman found me and took me in for a few days. But she secretly reported me to the authorities. They didn't know what to do with me after they arrested me, so they put me on a bus to New York City. City officials didn't know what to do with me either, so they put me on another bus to Albany.

When I arrived here, I hadn't bathed in several days and had eaten only a few small sandwiches provided by authorities at each stop."

I imagined her story being repeated in many small cities across the United States as coyotes dump hundreds of immigrants into Texas every day, and Texas shuffles its undocumented immigrant problem to every other state. "God bless America." I sighed.

"That's where I came in," Henry said. "I found Nadiya begging for spare change at the Happy Jack's across from the bus station in Albany. I offered her a free meal, and here she is."

"Yes," Nadiya continued, "Mr. Hawkes bought me a large meal, and we discussed my plight. When he learned of my skills in mathematics and computer science, he offered me a job tutoring his daughter Charity…a job including room and board. I had no better option, so here I am. The Hawkes have been wonderful to me. I hope someday to be able to repay them for their kindness."

"So, back to your grandfather…"

"I wrote to Grandfather, told him about Mother, and asked him to try to get word to Father and my brother. I gave him my address here in Altamont and the Hawkes' telephone number in case anyone could call me. I heard from nobody until Grandfather called me from a small motel in Willow Falls a few days ago. He said he traveled here through Canada. He said he needed to see me. He also told me he put something valuable in the mail to me."

"What did he send you?"

"I don't know. Nothing has arrived yet—"

Elizabeth interrupted. "Mr. Bodnar was supposed

to come visit Nadiya three days ago, but he never showed up. I drove her to The Ladysmith Motel, where he was staying. When we arrived, we found him in his room, beaten and shot. He looked terrible...possibly dead. We called an ambulance. The medics called the police. According to that lady police detective, nobody heard any shots fired and nobody saw anyone entering or leaving Mr. Bodnar's room."

"Where is your grandfather now?"

"He is in the Willow Falls hospital," Nadiya replied. "I go to visit him every day, but he has yet to regain consciousness."

"Probably loss of blood," Henry Hawkes speculated.

I nodded. "Maybe."

Elizabeth pointed at Henry. "I just want it on the record that you brought this problem into our home." She looked at Nadiya. "No offense intended, my dear. What I am about to say is directed at Henry and is not intended to cast any aspersion upon you." She turned back to Henry. "Like I have told you so many times, illegal immigrants always bring trouble, and when you bring illegals into our home, you inflict their misery upon us. This sort of thing must stop."

I turned to Nadiya. "Who was the lady police detective who came to the motel?"

Nadya dug a business card out of her jeans pocket and read it to me. "Helen Martin, Detective, Willow Falls Police Department." She looked at me. "From your expression, I think you must know her."

"Yes. We go back a long way. You're in good hands with Detective Martin. I'll give her a call and see if we can collaborate on finding who did this awful thing to your grandfather."

"We're going to the hospital to visit her grandfather this morning," Henry said. "He's been moved out of intensive care and into a regular room. I've arranged for him to recuperate in a private room. Care to tag along?"

"Sure. I'll follow you into town."

"Henry," Elizabeth said, "why not let Mr. Jones take Nadiya to the hospital so they can talk some more. There's no need for us to go, too."

"Mr. Jones?" Henry asked.

"That would be fine." I looked at Nadiya. "Do you mind riding with me?"

"That would be good. I wish to inconvenience as few people as possible."

Chapter 5

The registered nurse walked into Kuzma Bodnar's room, checked his vitals, and jotted them down on the clipboard at the foot of his bed. She removed the empty saline bag from its stand, hung a new one, and inserted the needle at the end of its plastic tubing into the IV port that was attached to Mr. Bodnar's wrist. Then she adjusted his pillow and pulled the white hospital blanket back up to his neck. Certain he was resting comfortably, she walked out of his room and attended to the next of her fifteen patients.

When the nurse departed from Mr. Bodnar's room, another one entered, unseen by the first. She pulled the hydration needle from his IV port, letting it drip onto the floor. Then she removed a syringe from her pocket, pushed it into the IV port, and pressed her thumb on the plunger until all the syringe's fluid had been dispensed. She removed the syringe, placed it back into her pocket, then reinserted the hydration needle into the IV port. The entire process had taken less than thirty seconds. She peered into the corridor to ensure her way was clear, then exited the room as quickly and as quietly as she had come. As she exited the unit, she nodded briefly to the man and young woman who were about to enter.

****

Nadiya and I arrived at Willow Falls Memorial

Hospital at 12:30 p.m. I parked curbside rather than pay the five-dollar fee demanded by the hospital's four-story parking garage. Then we strode up the sidewalk, passing an elderly couple who were enjoying the afternoon sunshine on a cement bench. They looked up as we passed. The hospital's main entrance doors opened automatically when our bodies reflected the beam from their operating mechanism.

Nadiya led me past the greeting desk and to the bank of D-wing elevators. We waited quietly until one opened. We entered it, and Nadiya pressed the fourth floor button. "They moved Grandfather to the fourth floor after he was transferred from Intensive Care."

When the door opened, we turned right and followed the hallway toward the private care unit. As we reached the unit's entrance, a young nurse hurried past us, lightly brushing my shoulder. "Good afternoon," Nadiya said to her.

"Yes, it is very good."

I thought her response was strange. Maybe something good had happened to one of her patients. Maybe she had just received word that she was getting a promotion or a bonus. I noticed her eyebrows were blonde, but her shoulder-length hair was deep brown, almost black. But that's nothing strange in today's world. Almost everybody colors their hair at one time or another, even men. In fact, I remembered when I met her last year, the director of the hospital's blood bank wore nose rings and had rainbow colored hair. Who would ever have expected that of a licensed physician?

Nadiya and I stopped at the nursing station. A heavy-set man was seated behind the counter reading something on his computer screen. I tapped lightly on the countertop. He looked up at me.

"We'd like to check on Mr. Bodnar's status," I said.

He looked back at his screen. "No change. He's still unconscious, but his vitals are improving. You may go down to his room if you're here to visit."

"He's in room 428," Nadiya said.

I ushered her around the nurse's station and followed her down the corridor. Without warning, a loud beeping signal erupted. Nurses and orderlies hurried past us and into a room ahead of us. "Some poor sap bit the big one," I said.

Nadiya froze. Her hands covered her mouth, and her eyes widened in alarm. "That's Grandfather's room."

We pressed against the wall in the narrow corridor as nurses, orderlies, and doctors came and went from room 428. After several minutes, two doctors emerged, their eyes cast downward. "I thought he was going to make it," one said aloud. The other nodded.

"Excuse me," I said. "This is Mr. Bodnar's granddaughter. Can she see her grandfather?"

"Sure, but don't stay too long. He's deceased. Please don't touch his body. We've ordered an autopsy."

Nadiya broke into tears. "He was my father's father...a good and generous man."

\*\*\*\*

After Nadiya said a prayer over her grandfather's body, we went to the basement, where the morgue and the hospital's medical pathologist's office were located.

I pulled on the steel door to the pathologist's office and held it open for Nadiya.

A young black man in a white shirt and green medical gown greeted us. "How may I help you?"

"My name is Bart Jones. This young woman is Nadiya Bodnar. We've come to request a copy of the autopsy on the body of her grandfather, Mr. Kuzma Bodnar. He passed away just a few minutes ago in a room on the fourth floor. His body is still warm."

The young man rifled through some papers until he found an autopsy request form and handed it to me. "Fill this out. Normally, once the doctor has ordered an autopsy, you should request a copy from his office. The fee for copies is twenty-five dollars, and you must pay him for obtaining a copy for you."

I pulled out my wallet and laid a twenty and a five on the countertop. "How about if we just pay you and save the hassle of going through a middleman?"

He tapped a few keys on his desktop computer. "There you go! Dr. Zeller just requested an autopsy. Next of kin are eligible to receive copies." He looked at Nadiya. "You're said you're his daughter?"

"No," Nadiya replied. "I'm his granddaughter and his only relative in the USA. The rest are in Ukraine. His son is fighting in the war against Russia."

"I see. Sad thing, that war. Because you're Ukrainian, I'll bypass the doctor and waive your fee out of respect for how your countrymen are standing up to the Russian forces."

"Thank you, sir," Nadiya replied.

I put my twenty-five dollars back in my wallet. "When do you think you'll have the report completed?"

"Once I receive the body, I'll get right on it. Maybe two days."

"Should I call?" Nadiya asked.

"Just leave me your contact information, and I'll call you when it's ready."

Nadiya jotted her name and telephone number onto a post-a-note and handed it to the young man. "Thank you, doctor."

**** 

Two days later, the pathologist called Nadiya and asked her to meet with him in his office. I met Nadiya at the Hawkes' front door, and we drove to Willow Falls. It was a cloudy day, and the air felt like it was carrying rain. We parked on the street again and made our way through the hospital's main entrance and then down to the basement and the medical pathologist's office.

That morning, the young black doctor was dressed in khaki trousers, a pink shirt, and baby blue tie. He seemed nervous. "I have some distressing news for you," he said, "and I'm not sure how you want to handle it, so I thought we should talk. That's why I asked you to come in today."

Nadiya uttered a quiet moan.

I tried to reassure her. "It's okay, Nadiya. I'm here for you."

She squeezed my hand. "I hope it's not something genetic."

The pathologist laid his report on the countertop. "You'll be happy to know your grandfather did not pass from a genetic disorder, Miss Bodnar, and he did not die from complications caused by the gunshot wound. However, I am obliged to inform you that he was murdered."

Nadiya gasped and stepped backwards. Her eyes opened wide in disbelief. "Murdered?"

"How can this be?" I asked.

"I don't know how it came to be. I can just report my findings. His heart was stopped chemically. Whoever did it used potassium chloride. Probably injected it into his IV port. His blood was full of it."

I knew that potassium chloride is used to euthanize convicted murderers in the United States and Japan, the only two industrial democracies which still execute prisoners. Usually in the U.S., the convicted are first given a sedative to render them unconscious. Then they are given a drug that causes paralysis of everything except the heart. And finally, they are injected with potassium chloride to stop the heart.

"You need to report this to the police," I said.

"I agree," the doctor replied, "and I already have. I was obligated to report the murder by law. But I wanted you to know about his murder as well. Certainly, as next of kin, you will be on the police department's radar as the possible murderer, Miss Bodnar, especially if you're the beneficiary of the deceased's insurance policy."

Nadiya burst into tears.

I touched her forearm. "I know the officer who has been investigating your grandfather's shooting. By police protocol, she is mandated to interview you, but you won't be charged with his murder. He was probably murdered by the same person who shot him."

Chapter 6

We were still in the pathologist's office when the door opened, and two uniformed police officers entered. One was Helen Martin. When she saw me, her expression changed to one of annoyance. "Should have figured you'd be here, Jonesy. You're always involved in my most curious murder cases."

Helen's eyes showed signs of fatigue, but otherwise she looked good, and it was great to see her again.

She turned her attention to the young pathologist. "Got a copy of your report. I've already requested security videos of the fourth floor for the morning of the murder. You sure about the diagnosis?"

"Absolutely. Do you want to see the body?"

"Nope. The photos were grisly enough. This guy was a foreign visitor. Have you established next of kin?"

"Helen," I said, "permit me to introduce the victim's granddaughter, Nadiya Bodnar."

Helen turned to Nadiya. "Sorry about your loss, ma'am. Does your grandfather have any other relatives in the US?"

"She's his only relative," I said.

"Let the woman speak for herself, Jonesy. You know the protocols."

Helen was right. I'd been away from police

protocols for too long. I sat back and let Nadiya speak for herself.

"Like I told you when you came to the Hawkes' home to investigate his shooting, I am my grandfather's only relative outside of Ukraine. He came to the US to see me unannounced, and I was surprised by his telephone call."

Helen gave Nadiya a stern look. "But now, my investigation has escalated to homicide. Don't you be leaving the capital region without first clearing it with me. You're on my short list of suspects."

I figured Helen had no list of suspects other than Nadiya, and she was frustrated that Mr. Bodnar hadn't regained consciousness before being murdered.

\*\*\*\*

I called Helen on Wednesday morning and arranged to meet her for lunch at Ruby's Red Hots, a place we used to frequent when we worked together at the Willow Falls Police Department. When I walked in, she was already sitting at our favorite place at the counter. She was dressed in her gray uniform with the dark blue stripe down her trousers leg. Her service belt was packed with her pistol, mace, cuffs, and all the goodies a uniformed detective wears when she's on official duty, like a funeral or honor guard ceremony.

"Funny, you asking me to meet you here," she said as I sat down. "It's like you want to make peace or something."

"What? Have we been at war? I know I haven't stopped by the see you lately, but you're still my best friend."

"That witchy woman throw you out yet? You must be looking for a place to lay your head at night."

The counter waitress broke into our conversation. "Haven't seen you two in a while. You want your usual?"

"Yeah," I replied.

"Me, too," Helen said.

The waitress turned toward the short order cook. "Two orders of two weenies all the way." She walked the fifteen feet to his station, and our orders were ready for pick-up before she got there. When she set them down in front of us, she slid over a jar of habanero sauce and winked at me. "I know you like it hot."

I grinned. "Thank you, sweetheart."

Helen rolled her eyes at me when the waitress turned away.

"What?"

"Either you already had a fling with that waitress, Mr. Hot Stuff, or she just offered you a chance to catch something you'll wish you never had. Which is it, you sleaze ball? Look what's sitting beside you...clean and upscale. Sometimes, I think you can't see beyond your trousers zipper."

"Whoa, Helen. All I said was, 'Thank you,' and you're accusing me of all kinds of unfair stuff."

"You don't call some woman 'sweetheart' like that unless you're hoping she'll hop into the sack with you...or she's already been there."

I put my forehead on the countertop. "Can we start over?"

"I s'pose."

"I'm working on the case of an elderly Ukrainian man who recently was murdered in the hospital."

"Mr. Bodnar? The one with the undocumented granddaughter?"

"Oh, you know about that?"

"Yeah, I figured it out pretty quick. But I haven't turned her over to ICE yet because I might need more from her to figure out who murdered him. What do you know about her, Jonesy? Is she into any kind of illegal shit?"

"Not that I know of. She seems pretty upfront with everything—you know, what you see is what you get. She's got a good job as a nanny for the Hawkes. There's no indication she's got any money other than what they're paying her, and that can't be much because they're including room and board. They say she hasn't received any phone calls except the one from her grandfather. I think she's legit."

"'Cept she's an illegal."

"Yeah, there is that. But she's not applied for any welfare or social services stuff. The only drain on our system will be the medical costs incurred by her grandfather, and I don't think the hospital will be able to collect anything from her because she's two generations removed. The Hawkes will probably advise her to throw any hospital bills into the trashcan. If they don't, I will."

"Well, promise me you'll keep me apprised of what you discover during your investigation." Helen raised a single eyebrow. "Don't do what you been doing to me recently…you know, like giving me tidbits but not everything I ought to know."

I took a bite of my hotdog. Meat sauce squirted out the back end of the bun and onto the countertop. I pulled a couple of napkins from the chrome dispenser and wiped up the mess.

"So, you're still under the covers with the Queen

from England?" Helen asked.

"Yeah. We both know it's not long-term, but neither one of us is looking for anything permanent."

"Jonesy, I don't think you're the kind of man who does well with that type of relationship. You need something permanent, something stable. Where you gonna go when the queen kicks you out from under?"

"Oh, I still have that penthouse at Mariaville Lake to call home."

"You mean that efficiency apartment over the garage at Joey Astor's new lake house?"

"Yeah. It's small, but it's all I'll need if things don't work out with Roxanne."

We finished our lunch and promised to keep in touch as our separate investigations unfolded. When I rose to walk out of Ruby's, Helen pointed at my face. "Wipe that meat sauce off your forehead, Jonesy. You're embarrassing me."

Chapter 7

Friday morning, Henry Hawkes called me. He sounded excited. "Nadiya received a package by courier this morning. It's from her grandfather. It came registered and she had to sign for it."

"What was in it?"

"We don't know. I suggested to Nadiya that you should join us when we open it in case something inside offers a clue to her grandfather's murderer."

I had stayed up drinking beer and watching Atlanta clobber Kansas City on a Thursday night sports channel. Out of basic decency, I needed to shower and brush my teeth before I dropped in on anybody. "I can be there right after lunch."

"We'll be waiting for you."

At one o'clock, I drove through the electronic gate and pulled up to the Hawkes' residence. I opened my car door and put my foot out, then I quickly pulled it back in. Two huge mastiffs leaped against the outside of my door and drooled all over my side window while barking and scratching at the door handle with their giant paws. I envisioned claw marks all over my door.

As quickly as they arrived, the beasts departed, running hurriedly toward a side door, where Elizabeth Hawkes stood holding a silver device to her lips. She opened the door, and the dogs followed her inside.

Henry appeared at the front door. "Sorry about

that. I hope our pups didn't scratch your paint. If they did, just let me know, and I'll cover the cost of re-painting your door.

I climbed out of my car and inspected the damage. There wasn't anything worth the cost of a paint job. "I think it'll be okay, Henry. But I'm glad Elizabeth called them off."

"Dog whistle. It works wonders, doesn't it?"

We walked inside, rode up the small elevator, and passed through the foyer to the great room. Nadiya rose from her seat on the sofa and greeted me. "I'm glad you were able to come today, Mr. Jones."

A shiny package lay on the coffee table in front of her. It was a handmade sandwich of cardboard, approximately two feet square, bulging in the middle and earnestly wrapped in three or four layers of clear packing tape. Nadiya's name and the Hawkes' address were scrawled on the tape in black permanent marker.

"Do you feel it would be safe to open the package, Mr. Jones?" Henry asked. "I thought perhaps latent fingerprints or other clues might be found on its exterior."

"Assuming Nadiya's grandfather constructed the package and then it was handled by the courier service, many hands would have touched it by now. Besides, if his killer had found the package, it would never have arrived here."

"I suppose you're right, but I was afraid to contaminate any possible evidence."

"May I open it now?" Nadiya asked. "I'm most interested in what Grandfather could have sent me."

I nodded.

Henry handed her a plastic razor knife. Nadiya

gently sliced three edges of the package, where the front and back had been taped together like pursed lips. Then she opened the package the way you would open a dictionary. On top was a small stack of papers and photographs. Nadiya spread the papers on the tabletop. Most were notes handwritten in Ukrainian. Several photographs were of German military officers and civilians dressed in old fashioned suits. I slid them to the side and flipped them over. Written in pencil on the back of each photo appeared to be the name of the character on the glossy side: Rudolph Hess, Dietrich Eckart, Dr. Winfried Schuuman, Rudolph Von Sebottendorf, and Maria Orsic. But I would have to wait for Nadiya to translate the hand-printed information on the back of each photograph.

I handed the five photographs to her. "Would you tell me what it says on the backs of these pictures?"

Nadiya leafed through them quickly and then began translating them for me. She held up the photo of a guy with a square face and bushy eyebrows. "This man is Rudolph Hess. It says that he served as Deputy Führer of the Nazi Party and that he co-authored *Mein Kampf* with Adolph Hitler. He was good friends with Maria."

Next, she held up the photo of a bald guy with a full trapezoidal mustache. "Dietrich Eckart. He was founder of the German Worker Party. After his death, he channeled plans to Maria while she was in a trance. He claimed Sumerians came to Earth half a million years ago from the Aldebaran star system. Original Aryans."

Nadiya shook her head. "This is kind of crazy, you know, Mr. Jones."

The next photo she held up was a guy with a wide forehead and a pointed chin. He was wearing glasses. "Dr. Winfried Schuuman, aka 'Otto.' High voltage expert. Helped Maria decipher drawings and develop prototype Munich Device. After war, he was taken to Wright-Patterson Air Force Base in USA—Operation Paperclip."

Then Nadiya held up a photo of a guy who looked like an overweight banker. "This is Rudolph Von Sebottendorf...aka 'Erwin Torre'...aka 'Adam Rudolf Glauer.' Founder of the Thule Society, which merged with Maria's Vril Society. Disappeared with Maria after war."

The last photo was of an attractive young woman with long, possibly blonde hair. "Last but not least is Maria Orsic," Nadiya said. "Founder of the Vril Society. Psychic. Received drawings in a trance. Close friend of Hitler. SS wanted Munich Device for warfare. Maria and the device disappeared."

"That's it?" I asked.

"That's all that is written on the photos, Mr. Jones. But the papers and the drawings may have more. What do you think so far?"

"It sounds as though the Germans had some kind of new weapon near the end of World War II, and maybe these drawings are the plans for it."

Henry shook his head. "I don't think the Germans ever got the plans." He pointed at the photo of the young woman. "It sounds like they tried to get them from this Orsic woman, but she and her Munich Device disappeared."

Nadiya pulled out a small box which had been hidden beneath the photographs and her grandfather's notes. "Look, Mr. Jones. It's an old cassette tape. I wonder what's on it?"

I turned to Henry. "You wouldn't happen to have a cassette player would you?"

"I haven't seen one in years."

Nadiya shook her head. "Me neither."

"What about Harvey's Electronics?" Henry asked. "They have all sorts of stuff."

"It's worth a shot," I said.

"I'll be right back."

Henry grabbed the keys to his sedan and disappeared into the hallway. I heard the front door close.

Nadiya began sorting through the papers.

"What are they?" I asked.

"Technical papers and schematic drawings, like for an engineer or a scientist. I don't really understand them." Then she uncovered six pages of drawings and held the first one in the air. "This is what the papers describe. It's some sort of machine."

I took the drawing from her and examined it. The schematic was written in German, which was no help to me. Hell, I barely understand English. But when I turned the drawing right side up, there was no question what it displayed. "It looks like a flying saucer, Nadiya. It's a goddamn German flying saucer."

"This is all very strange, Mr. Jones. Why would Grandfather send something like this to me?"

"That's to be seen, isn't it? We'll have to figure that one out."

Clearly, her grandfather's behavior had been strange. He hadn't called Nadiya before he arrived, and he hadn't come directly to her home in the Helderbergs.

He had been beaten, left for dead, and ultimately murdered by somebody. And now this mysterious package had been delivered to the Hawkes' home. The package was of value to somebody. We needed to discover why. Maybe we already had.

Henry was back home in less than an hour, waving a battery-operated cassette player from Harvey's. "I got it for less than twenty dollars."

He set a small box on the table and pulled the recorder from it. Then he popped its back open and shoved four D-cell batteries into place.

"You got that tape, Nadiya?"

"Yes."

She removed the cassette from its clear plastic container and handed it to him. Henry put it in the small lavender player, shut its lid, and hit PLAY. An old man's voice came out of the speaker. I couldn't understand anything except his first words: "Privet, Nadiya."

Nadiya listened intently to her grandfather's message, which lasted almost five minutes by my reckoning. When it ended, she pushed the OFF button on the player.

"So, what did he say?" I asked.

Nadiya cleared her throat. "He said he found the drawings in a secret compartment in a desk he purchased at an estate auction, and that the drawings will change the world."

"Is that all?"

"He said I should sell them to the highest bidder among the American aerospace industries."

"Really?"

"Yes. He told me not to give them to the big oil

companies or to the American government because the machine in the drawing would disappear or probably be militarized."

"What did he mean by that?" Henry asked. "Where are the drawings?"

I forgot he hadn't seen them, and I was interested in what he would see when he looked at them.

Nadiya slid the drawings out from beneath the pile of pictures and pages of notes. Henry held them in the air and examined them, one at a time. "The first page clearly tells us what this device is supposed to do. See where it says 'Antigravitationsmaschine.' Loosely translated, that means "Anti-Gravity Machine.'"

"Yes," I said, "and doesn't it look like a flying saucer? Clearly, Mr. Bodnar thought the machine in these drawings would revolutionize the transportation industry or else make our military invincible."

Henry tilted his head. I think he was trying to wrap his head around the pile of materials lying on his hassock.

"When I was a kid," I said, "I heard somebody had invented an engine that would run on water. He sold the plans for the engine to the oil industry, and they hid them away so their industry would not become a thing of the past and their profits would not disappear."

"Who was that man?" Henry asked.

"I don't know. Maybe it was just a conspiracy theory. At the very least, it was a rumor."

"But was it possibly the truth?" Nadiya asked.

"Yes, it's possible. Think about things which have gone away because they have been replaced by something better."

"Like the typewriter?" she asked.

"More like the horse and buggy," Henry said.

"Exactly," I replied. "If the buggy-making industry could have purchased the plans to the automobile, would they ever have released them to the public? Once the automobile arrived, buggies quickly found their way to the junkyard."

"And roadmaps," Henry added. "Now that we have GPS, who uses a roadmap anymore?"

"Yes," Nadiya replied. "And the camera. Everybody takes pictures with their cell phones."

"That's my point," I replied.

"So, Grandfather thinks the machine in this drawing will threaten some industry?"

I nodded. "Yes...or else he thinks the military will turn it into a weapon and the general public will never get their hands on it."

Henry groaned. "Maybe it's not so good that we have these drawings. Somebody already knows your grandfather had these plans in his possession, and they tried to steal them from him for their own benefit." He turned to me. "Do you think it's the military, or is it someone from private industry?"

"One or both. It's too early to tell. Whoever it is, they mean business. We need to hide these drawings someplace where they cannot be stolen."

"Before we do anything with them, I'd like to study them carefully," Henry said. "I'm going to have to find someone who can accurately translate German into English."

"Yes, that's an excellent idea."

"However, the bilingual folks I know are all connected to the company I sued, and I wouldn't want the higher-ups to get wind of this device."

I turned to Nadiya. "Officially, these documents all belong to you, and here we are making decisions as if they're ours. Do you mind if we have them translated to see what they really describe?"

Nadiya shrugged her shoulders. "Not at all. I never studied German, and we definitely need a translator to discover if Grandfather has found something truly special."

"What he said to you on that tape makes it sound especially valuable."

"Do you know what else Grandfather told me on that tape?" Nadiya asked.

"I'm all ears," I replied.

"Watch out for Maria Orsic."

## Chapter 8

It was almost noon when Roxanne and I woke. We showered together. Then Roxanne poached a couple of eggs for breakfast and served them over toasted brioche bread onto which she had slathered a layer of unsalted butter. As a side dish, she served frizzled scrapple, which we washed down with hot green tea. I'm more of a bacon, fried eggs, and home fries man, but she did all the cooking, and I wasn't about to give her menu a bad review, especially after she had facilitated the athletic event which kept me up until three in the morning.

After I helped her rinse the dishes and place them into her dishwasher, we reclined on her plush velvet divan. I was against the backrest and she in my arms. It was almost heaven, except my cell phone rang. Roxanne sat up so I could dig it out of my pants pocket. Caesar French was reaching out to me.

"Good morning, Jones. How are things today?"

"Not going as well as I had hoped. What's up?"

"Can you meet me in my office at two? Henry Hawkes brought me photocopies of the paperwork his Ukrainian house guest received from her grandfather. I have a multilingual friend coming to review the drawings and their accompanying papers."

"Okay, I'll see you then. Do you need me to bring anything?"

"Just your detective's inquisitive mind."

I turned to Roxanne. "I have to be at work at two." I shut down my cell phone and powered it off. "There, no more interruptions while I'm holding you in my arms."

She lay back down, her head resting against my chest. "I could get used to this, Barty…at least on days when I don't have to go to work. Will you stay with me tonight, too?"

I thought about it, but not too long. "How about we do dinner at Chez Nicole's and then come back here for an encore of last night's performance?"

"Excellent. You're such a romantic. I just don't understand why your wife ever left you."

"She wasn't like you, Roxanne. She didn't bring the same things to the table, if you know what I mean."

Roxanne kissed me. It was deep and passionate. I might have acted on my inner urges, but I needed to save some energy for after dinner.

****

Caesar was standing outside, waiting anxiously for me when I pulled to a stop in front of his office at five after two. He was dressed in designer jeans and a white silk shirt. Caesar opened the building's door and signaled for me to enter first. We walked quickly to his office. The usual things on his desk—the lamp, the phone, a blotter, and his name plate—were gone. In their place were the mechanical drawings and all the papers that had been mailed to Nadiya by her grandfather. A Hispanic man wearing yellow sunglasses and a green tee shirt was typing into a laptop computer.

"Jones, I'd like you to meet Juaquin Fajardo. Henry Hawkes called me to ask if I knew any translators who are trustworthy. Juaquin is translating German into English for Hawkes."

"Nice to meet you, Juaquin. You can call me Bart."

We shook hands. "Everybody calls you 'El Gringo.'"

"I'd prefer Bart."

"'El Gringo' is a name of respect, like 'El Escondido.' If you don't mind, I'd rather call you what the peons do."

El Escondido was French's nickname. His predecessor, Diego Cisneros, had endowed me with the name "El Gringo." For me, it was too close to some kind of gang name, but I was finding a way to live with it. "Yeah, okay, I guess so. I'm getting used to it." I pointed at the paperwork. "What do you think of this stuff thus far?"

"There's a lot of scientific jargon." He held up a German dictionary that sat on a shelf to his right. Beside it lay a Spanish dictionary. "When I'm unsure of a scientific word, I do my best to find its meaning. Some of the terms aren't included in the dictionary. I've highlighted them. You may need to visit a university physicist or a mechanical engineer to understand some of the technology that's described here."

"So, what do you understand thus far?"

"It's some kind of antigravity machine which operates by spinning shallow vats of mercury in opposite directions through a strong magnetic field."

"Will it fly?"

"Beats me. If you got enough bucks, maybe you should build a prototype. But I don't know where you would go to buy a couple of thousand gallons of mercury. They don't sell it at the hardware store, except in those little thermometers."

"Yeah, except the manufacturers of those little thermometers buy the stuff in fifty-gallon drums. Somebody somewhere has a stockpile of it. But I think a prototype is out of the question unless Mr. Hawkes wants to spring for it."

Caesar sat in a chair normally intended for visitors. He drummed his fingers on his knees. After two minutes, he stood. "Excuse me for a few minutes." He left the office.

"How did you become multilingual?" I asked.

Juaquin looked up from his work. "My mother is from Argentina. Her mother was a native Argentinian, and her father was German. He refused to learn Spanish, so she grew up speaking both German and Spanish in her home."

"That explains the Spanish and the German. What about English? Learn it here?"

"I'm one hundred percent American made. My mother learned English in school. She came to the United States to go to college, but she never graduated because I came along. I learned languages from her. My father worked on the offshore oil rigs. Still does. I learned the roughneck trade from him."

I nodded. "How come you're not on a rig yourself?"

"Contract work is hard to find right now because of the governmental push for solar and wind power, and because of the recent series of hurricanes."

"You mean those hurricanes which damaged the rigs?"

"Yeah. Rig repair isn't my specialty. I'm a derrickman. I monitor mud flow when the rigs are operational. When they're shut down for any reason, I come home. So, here I am."

I let him get back to work and went to find French. Caesar was busy on his cell phone when I found him. He motioned for me to give him some space, so I wandered into the warehouse and inspected the Scentless Waste trucks which were still dripping water from being hosed off after their morning runs.

A few minutes later, Caesar approached me. "We're going to go to a meeting, Jones. You and me."

"This afternoon?"

"No, on Tuesday. My secretary is arranging our flight details. The meeting is Wednesday morning."

"Mexico?"

"No, I don't want to leave the US. We're going to Vieques."

"Where's that? Texas somewhere?"

He rolled his eyes and shook his head. The gold cross on his neck chain slipped out of his silk shirt beneath its top button. "You really got to get out more. Vieques is part of Puerto Rico. It's a small island where our meeting won't be disturbed. It's a quiet place. No media, no tourists to speak of, and no trouble with the *policía*."

"And no passports needed because Puerto Rico is an American trust territory?"

"That's right. We just show our driver's licenses if asked. But we won't be asked."

"Suits or casual attire."

"Casual, but upscale. No jeans or cutoffs."

"Who are we meeting with?"

"Some friends of mine. Decision makers in a professional organization I belong to."

I knew this was going to be an important meeting, especially if it included decision makers. "What's on the agenda, Caesar?"

"You'll have to wait to learn that. You just come along and listen to the discussion. I'll be sure you have an interpreter."

We walked back into Caesar's office. Juaquin looked up as we came in.

"How's it coming, my friend?" Caesar asked.

"Another couple of hours and it should all be ready for your inspection."

"Including both the Spanish and the English versions of the drawings?"

"Yes. I enlarged the plans and created both Spanish and English versions. I pasted paper tape over the words I could translate and wrote them in English on the tape. Some are still in German. You'll need an engineer for most of those."

"That's okay. Jones and I can take it from here. Laverne will have your money when you're done for the day."

"Thank you, Mr. French. Anytime I can be of assistance, it's my pleasure to serve you."

Chapter 9

Caesar was up to something clandestine. Why else had he had Nadiya's materials translated into both English and Spanish? And I wasn't sure if Henry Hawkes was aware of Caesar's activities. I felt as though I should say something to Henry, especially since anything Caesar did with the mechanical drawings could possibly affect Nadiya. But Caesar was my primary employer, and I had a certain amount of loyalty to him. Until I could question him, I couldn't jump to conclusions. Still, I'm talking about Caesar, and he hasn't always been up front with me.

On Tuesday, I met him at five thirty in the morning at Cabrillo Construction. I was dressed in blue pocket pants, a green golf shirt, and baby blue sneakers. My eyes were heavy from waking so early, and I hoped I could catch a nap on the plane.

Caesar was in a tan business suit, but he wasn't wearing a tie. He introduced me to Paolo, a subordinate who would be driving us to Boston for our flight to San Juan. I had never seen Paolo before. He was young, handsome, and small framed. Unlike most of Caesar's employees, his arms were free from tattoos, and his only bodily embellishment was a St. Christopher's medal dangling on a silver chain.

"Hola. It is my pleasure to meet you, El Gringo. My sister says she owes her life to you."

Caesar handed his suitcase to Paolo. "Juanita rode back from Canada with you."

I nodded. "Yes, thank you, Caesar. I remember her now."

Juanita was one of two women I had picked up in Canada and brought back to the United States through the St. Regis Mohawk Reservation. Before she flew from Sinaloa, Mexico, to Toronto, a Mexican drug lord had forced her to swallow more than forty balloons of heroin laced with Captagon. One of the packets began leaking inside her intestines during the trip. She was very sick upon arrival, and I wasn't certain I'd reach Willow Falls in time to save her life.

I handed Paolo my suitcase. "How is she enjoying life in the United States?"

Paolo stuffed my suitcase beside Caesar's in the rear compartment of Caesar's SUV. "Ha! Like most of life in the U.S., living here is a double-edged sword, El Gringo. She hates the cold and mourns for her friends back home, but she has a good job at the supermarket and has enrolled in a citizenship course at the community college."

"You sound proud of her."

"Oh, I am. She is going to be a first-class American citizen someday. She even pays taxes with every paycheck she receives."

Juanita probably was earning minimum wage and probably would get a full tax refund from Uncle Sam. "I'm sure she'll get all her money back in April," I said. "Be sure she files a claim in February or March."

"We take care of that, my friend," Caesar said. "Our accountants complete tax returns for all employees and their family members. All they need to do is sign the bottom of the forms."

"They didn't do mine this spring."

"You're a special case. You're already an American citizen and know how the system works. You don't need those services. Besides, I don't want to offend you by taking a ten percent commission from your refund."

We rode in silence for most of the three-hour trip to Boston. Caesar concentrated on articles in two Mexican newspapers. Every now and then he shook his head and muttered something incomprehensible in Spanish. At one point, he offered me the comics, but I refused. Hell, I couldn't read them, anyway. Occasionally Caesar received a text message, and his thumbs rapidly tapped out a reply to an unknown recipient. Unknown to me, anyway. Bored when I wasn't dozing, I watched the wooded mountains of the Berkshires and the cityscapes of Springfield, Worchester, and Framingham pass by as we sped east on the Massachusetts State Turnpike.

Paolo dropped us in front of the entrance at Logan International Airport and then he headed back to Willow Falls. Caesar and I walked to the ticket counter, where our tickets were waiting for us in Caesar's name.

"I thought we'd be flying a major airline," I said.

Caesar shrugged his shoulders. "This is the only airline offering direct flights to San Juan from Boston. I didn't want the annoyance of a layover or a possible missed connection. Maybe we should have flown out of Newark."

"This is going to be fine. But before we board, maybe we should stop in a liquor store and buy a couple of mini bottles for the flight. They'll probably offer us cola on the plane, and if we buy rum we can make our own Cuba libres."

"I like the way you think, Jones."

We waded through the security checkpoint and then found a tax-free store, where we each bought two mini bottles of 151 proof rum. Then we found Gate C26 and sat for twenty minutes on hard plastic chairs until all passengers were called for boarding.

We entered the plane at the midpoint of a long line of travelers. Caesar moved his head back and forth as he looked over the available seats. Then he handed a stewardess a one-hundred-dollar bill and whispered something into her ear.

The stewardess looked down the crowded plane and then forced her way through the standing passengers to the exit doors near the wings, where two women already had settled into two of the three available seats. She said something to the women. One looked in our direction with disdain. The two women then stood and moved toward the rear of the plane. The stewardess waved to us and protected the seats until we were able to reach them.

"Here you go, gentlemen. If I can be of any other service on your flight, please don't hesitate to call upon me."

"*Gracias, señorita. Estos son excelente*," Caesar replied.

We sat down and buckled up. "Does she understand Spanish?" I asked.

Caesar winked. "She understands Ben Franklin, Jones." Then he stretched out his legs and wiggled uncomfortably in his seat. "As bad as they are, these seats offer the most leg room on the plane. Next time, we fly on a major airline out of JFK."

We arrived in San Juan during a sun shower. Droplets of water streaked across our rectangular porthole as the plane sped toward touchdown in the bright Caribbean sun.

"Prepare yourself, my friend. It's going to be hot and humid," Caesar said.

We disembarked and followed the crowd ahead of us into the terminal of Isla Verde International Airport. I expected it to be mobbed, but the crowd was modest, probably an aftereffect of the coronavirus pandemic.

We found our luggage, and then Caesar led the way to Gate B-3, where a twin-engine plane awaited us. Four other passengers had already boarded, leaving us the two seats at the very rear of the cabin. We hunched over and maneuvered through two sets of opposing elbows to reach our seats.

We sat down and buckled up. Then Caesar pointed to a man in an island shirt who was seated in the front row. "That hombre is your interpreter," he whispered. "His name is Jorge Valenzuela. He's flown in from San Diego."

"Why didn't you introduce me to him when we came aboard the plane?"

"Our eyes met, and that is all. In this line of work, it is best everyone believes us to be strangers."

I nodded. I realized that my suspicions were correct. Caesar was slowly introducing me to a side of his world that he never exposed in New York—the world of an international cartel. I could see where pretending to be strangers would make sense in Caesar's world. If anyone is being tailed, the other party wouldn't be noticed or identified as a possible accomplice. All interactions in public should be discreet.

The pilot taxied the plane to the end of the runway and then accelerated to full speed. As we lifted off the ground, the trade winds pushed the plane's tail sideways. I gripped the armrest until the plane straightened out.

Vieques lies six miles southeast of the main island of Puerto Rico. Our flight from San Juan took only thirty-five minutes. Most of those were spent flying above the main island's famous rain forest, El Yunque.

Caesar pointed out the thick green vegetation below us. "Get lost in that mess of bamboo and razor palms and nobody will ever find you. It's the home of the Chupacabra."

"You don't believe in that malarky, do you?"

"Two of my Hispanic employees have seen it, Jones. It's a hairless beast that the locals call 'the goat sucker.' It frightens them to talk about it, even today."

"Come on, Caesar, this is the twenty-first century."

"If you ever meet someone who has seen El Chupacabra, he'll make a believer out of you."

We touched down and stepped out of the plane onto a short runway which could never welcome a large jet airliner. If possible, it was hotter on Vieques than it was on the main island. The sun beat down on us and the breeze we had enjoyed in San Juan was absent.

Our pilot handed us our suitcases from the hatch behind the plane's seating area, and we walked to a small tin-roofed concrete building which served as the airstrip's terminal. Outside the building, three taxis waited in anticipation of carting paying passengers to their destinations.

Caesar selected our cab, a yellow and green 2010 four-door sedan. We put our luggage into the open trunk, closed the hatch, and climbed onto the taxi's hot plastic seats. Caesar tapped on the driver's shoulder. "Take us to Casa del Sol."

"You sure you want to go there? They got some kind of private party there this week. Nobody can drive within a hundred yards of the Casa."

"That's where we need to go, please."

The driver started to pull away. Suddenly, a man's voice shouted, "¡Espera! ¡Espera! ¿Puedo coger un aventón?" It was Jorge Valenzuela.

"What's he want?" I asked.

"A lift."

Caesar tapped on the driver's headrest. "Driver, let's give this man a ride, too."

The cab driver stopped and exited his car. We heard the trunk open and close. Then Jorge Valenzuela climbed into the front seat beside the driver. He turned to look at Caesar and me. "Gracias, señors. It would have been a long walk without your generosity."

Caesar nodded. "No problemo. Where are you headed?"

"To Casa del Sol."

"Then you're in luck. This may be the only cab on Vieques that will take you there."

Caesar tapped on the driver's shoulder. "It seems our new passenger is going to the same place. ¡Vamos!"

The highways on Vieques were nothing more than two lane roads at their widest. Sometimes they narrowed to little more than a single lane. Bougainvillea vines sporting bright red and purple flowers climbed the fenceposts on both sides of the roads. The small concrete and block homes we passed were painted in bright tropical colors—aquamarine, tangerine, banana, and watermelon. At one point, our driver came to an abrupt stop. I was stunned to see a small herd of Brahman cattle pass on both sides of our cab, driven down the road by two men on horseback. I don't know where I would have leaped for safety if I had been walking along the road because both sides were fenced in rusty barbed wire.

"Where are the cattle being taken?" I asked the driver.

"To the harbor in Isabel Segunda. From there, by boat to the slaughterhouse in Fajardo."

"Isabel Segunda is the largest town on the island," Caesar said. "Maybe fifteen hundred people. A few small cantinas and bars. But we'll be staying on the other side of the island where *turistas* don't go."

Five minutes later, we pulled to a stop at a temporary barricade set up at the end of a very long crushed coral driveway. Brahman cattle grazed in the pasture to our right. White tropical birds rode on the backs of two bulls. Half a dozen horses grazed to our left. At the top of the hill stood a creamy yellow two-story house with a dozen screenless windows and a blue steel roof. It was surrounded by tall palm trees. I assumed it was Casa del Sol.

Two men approached our taxi, one carrying an assault rifle, maybe Russian or Turkish. The other sported a bulge on his hip. No doubt it was a large pistol.

"Ola," the pistol-bearer said. He stepped closer to the driver's window. "What is your business? This is a private party."

The cab driver pointed his thumb over his shoulder toward Caesar and me. "Ask these señors. They asked me to bring them here...but we don't want no trouble."

Caesar rolled down his window and handed the guard a Ben Franklin. "I am El Escondido. We are expected."

The cab driver stared at Caesar in his rearview mirror. His brow was covered with beads of sweat, and his face was painted in stress. Then he looked at me. When our eyes met, his quickly returned forward.

"Si. You are the last, El Escondido. The others in your party are enjoying the pool this afternoon. They tell me the water is cool and refreshing."

"Any *mujeres jovenes*?"

"No, señor. They tell me it is business only."

"Good."

The two sentries moved three yellow sawhorses and waved us through.

"What did you ask him?" I whispered.

Valenzuela turned toward me. "El Escondido asked if any young women were staying at the Casa. The answer was 'No. This is a business meeting.'"

The cab driver stopped in front of the entrance to Casa del Sol. He exited the car and opened Caesar's door. Then he opened the trunk and removed our bags.

Caesar stepped out and approached the driver. "How much do we owe you, señor?"

The driver gestured nervously and bowed his head. "Oh, you owe me nothing, señor. Nothing at all. It was my pleasure to bring you here today. Welcome to Vieques."

Caesar handed him a fifty. "This is for your driving skills, especially for not getting us killed by that stampede of Brahman bulls."

"Oh, *gracias*, señor. You are very generous."

Caesar then handed the driver two Ben Franklins. "And this is because you have heard my name, and you are a very wise man who will not mention to anyone that I am on Vieques for a few days."

Streams of sweat ran down the driver's face. He bowed again, his belly bulging at his belt. "Oh, have no fear, señor. I already have forgotten the name you told the gatekeeper."

"*Bueno*. Can you be here at nine o'clock on Thursday morning to take me to another destination?"

"Si, señor. As you wish, it will be my pleasure to be here at nine o'clock Thursday morning."

"Then we have an appointment. Do not forget. We will see you then."

"*Gracias*, señor. *Muchas gracias*."

I whispered into Valenzuela's ear. "What does 'El Escondido' mean?

"The Hidden One."

Chapter 10

Casa del Sol was set up perfectly for small group events and entertainment. The ground floor included three sitting areas and a small concierge desk where check-in/out procedures were accomplished. Its ceiling vaulted two floors to a glass pyramid which was filled with palm fronds from a tree which was rooted in the ground in the center of the room. A handrail encircled the entire second floor balcony, where each wall was home to two bedrooms for guests. Assuming two guests per room, the Casa maxed out at sixteen guests, though I assumed a closet somewhere held folding cots for overflow.

The natural flow from the main room led through a small dining room and bar to an outdoor patio with shaded tables and chairs. In the center of the patio, a small swimming pool rippled with turquoise water. Three men were standing waist-deep in the water when Caesar and I found the patio.

"Hola, El Escondido," one swimmer bellowed deeply. He was distinctly taller and appeared stronger than the other two swimmers. His muscular chest was tattooed with the Los Equis logo.

Caesar gave the man a "thumbs-up."

"Who's that?" I asked.

"Just a man to be cautious of. His name is Orlando. When he is near you, he holds your life in his hands and can snuff it out in less than a second."

I memorized the man's face. When his eyes met mine, I nodded respectfully. He nodded back, undoubtedly memorizing my face, too, and wondering why I was accompanying El Escondido. I was beginning to wonder the same thing. I didn't belong at this assembly of cartel heavyweights.

"Come, Jones. The man I had hoped to see must be napping. Let's settle into our room."

We climbed the stairs and found room seven. Our luggage already had been brought to the room by Casa staff and had been placed on small folding stands at the foot of each bed.

I had never been to the tropics and was amazed at the room's decorative theme. Its floor was wide-plank wood which had been stained mahogany and waxed heavily. The wooden ceiling had been painted creamy white and, in its center, the deep brown blades of a fan rotated gently. The walls were papered in thin sand-colored grass that I had seen before in a Polynesian restaurant. Our three windows were screenless and opened onto a vista of grassy hills which spilled into the distant ocean. As I stood engrossed in the view, a small green lizard climbed onto the sill from the outside and ran across the wall.

I pointed at the tiny reptilian visitor. "Look, Caesar. We have a visitor."

He chuckled. "In Mexico, children catch them and hold them near their earlobes. When the chameleons clamp on, the children let go and wear them as earrings until they drop off."

Caesar disappeared into the bathroom. A few minutes later he reappeared, wearing a blue swimming suit, an island shirt, and sandals. "Stay here for a few minutes and then join me at the pool…maybe in twenty minutes. The men below need to know you do not speak or understand Spanish and that you are my special guest."

That suited me just fine. I knew I would hear a lot of conversation during our stay and most of it would be meaningless gibberish to me. That's why Caesar had arranged a translator.

I lay down on my bed and watched the fan spinning above. Soon I heard a knock on the room door. I rose and opened the door. It was Jorge Valenzuela. "El Escondido sent me to see if you are okay. You've been up here for more than an hour and a half."

"Thanks, Jorge. I must have dozed off." I had done that before. Back in seventh grade, I took over a friend's paper route. One morning, I lay back down after the alarm clock shook my nerves. I thought maybe a minute had passed by, but when I sat up to fold the papers and begin working the route, I saw that two hours had elapsed. I delivered the papers, but the circulation manager received many complaints from customers who had expected their papers to arrive in time to read with their morning coffee.

"Well, get into your swimsuit and come down to the pool, pronto."

I tried to be ethnic. "Si, amigo."

"Don't talk no Spanish while you're here, El Gringo. You're not supposed to know any Spanish."

"I don't. I know cerveza, taco, burrito, and hola. It's just enough to get by when I'm at Taco Bell."

"These are big hombres you are mixing with today and tomorrow. Don't say nothing to offend them. You tell me what you want to say to them, and I'll convey the message back and forth. *¿Comprendes?*"

"Yeah. Thanks for the reminder."

"Well, get dressed and come down pretty quick. El Escondido wants to introduce you to La Cabra."

I knew that name. In a conversation with me last year, Caesar had recited the line of succession in Los Equis' leadership. La Cabra is seated atop the organization for the time being, but he is supposed to be in hiding while recovering from a gunshot wound. For a moment, I was tempted to call Helen and have her alert the FBI as to La Cabra's present location. Then I snapped back into reality. These guys on Vieques were my meal ticket, especially Caesar. And, so far, he'd never asked me to do anything too illegal. Well, other than escort two illegal immigrants and their cargo of heroin and Captagon across the Canada-USA border.

"Tell El Escondido I'll be right down."

I splashed cool water on my face and changed into my navy-blue swimsuit. I hadn't thought to bring sandals, so I walked downstairs barefoot with a towel draped over my shoulder.

"Over here, Jones."

It was Caesar, sitting in a yellow plastic beach chair beside a man who appeared several years younger. The man had greying temples, and a small Los Equis logo tattooed on his left shoulder. Several gold chains hung from his neck. A two-inch tall letter X hung from the thickest chain.

Caesar said something to the man, who nodded. "Amigo, I'd like you meet the leader of our organization, La Cabra."

"My pleasure, sir." I shook hands with the man.

His grip was stronger than I would have expected of a man who was recovering from a gunshot wound. I saw no evidence of a wound on his chest or legs. I wondered if he had been shot in the back by some coward.

La Cabra said something to Caesar. Caesar turned to me. "From your inspection, he suspects you're wondering about his wound. He wants you to know the rumor of his injury was only that, and it was developed by his press agent to prove he is invulnerable to bullets. The peasants believe that to be true."

"Have you two been in the water?"

Caesar translated my question to La Cabra. Both men laughed.

"We're not here to swim. We're here to consider a new venture, which you will learn about at tomorrow's meeting. La Cabra says you are welcomed to listen to what is being said, but only from behind a screen, where you and Señor Valenzuela will be able to hear voices but not see who is speaking."

I spoke directly to La Cabra. "I'll abide by any rules you establish, sir."

Caesar translated for me. La Cabra looked me in the eyes. "Good."

So, he knew a few words of English, too. I suppose most foreigners, especially those who do business in the United States, know more English than they will admit. It allows for a little eavesdropping on private conversations.

I sat in an aluminum framed lounge chair while Caesar and La Cabra conversed in Spanish for the next hour. I guess I drifted off to sleep again because Caesar tapped my shin with his sandal.

"Wake up, Amigo. You're snoring."

I sat up. "Sorry, gentlemen." I rose and plunged headfirst into the pool. The water was very warm, almost like a bath.

Caesar laughed. "You were expecting a cool experience? This is the tropics. The best time to swim is after eleven at night."

I brushed the water from my face. "I'll remember that."

Caesar and La Cabra both chuckled.

As I climbed out of the pool, the gentle island breeze cooled my skin. "That's the secret, Caesar. Get wet and let the wind cool your body by evaporation."

La Cabra turned to Caesar. "This El Gringo of yours…he learns fast."

\*\*\*\*

Dinner was served at seven. I sat with Jorge Valenzuela at an intimate table for two. Caesar and La Cabra sat at a table with nine other men. Occasionally, Jorge would tell me what they were talking about, but mostly we spoke about baseball. Jorge's passion. Not mine.

Dinner consisted of langosta, the clawless lobster of the Caribbean, served with fried plantains, and Puerto Rican rice. The rice was yellow in color and filled with sliced olives, red beans, and an assortment of finely chopped vegetables. I sprinkled it with Sombrero Negro hot sauce. To quote Helen, "It was to die for."

Without warning, a man threw a dinner roll at Caesar, stood up, and yelled at him. I feared for Caesar's safety. I stood and quickly approached the table near Caesar's seat. Suddenly, I was lifted into a full nelson head lock and returned to my place. The man who carried me like a feather was Orlando, the large man who easily could snuff out my life if provoked.

He pointed a finger at me. *"Siéntate, y collate."*

I didn't understand his words, but I knew I was supposed to sit down. I did.

Jorge leaned forward. "That was a dangerous thing you just did. The argument you saw was not your war."

"But he threw a hard roll at Caesar."

"He accuses El Escondido of being greedy and not sharing the Captagon trade with his compadres."

La Cabra was speaking to both men, first the assailant and then Caesar. Then he spoke to the entire table. All the men murmured and nodded in agreement.

"What's going on?" I asked.

"El Escondido has agreed to let La Araña control the sale of captagon on the west coast...California, Oregon, Washington, Arizona, New Mexico, and Texas. However, La Araña must acquire the capsules through El Escondido and may not manufacture them himself. Both men have agreed to the plan. The other chapter leaders have agreed the solution is fair."

Orlando was still standing beside me. He pushed my shoulder with his huge hand. I looked up at him. "See?" he said. "La Cabra is in control. Both men have won something."

I noted he spoke English. I also realized I had misjudged him. He might have been huge in size and physical in professional function, but he wasn't stupid.

Orlando walked away from my table and stood in the shadows where he had been protecting La Cabra from any unwanted assault.

Caesar lifted his glass of wine and tilted his head at La Araña. La Araña lifted his glass and nodded to

Caesar. Both men drank. The problem had been identified, and an amicable solution had been reached. Caesar and La Araña were now in business together. Both would profit from the partnership.

Chapter 11

When I woke the next morning, Caesar was showering and singing something in Spanish. I checked the time. It was seven, but my head felt like it should have been five. Soon, Caesar finished and walked into our room wearing a towel around his waist. I rolled out of bed and into the shower. By the time I was finished cleaning up, Caesar had already gone from the room. I quickly dressed and joined him downstairs for breakfast.

I sat between Caesar and Jorge. The breakfast options included *tetelas*, huevos rancheros, or eggs. I opted for scrambled eggs, which arrived with chopped white onions, Serrano peppers, and diced tomatoes—the colors of the Mexican flag.

After breakfast, the morning meeting began. Armed sentries were posted at the two entrances to the room. A security guard scanned the room for listening devices, and when he gave the "all clear," Orlando stationed Jorge and me at the rear of the room behind a rattan screen over which somebody had thrown a white bedsheet to ensure we couldn't see who was speaking. Once we were seated, Orlando stood beside us while cartel members entered the room and took their seats at the rectangular table.

I recognized La Cabra's voice as the first speaker. Jorge translated. Well, he summarized without giving me the names of the voices I was hearing.

"That speaker is just welcoming everybody and thanking them for finding time away from their businesses to consider a new venture."

I nodded. This was going to be an exercise in trying to keep everybody straight in my head.

But then I heard Caesar's voice, and Jorge began summarizing again.

"The new speaker, he is speaking about how Los Equis are always interested in expanding business, even though business is good. He wants Los Equis to do business where no man has gone before."

A loud voice said something unintelligible. The group laughed.

"That hombre said something about opening up Russia. Everyone thought that was funny. Russia has its own cartels, and they would never let Mexicans in."

Caesar began again, but he was interrupted by another voice.

"The speaker must have made a gesture."

"Why's that?" I asked.

"Because the speaker said he wanted to do business there, and the other guy asked him why he was pointing at the ceiling."

I wished I could see what was going on, but I knew there was no way Orlando would let me stand up. Doing that would have been immediate death.

Caesar spoke again. Several members of the group gasped.

"Now the speaker is explaining that he wants to do business in outer space."

My eyes opened wide. "No wonder they're gasping."

"The speaker says that the USA, Russia, China, and Japan are already flying in circles above us. And SpaceX and Amazon have already begun opening space for private companies and are planning installations on the moon and Mars. He says that Los Equis should be next. We should open up space for sales of our most precious commodities to space warriors."

I could hear commotion from the men around the table.

"What are they mumbling?"

"Some think the speaker is crazy. Los Equis doesn't have the technology or the trained astronauts."

Caesar continued talking.

"The speaker has addressed several hombres directly. He pointed out to one that Los Equis already has plenty of money, enough to buy the technology and to hire scientists to perfect it. He said to another that we have to quit hiding our money in the walls of our houses and, instead, put it to good use making more money and opening up new markets."

I heard another voice say something.

Jorge continued summarizing. "That guy said there's not enough people up in space to make it a good marketplace. The speaker reminded him that Mexico was once a barren desert, but it is now full of cities and villages where money can be made. Soon space will be full of people, and Los Equis should be first in line when the markets open."

Then the voice said something else, followed again by Caesar's voice.

"He asked what commodities the speaker envisions selling up there. The speaker said we'd do everything we do down here—general smuggling of forbidden items, like whiskey, drugs, weapons, protection, and women."

"El Escondido is thinking waaay ahead of the other cartels," I exclaimed.

Orlando pushed on my shoulder. "No names, hombre. Last warning."

I looked up at his massive face and shrugged. "Sorry."

Yeah, I was sorry to have said Caesar's nickname aloud, but I was excited about his plan. As narrated at the beginning of every episode of my favorite sci-fi series, space is the last frontier, and Caesar was challenging the cartel's leaders to go there. It was a brilliant idea.

Caesar said something again.

"The speaker says all Los Equis needs to do is build the vehicle to get into space and then we can open up business. We can even contract with governments around the world to carry important stuff to their space stations and planetary colonies."

Another voice spoke. The group began mumbling again.

"That hombre asked, 'How do we expect to build us a rocket ship?'"

Caesar answered his question.

"The speaker says he has plans for a spaceship like none other. It's a flying saucer designed by the Germans, but they didn't have time to build it before they were defeated in World War II. He says Los Equis should build it. Nobody else has anything like it, except maybe the little green men."

The group laughed and mumbling erupted again. A man's voice shouted out a question.

"That hombre asked how much this venture would cost each of us. He said, 'Not everybody has houses full of money.'"

Caesar began again.

"The speaker says that if Los Equis moves forward with this plan, La Cabra has agreed to oversee the collection of money from each chapter, according to what each can afford. Profits from the venture will be divided according to the same percentage of investment."

Another voice asked a question.

"That man wants to know what happens if the spaceship explodes or the venture fails?"

I heard another voice. I thought it was La Cabra's.

"That hombre says if the spaceship doesn't fly, El Escondido will reimburse each chapter from his own chapter each month until the debt is paid."

I winced at the thought of repayment. I knew Caesar was going out on a very thin limb with his proposal. If the venture failed, he probably would be pushing up daisies in some unmarked ditch, and Cabrillo Construction would be assigned another new manager.

The meeting continued throughout the morning until a vote was about to be held. But before the chapter leaders cast their ballots, La Cabra spoke. Jorge translated what he told his captains: "You know I support this concept brought to us by our compadre from New York. I wouldn't have called you together if the idea didn't have merit. Yet, I know it will cost each of you millions of dollars, so I won't blame you if you vote against it."

Each man was given a turn to explain his vote. All

but one chapter agreed to Caesar's plan, yet its captain was reluctant to disagree with the other nine. According to Jorge, that captain said, "I know you all expect to reap great profits in the future, and perhaps you see Los Equis becoming a legitimate player on the interplanetary stage, but in my chapter my soldiers are still fighting daily with the Marines, and our numbers are dwindling. When I came to this meeting, I had hoped for immediate support for our cause, not some distant reward I may never see."

La Cabra's voice took on a fatherly tone.

Jorge translated. "The Leader asked what might sway this captain to make the vote unanimous. The captain asked if some of the others around the table would send some soldiers to help in his war with the Marines. And he said if someone could convince the Mexican Marines to back off, he could be encouraged to change his vote."

I heard La Cabra speak again, and Jorge translated. "The leader has asked the other captains to send four soldiers each to assist with the problem of the government's Marines."

I heard murmuring, and then La Cabra spoke again. "They all have agreed," Jorge said. "And our leader asked one of the other captains if he would use his personal influence to assist this chapter with its problem with the Marines. The captain has agreed to do so."

I heard the voice of the naysayer. Jorge translated: "*Gracias*, amigos. Because of my compadres' support, I change my vote to 'yes' on the space initiative."

I thought he was a wise captain...and he probably wanted to avoid an early demise.

The group broke for lunch at the small tables

around the pool. Jorge and I sat together, which seemed appropriate because we had been together all morning. Lunch was a Mexican platter—refried beans, chilis rellenos, and quinoa pilaf with nopales. I was in the mood for a burger, but I didn't complain. Besides, my trip had been fully funded by Caesar, so how could I complain about the food?

In the afternoon, the conversation considered different variables, such as how much money each chapter would donate per month, identification of aerospace engineers to impress into employment, and the location of the spaceship construction facilities.

I was surprised when Jorge said, "They have decided that El Escondido will construct a new fieldhouse in rural New York, and assembly of the spaceship will occur there, where he will be able to keep a watchful eye on the process. La Cabra expects a monthly report, which he will forward to all the chapter captains."

It was clear Caesar had much work to do when we returned to Willow Falls, but because he operated Cabrillo Construction, erection of the fieldhouse would be easily accomplished.

At nine o'clock on Thursday morning, a nervous cab driver met us at Casa del Sol and returned us to Vieques' small airstrip. Caesar tipped him well for his silence. From there, we flew to San Juan and then back to Boston, where Paolo was waiting for us when we touched down. Caesar and I both slept in the back seat of his SUV during the ride back to Willow Falls. But my sleep was fitful because my suspicions about Caesar's connections to Los Equis had been confirmed.

Also, I knew I had to find Mr. Bodnar's killer—and soon.

Chapter 12

Caesar and I arrived at Cabrillo Construction at eleven at night.

"Enjoy your weekend, Jones. We have much to do beginning Monday."

"Yes, and I still need to identify Mr. Bodnar's killer."

"Yes, you do." He touched his forehead with his finger and then pointed it at me. "See you Monday."

"Caesar, before we go to our respective homes, may I ask a delicate question?"

"Yes."

"I learned that you are handling the national distribution of captagon. Why did you give away the west coast territory?"

"You have big ears, my friend. But I trust you. I did not set up the distribution strategy. Diego Cisneros did. But he hasn't been seen for over a year. I don't mind sharing the profits with La Aranya. He is already on the west coast, and I do not wish to be in competition with him. By sharing with him, I have avoided a small war. Besides, I still earn profit from every pill he sells. He does all the work, and I get wealthier. How do I lose?"

I bid him farewell. What he said made perfect sense. That's why he's in a power position.

\*\*\*\*

Roxanne had texted me while I was on the way back to Willow Falls with Caesar. I couldn't pass up her invitation to stay on permanently. Initially, she called it a trial relationship, but now she seemed more serious about us. Besides, she told me she had news for me, something about my current investigation.

Gravel popped under the weight of my tires when I pulled into her driveway at eleven thirty. Four cars were parked on the edge of her front lawn. I didn't recognize any of them.

Chatter and laughter came from behind her home. Maybe she had a party going on. I walked around the side of her home and onto her marble patio. The laughter became louder. All the voices were female.

I stopped dead in my tracks beside a potted hydrangea bush. Roxanne's hot tub was full of naked ladies, all holding drinks in their hands. Roxanne was among them. Her eyes sparkled when she saw me. "Boobies in the drink, ladies," she squealed.

All the women dropped up to their necks in the water. One turned to look at me. I'd seen her before somewhere. I think at the sanguinarian's Halloween party last October. "Is this your lover, Roxie? Can we share him?"

"When I'm done with him, I don't think he'll have enough reserve to service you, Gloria. You'll have to find your own stud-muffin."

"Too bad…"

Roxanne pointed toward the kitchen. "Barty, be a good boy and find something to do for half an hour. When the ladies leave, I'll come find you."

That suited me just fine because I wasn't in the mood to be a spectacle or the brunt of girlish jokes. I walked through the kitchen and then upstairs, where I took a quick shower. Then I lay down on Roxanne's bed with the towel wrapped around my waist.

I woke at eight in the morning, still wrapped in a damp towel. Roxanne's guest bathrobe was hanging in her closet, so I threw it on and went downstairs to find her. I probably looked silly in its lavender floral print, but I really didn't care.

I staggered into her kitchen. "Good morning, handsome," Roxanne said. "I didn't have the heart to wake you last night. You were heavy into REM."

As early as it was, she was gorgeous. She was dressed in tangerine silk lounge pajamas with matching slippers. The skin on her cheeks softly reflected the light from overhead.

I gave her a gentle kiss on her lips. "It was a long trip."

"I can see that. Your eyes tell me how tired you are. Take it easy this morning and catch an early afternoon nap. Then I'll welcome you home."

Roxanne poured me a cup of coffee.

"What's with the strange back taste?"

"Toasted betel nut from the tropics. This batch comes from Malaysia, where they call it 'areca catechu.'"

"You're into some weird stuff. Is it going to give me the runs?"

"Oh, Barty, sometimes you're such a nudge. You know I wouldn't give you anything that could hurt you."

I guess she was right. I'm not very accepting of anything new. I like my world to be as I expect it to be, and I'm slow to adapt to new stuff, including foods, flavors, clothing styles, music, and technology—not to mention new ways of doing anything. I'm happy with the old tried and true.

I took another sip of the strange coffee, and then I changed the subject. "You said you had some new information about the case I'm working on?"

"My group of ladies divined a strange message for you: 'the woman deceives you.' Does it ring a bell yet?"

I shook my head. "That's as clear as a summer night's windshield."

"When the time is right, you'll know exactly what it means. In the meanwhile, my girls will keep searching the ethers for more clues."

We walked into Roxanne's sitting room. She picked up her remote. "Let's find something interesting on the telly."

I sat beside her and watched the screen as she clicked from channel to channel. Finally, she stopped at an old black and white movie. It was innocent and mindless, which was exactly what I needed. I laid my head on Roxanne's lap and dozed off amidst the mild aroma of chlorine from her hot-tubbed skin.

\*\*\*\*

Roxanne gently shook me. "Barty, your phone is ringing upstairs. Would you like me to go get it?"

I lifted my head from her lap and sat up. "Damn, I hope it's not one of those robocalls."

I climbed her stairs and looked at my list of calls. The most recent was from Caesar French, only two minutes ago. I tapped on the number to return his call.

Two rings later, he answered. "French here."

"Caesar, it's Bart Jones. You called?"

"Yes. Can you come in this afternoon, maybe twelve thirty? There have been some developments in your investigation."

I knew he wouldn't give me any particulars over the phone, especially if he suspected that his phone was tapped or if someone was standing nearby, listening to his conversation.

"Sure. I'll be there before one o'clock."

"Good. See you then."

Roxanne came into the bedroom. "Is it work?"

"Unfortunately, yes. I need to leave for work around noon."

She pushed me backwards onto her bed and landed on top of me. Her hair brushed across my face and tickled my neck.

"Then I have only two hours to welcome you home," she said. "Will that disappoint you?"

"Nothing you do disappoints me, Roxanne."

She kissed my cheek and then ran her tongue down my neck.

I felt tingling down my spine. "Nice," I whispered.

"Yessss," she moaned.

We kissed passionately. And when our tongues intertwined, I noticed a hint of betelnut on hers.

\*\*\*\*

I pulled into Cabrillo Construction at twelve thirty. The parking lot was overflowing with a mishmash of four-cylinder foreign vehicles. Most of them sported dents and were adorned with left-wing bumper stickers like "I voted for her," "Got social security? Thank a Democrat," "Marx was right," and "Abolish the Police." That last one irked me because I was happily a cop until Defund the Police came along.

I walked into the main office. Laverne looked up. Her hair was pulled back into a ponytail and her lipstick was glossy purple. "He's in Building Four. I think the meeting ran longer than he expected."

"Who's he meeting with?"

Laverne held up a postcard and read from it. "CRAANA, the Capital Region Association for the Assimilation of New Americans."

"Never heard of it."

"Me neither until yesterday. Mr. French told me a little about it. I guess we are one of six employers offering housing, good salaries, and job training skills to our new employees. You know… the undocumented immigrants."

I nodded. Caesar probably was involved in CRAANA to deflect suspicion that he might be involved in other, questionably legal activities.

Laverne pointed to the doorway to French's office. "There's a couple of tables set up with refreshments in the warehouse. I don't think Mr. French would mind if you go help yourself. When the meeting breaks up, most of the attendees will drift into the warehouse for a handful of free cookies and a drink."

I did as she suggested and walked into the warehouse area. The aroma of bleach let me know the concrete floor had recently been washed, probably because of today's meeting. Nothing will kill a guest's desire for refreshments more than a room that smells like a garbage truck.

I poured myself a cup of coffee and was perusing the donuts when a group of people came into the warehouse.

"How'd you beat me here?" a man asked. He was

shorter than I am, maybe five foot five. The jacket of his tan suit was wrinkled, and his ten dirty toes protruded from his sandals the way the shoemaker had intended.

"I got here too late to walk into the meeting."

"Are you with CRAANA?"

"I'm with French. I'm still trying to figure out his interest in this organization."

"I'm with Cooperative Extension," he said. "We offer shopping and budgeting skills and nutrition and food preparation skills to women, especially mothers. Our federal WIC program offers cheese, milk, and childcare training and cooperates with the county in the distribution of food stamps."

"To the illegals?"

He gave me a look of disgust. "To the new Americans." He plopped a couple of tablespoons of crème cheese on half a poppy seed bagel. "We do a lot of work with the county. They offer free medical and dental care, and through their housing office, they help locate affordable housing, much of it provided for free."

Another man joined us. He was wearing a flowery Hawaiian shirt, and his face was obscured by a large graying handlebar mustache. "Hey, Mel," he said to the guy with the bagel.

"I didn't catch your name," Mel said to me.

"Jones. Bart Jones."

"Zeke, this is Bart Jones. Bart and I were just discussing our roles in CRAANA."

"I haven't seen you before," Zeke said. "New to the group?"

"Just learning about it," I replied. "I work for Caesar French.

"Oh, great guy…French. I'll bet you didn't know he and his colleagues used to fly into war-torn countries under the cover of darkness to evacuate homeless orphans and relocate them to new families around the globe."

"Sounds harrowing. And no, I didn't know that."

"The planes were always unmarked, and all participants could carry no personal identification on their person. It was all done with full cooperation of our federal government and the host countries, but if there was an accident or if the clandestine operation was discovered by the enemy, our government would disavow any knowledge of it."

Now I was completely intrigued by French. I had just recently learned my suspicions about his involvement in illegal cartel activities were correct. But now, I saw him involved in international humanitarian efforts to assist orphans and immigrants to create new lives in new countries. He was a man of two distinctly different identities, his feet deep into two oppositional worlds. No wonder he was known as El Escondido, "The Hidden One."

Twenty minutes elapsed before French's warehouse emptied of the meeting's guests. Then he approached me. "Glad you could make it, Jones."

"Wish I had attended the entire meeting. What you folks are doing is impressive."

"Maybe you should come along on one of our missions. You might find a new calling."

"Do you sit on flak jackets when you fly into war zones?"

"Sometimes…"

We walked to his office. I sat in the plastic chair

across from his desk. "You said have an update for me?"

"Well, it's just some interesting information which came to me from a contact in Romania."

"I'm all ears…"

"There's a young woman in Romania who has been presenting herself as Maria Orsic, the young psychic whose work was of interest to Hitler. The police are searching for her because she has been implicated in several low-level criminal incidents."

"Then she isn't Maria Orsic…she's an imposter?"

"Yes, she's an imposter. My contact believes she's a distant relative, perhaps a great granddaughter or a distant cousin who bears an uncanny resemblance to Orsic. She's been using her appearance to claim that she is Orsic and that she's been living in the Pleiades since her disappearance near the end of World War II."

"Interesting scenario. It takes full advantage of Einstein's explanation of time travel…that you don't age when you travel at the speed of light."

"Exactly. I suspect if she's now in the United States, she may have killed Nadiya Bodnar's grandfather."

Chapter 13

My phone rang at ten in the morning. It was Henry Hawkes. "How are you doing in your search for Kuzma Bodnar's killer?"

"There's not much to report. I've been out of town for a few days on other business, but I am making a little headway." *Very little*, I thought. I needed to refocus on solving this riddle by putting Caesar's subterfuge out of my mind.

"Well, I've been doing some research of my own, and I wanted to share it with you. Can you come by this morning?"

Henry's home wasn't too far away from Roxanne's, where I was now a permanent resident. "Sure. How about eleven?"

"Great. See you then."

When I pulled up to the Hawkes mansion, a convertible 4X4 was parked in front and the "pups" weren't out, so my car door was safe for the moment.

The front door opened as I got out of my car. "Good morning, good morning," Henry said. He ushered me into the foyer, up the elevator, and then into the family's large eat-in kitchen. I had never seen that part of the home before. The floor-to-ceiling cabinets were dark cherry, which surprised me because the remainder of his home featured lighter colors. All the appliances sported cherry doors, so they were invisible unless you sought them out. Spreading down the middle of the expansive room was a green granite wet island with stools to seat twelve. I wondered how often they were all filled at once.

A young man, probably in his early twenties, was seated closest to the stove, finishing a late breakfast of scrambled eggs and an everything bagel. He was dressed in a white tee shirt and long-legged cotton pajama bottoms.

"This is my son, Cooper," Henry said. He turned to Cooper. "This is the gentleman I mentioned, Detective Jones."

Cooper and I shook hands. He then squeezed a puddle of antibacterial handwash into his palm and rubbed his hands together briskly. Now I knew what he thought of private detectives.

I turned my attention to Hawkes. "So, what's new and interesting, Henry?"

"Let's talk in the living room so we don't bother Cooper. Elizabeth and Charity have gone to the market. Nadia is showering. So, it's just us for the moment."

Once we sat down, me on Henry's white leather sofa and him opposite me, he opened up. "First, I assume you know I contacted Caesar French for assistance in locating a non-scientist who can translate the German documents Nadiya received from her grandfather. Caesar assures me he has someone in mind, and I've entrusted him with photocopies of the original documents."

*That was your first mistake*, I thought. I didn't let on that Caesar was already well ahead on that front and had taken me to Puerto Rico to enlist the assistance of the entire Los Equis cartel in developing the machine in the plans. Instead, I deflected the direction of our conversation. "Speaking of Caesar, he shared a little of your story with me. It is an amazing tale of successful creativity. You have achieved the great American Dream."

"Yes, you see the obvious all around you. But it comes at a great cost. Although I have friends, Caesar among them, I have come into contact with many charlatans who would like to relieve me of the burden of managing such wealth. My wife, son, and daughter are always under the watchful eyes of bodyguards. My home is an electronic castle—the electronics intended to provide security for me and my family."

"I'm sorry to have digressed. You have more to tell me, don't you?"

"Where did I leave off?"

"You were telling me about giving photocopies of the plans to Caesar."

"Yes. But you already knew about that, didn't you?"

"Yes, Caesar shared some of that information with me in the strictest confidence."

"Good. Well, part two of why I asked you here today is I have been doing some research on the characters in the photographs. This Maria Orsic was an interesting duck. I'm not sure if she was legit or a complete fraud. However, it seems she had Hitler wrapped around her pinkie."

I nodded.

"Hitler was highly interested in psychic phenomena and sent teams of men all around the globe to bring rare spiritual and metaphysical antiquities to him...stuff like crystal skulls, the actual Book of the

Dead, the Ghent Altarpiece, and the Holy Grail."

"I've never heard of the Ghent Altarpiece."

"It was the first masterpiece using oil paints, and it supposedly included clues—perhaps a map—to the whereabouts of the Arma Christi. You've probably never heard of that either…"

He was right about that. I shook my head.

"It's a trove of Catholic treasures, including the Ark of the Covenant, the Holy Grail, and the Crown of Thorns. Hitler believed if he possessed these, his armies would be invincible. Maybe he was a little crazy…"

"So how does this relate to my investigation?"

"According to several sources, Maria Orsic received the plans for a new device while in a psychic trance. Some of the details were in languages she didn't know, but they came through her and needed to be translated by experts in languages of antiquity. Anyway, she was friends with Hitler and told him about the plans for the device. He asked her for the plans. She failed to deliver them to him. Then he demanded the plans. When she didn't deliver them, he sent Nazi officials to her home to retrieve them. When they got there, she was gone. Her secretary told Hitler that Miss Orsic had flown to the stars with the Pleiadeans. Hitler had the secretary executed."

I had heard this scenario just the day before from Caesar French, but I played dumb. "Wow, that's some story."

"Yes. And now Nadiya's grandfather has warned her to beware of Maria Orsic. What could that possibly mean?"

There definitely was a connection between the information Henry had gleaned from his research and the information Caesar had obtained through his Romanian connection. I suspected this Maria Orsic impersonator was here in New York and was looking for the documents Nadiya had received from her grandfather. I had to find this young woman.

****

I rolled out of bed at eight in the morning. Roxanne still lay in bed, snoring mildly with a light wheeze when she exhaled.

I dressed quietly and then went downstairs to the kitchen. I popped a generic k-cup into the coffee maker and then unplugged my cell phone from its charger and checked my messages. I had only one. It was from Nadiya Bodnar: "Hello, Mr. Jones. I'm sorry to bother you, but I am worried for my safety. Please call me as soon as possible."

When my coffee was ready, I stepped outside onto the stone patio, sat down in an Adirondack chair, and returned Nadiya's call.

"Mr. Jones," she said. "I think we may have a problem. Pyotr Berezovsky has moved in next door."

I had never heard of him, but I am no expert on international affairs. "Who is he?"

"He is an oligarch...a Russian oligarch. Among other things, he owns sixty percent of Uleigaz, Russia's sixth largest gas and oil producer."

"Why is this a problem?"

"Don't you see the connection? He is Russian, and he has moved in next door to me, a Ukrainian refugee. I fear when he learns of my presence, he will have me killed the way the Russians are killing so many Ukrainians."

"Have you asked Henry about him and told him of

93

your fear?"

"Yes. He says he has met Mr. Berezovsky, and they have spoken about his relocation to the United States."

"So that's a great question: Why would a rich Russian move to the USA? You would think he would stay in Russia so he could manage his wealth."

"He told Mr. Hawkes he relocated here so he wouldn't be sanctioned by the American government. He has purchased the Rockefeller Retreat and has applied for citizenship to prevent seizure of his 300-foot yacht, which is moored in Key Largo."

"All that makes sense, I suppose. Maybe there's more to it, but we'll have to see how he behaves."

"Do you think he knows about Grandfather's plans for the German anti-gravity machine?"

"I doubt it, Nadiya. But I'll see what I can learn. Just continue to express your concerns to Henry and Elizabeth. I'm certain they will protect you."

Later in the morning I called Henry and told him of Nadiya's fears.

"I don't think she's got anything to worry about," Henry said. "Soon, Nadiya and Pyotr both will be American citizens. Besides, he's busy fortifying the old Rockefeller Retreat. Bulldozers have been working for three days. A wagon train of concrete trucks passed this way just yesterday. He's probably making bunkers in case we go to war with Russia. Since his defection, I think he lives in fear of reprisal by the FSB. That's the organization which replaced the KGB when the Soviet Union collapsed at the end of the Cold War."

"Well, maybe you or Elizabeth should speak with Nadiya and try to calm her fears."

"Will do. By the way, I've invited Pyotr and his wife to dinner next week. Would you like to join us?"

"Thanks. I appreciate the offer, but I have other plans."

Chapter 14

I turned at the sound of sandpaper on concrete. It was Roxanne shuffling her feet in leather-soled slippers on the patio's stone surface. "Was that your new squeeze?"

"No, that was Henry Hawkes. Some rich Russian big wig has moved in next door, and Nadiya is afraid he's there to torment her."

Roxanne kissed me and then looked at my cup of drip coffee. "Pour that stuff out. Let me make us a cup of better stuff."

I did as she asked and watched my coffee slowly sink into the soil beneath an evergreen bush. I hoped the shot of caffeine wouldn't kill it.

We went back inside. Roxanne pulled a chrome percolator from a lower cabinet and filled it with water from a container in her refrigerator. Then she removed two canisters from her refrigerator's freezer and shoveled a couple of scoops of ground coffee from each into the percolator's metal basket. "It's best to start with cold filtered water," she said, "and freshly ground coffee." She could see the skepticism on my face. "I use a mixture of arabica and Kona coffees. It makes a good cup of joe."

"You sound like a Marine, Roxanne."

"I thought I should use vocabulary you would understand."

I smiled and gave her another kiss. "You're always thinking of me."

When the coffee was ready, Roxanne poured us both a cup, and we sat on the stools at her kitchen island. "Will you be home early tonight?" she asked.

"I hope so."

"The girls are coming over. They want you to participate in our divination exercise. You should find it interesting."

I sipped at my coffee. It definitely was better than the stuff that trickles out of the drip machine. "I thought you told me men are forbidden at your all-female ceremonies. You said something about how our testosterone interferes with the natural order of the cosmos."

"Yes, I did tell you that. But I was talking about our ceremonies. This is an exercise, not a ceremony, and we need you present in the room so we can draw images from the energies which are swirling around you. We feel it's the best way to help you solve the murder case you're working on."

So far, Roxanne's ladies hadn't given me much help. "The woman deceives you" meant nothing at all. I knew too many women: Helen, Nadiya, and Elizabeth among them. Maybe they could clarify that clue for me. "Okay, I guess it wouldn't hurt. I don't have much else to go on."

"Good. Don't drink anything alcoholic today. Alcohol interferes with the process."

I rolled my eyes. "Not even a beer?"

She gave me a stern look. "Not even a beer."

\*\*\*\*

Roxanne and I had finished a light dinner, and I

was cleaning the dishes when five women arrived in two cars and entered Roxanne's home without knocking. Each one carried a brown paper bag and placed it on the dining room table. The gathering had begun.

I tried to stay out of the way while the ladies squealed and hugged Roxanne the way ladies do when excitement is in the air. But one woman, a slightly rotund brunette with bright blue eyes saw me standing against the wall and pulled me into the center of the small crowd.

"Here he is, ladies," she squealed, "our guest of honor."

I hoped they weren't planning to roast me and eat me for supper.

Quickly, I felt hands touching me from all directions and heard embarrassing comments from some.

"Oh, he's not so hard on the eyes, Roxanne. Can we share?"

"He's a little meaty around the middle...are you over-feeding him?"

"Not bad for used merchandise. How much did he cost you?"

"You're certain he's not a breeder? Better watch out...even an unproven stud can occasionally undo an egg."

Roxanne's face was flushed, and her embarrassment was ear to ear. "Now don't get carried away, girls. He's all mine unless he does something to annoy me. Then I'll throw him out, and you can do with him what you will."

Another barrage of squeals erupted.

Roxanne poured non-alcoholic fruit drinks for her guests, and then the ladies each took a chair from around the dining room table and moved it into the living room. They formed a circle and placed Roxanne's white leather Ottoman in the center.

Roxanne pointed at the Ottoman. "You sit there, Barty. Face the window." I moved through the chairs and sat as directed. She turned toward the women. "Ladies, don our apparel."

The ladies moved back to the dining room table, and each opened the bag she had carried into the house. Out came five sanguine robes. The ladies slipped them over their heads and raised the hoods until only their faces could be seen.

Roxanne removed her robe from a hook behind the dining room door, and quickly slipped it over her head. She adjusted her hood. "Just a reminder, girls: Our guest is seeking our help to solve the mystery of who killed an elderly gentleman from Ukraine." Then she pointed toward the living room. "To the enchanted circle, ladies."

The women followed her into the living room and stood in front of their respective chairs. They all looked toward the chubby one who had pulled me into the group. Standing directly in front of me, she raised her hands toward the ceiling and then brought them to her waist. The ladies all sat in unison, drinks still in hand.

Roxanne began the ritual. "Position your drink between your legs and hold the glass with both thighs." She paused a moment and then began guiding the ladies through a relaxation exercise. "Ten deep breaths, girls. Inhale slowly through your noses and exhale even slower through your mouths. As you're doing this, empty your minds of everything. Remove all the clutter. If you find yourselves drifting, recenter your concentration upon thinking of absolutely nothing."

I fixed my eyes upon the chubby woman. Maybe my mind was playing games with me, but as she inhaled and exhaled, her face seemed to relax.

Roxanne's voice became gentler. "Focus on the male entity in the center of the circle. See the colors swirling around him. Feel them. The reds and yellows are warm. The blues and greens are cool." She waited thirty seconds and then spoke again. "Sense any other colors or vibrations that seem to emanate from outside his aura. Listen to them with all your senses. What are they saying to you?"

The chubby one leaned backwards, her face raised toward the ceiling. Her lower jaw trembled. I hoped she wasn't having a seizure. To her right, a woman with bushy red eyebrows and pock-marked cheeks seemed to be in REM sleep. Her eyelids flickered as, behind them, her eyes moved quickly right then left, then back again.

Ten minutes elapsed. Finally, Roxanne spoke. "When you are ready, open your eyes and be in the present again. Take small sips of your drink." Roxanne moved around the circle placing a small notebook and a pencil on each woman's lap. "Whenever you're ready, jot down notes of what you saw or heard. Draw sketches if you'd like. We'll share when all are done."

Ten minutes passed while all the women wrote or drew on the pages in their notebooks.

"Who'd like to begin? ...Marian?"

A thin woman with short yellow hair turned a few pages in her notebook. "Oooh, he is a busy one, this one. He's got worries, some of them about himself and his finances, but some of them about others...maybe a foreigner or a group of foreigners. They've got problems, too. I see influences from south of our border playing tricks on him, playing with his mind."

"Excellent work," Roxanne said. "Does anyone agree or disagree with Marian's reception?"

The woman with the pockmarks raised her hand to her shoulder. "I think I'd like to try, Roxanne."

Roxanne nodded.

"This is your lover, but I suppose we all knew that without having to learn it from the ethers. There's a tie which binds the two of you, like you had something going on at an astral level before he came into your life in the physical. He needs your support...all our support...to find victory against evil ones who seek to befuddle him. They're using descendants of the Conquistadors to steal away something powerful. It's a tool or a weapon of some kind. Your fella must be careful. I see him looking down on Earth, like from another planet or from the spiritual realm."

This woman's perception amazed me. She saw Caesar or maybe the cartel as descendants of the Conquistadors, and she saw me looking down on Earth. I hoped she didn't see me dead, but maybe circling the globe inside the flying machine Caesar was planning to build.

"Interesting, Brenda," Roxanne said. "I believe that the foreigners Marian saw connected with the Hispanics you saw. We'll leave the rest until we've heard from our other sisters. ...Next?"

Without hesitation, a woman with carrot-colored curls and a couple of facial growths spoke up. "I saw the evil one that Brenda saw. She's a young woman. I see death hovering around her. Also, I saw a woman crying in terror in a small room with a locked door. Her plight will arrive soon. She spoke…it was not English…perhaps Slavic?"

"Interesting, Louise," Roxanne said. She motioned in the direction of a black woman with dreadlocks. "What did you see, Phoenicia?"

"I saw a black sister angry at this dude. He hasn't been honest with her. She loves him but can't act on her feelings."

"Did you see anything else? Did you see the evil woman?" Roxanne asked.

"No. But the sister I saw could help him on his quest, yet he's afraid to let her know too much. There's something dishonest in the shadows, perhaps dishonest about him…perhaps dishonest with the others he's hanging with. He's walking a tightrope of his own making. When he falls, she will try to catch him. His weight may crush them both."

Great. This one was locked in on my relationship with Helen. And Roxanne was giving me the onceover, as though I were hiding a girlfriend from her. I wanted to crawl into a hole.

Roxanne looked at the last woman, the chubby one who had begun the psychic exercise. "Can you help us pull all this together, Bernadette?"

"Yes. The young woman is definite. She's not evil, but deceptive. And I, too, saw the hand of Death hovering above her. Also, I felt the presence of this gentleman in space…not so much that he was looking down on Earth, but that his work will enable others to do so. And I saw the Great American Land Rush…but the wagons were racing not across the prairies but among the stars. I must have seen that incorrectly…it was all so confusing."

It was Roxanne's turn. She cleared her throat and then took a sip of liquid from her glass. "I saw the death of an elderly foreign gentleman at the hand of a young woman who soon will die as the result of her own deceptions. I felt an airplane signaling distress, but salvation with no deaths. I felt new life growing in a woman's womb."

The chubby woman gasped. "Yours, Roxy?"

Roxanne placed her hands on her abdomen. "I think not, but greater surprises have occurred."

The stuff Roxanne said about the airplane made no sense to me. I'd have to wait and see. Clearly, Kuzma Bodnar had been poisoned by a young woman. Maybe a nurse? I wasn't sure. But I knew I'd have to be on the lookout for an evil or deceptive young woman, most likely the Romanian who was impersonating Maria Orsic. Could the deceptive young woman be Nadiya? And Roxanne couldn't be pregnant. She was taking birth control pills—I think. I'd have to wait and see about that one, too. I was also amazed that the ladies picked up on the space initiative Caesar and his cartel were launching. I could see a land rush in the form of SpaceX, NASA, Amazon, Russia, China, and Los Equis, all attempting to establish footholds on the moon, Mars, and every other planet in our solar system. Quite possibly, the future was going to be a competitive calamity.

Chapter 15

Father Eamon Shea sprinkled holy water on the casket and then extended his hand like a karate expert prepared to split a board. "As with all who have gone before us marked through holy baptism with the sign of faith, our departed friend and grandfather Kuzma Bodnar awaits the glory of the Resurrection. We commend his soul into the protection afforded by our Lord and savior Jesus Christ." He made the sign of the cross with sweeping movements of his arm. "In the name of the Father, the Son, and the Holy Ghost. Amen."

It had been a small funeral, more of an interment than a religious ritual, and it was attended by only the Hawkes, Nadiya Bodnar, funeral home staff, and a Roman Catholic priest, who read the ritual's prayers from a small black handbook—words he had not put to memory.

Four men, all employees of a small funeral home and dressed in black suits and white gloves, grasped the ends of hemp ropes and slowly lowered the pine coffin into the freshly dug grave. When the coffin was resting on two four by fours at the bottom of the grave, they retrieved the ropes, coiled them, and placed them on a green plastic tarp which lay beside the grave.

Nadiya Bodnar bent modestly to the ground, grasped a handful of dirt, and tossed it onto the coffin below her. Then Henry Hawkes helped her rise to a standing position. She pulled a white cotton handkerchief from her pocket and wiped her hands. Behind her black veil, her eyes were full of tears.

Father Shea approached the mourners. "I didn't know your grandfather, Nadiya, but if he was anything like you, he was a devout Catholic and a loving man."

Henry pulled an envelope from his coat pocket and handed it to the priest. "Thank you for your services this morning, father. And thank you for helping us to find an empty grave in this holy cemetery. Nadiya loved her grandfather very much, and now she will be able to visit here to pray for his soul."

"It was my pleasure, Henry. I hope to see you at Mass more often."

"Yes, I will be there often, if only to support Nadiya and her love of family."

Father Shea turned and walked to his new black executive sedan.

Henry said a few words to the funeral home staff who had coordinated the internment ceremonies, and then he escorted Elizabeth and Nadiya toward their steel gray sedan. He opened the door for his wife, and then for Nadiya. As Nadiya bent down to climb in, a man's voice asked, "Miss Bodnar?"

Nadiya looked up and then straightened her posture. "Yes?"

A tall gentleman in a navy-blue suit and dark sunglasses was standing beside a green SUV which was parked in front of the Hawkes. His left hand was on the top of its door frame and his balding head reflected the sun's glare. "Miss Bodnar, my name is Special Agent Walter Flynt. I'm an FBI agent on assignment to the

United State Department of State. Is there someplace we could speak in private?"

Henry puffed his chest and positioned himself between the young nanny and the tall stranger. "What business do you have with our nanny? This is a sad day. She has just buried her grandfather. You should have better sense than to harass her on this day."

"I'm not trying to harass anyone, Mr. Hawkes. We just have a small international problem that your employee may be able to help us put to bed."

Nadiya touched Henry's bicep with her right hand. "It is okay, Mr. Hawkes. This man is with the government. Perhaps I should hear what he has to say."

The agent nodded. "That's right, ma'am. We wouldn't want anything to interfere with your citizenship application, would we?"

Nadiya froze at the serious tone in his voice and the threat in his words. How did he know she recently had applied for citizenship? Could he possibly have the power to have her application denied?

"How about your home, Mr. Hawkes? Can Miss Bodnar and I meet there?"

Henry stiffened. The veins in his neck and forehead stood at attention. "There is a coffee shop at the intersection of VanDerwald and Onondaga Streets. We'll meet you there in five minutes."

"If you don't, I'll see you at your home later today with a team of FBI agents and State police."

"Enough with the threats, sir. This is a sad day. There is no need to try to intimidate us. Besides, friends are expecting us at home to offer Nadiya their condolences. You are going to make her late. This meeting could have waited until tomorrow."

When they entered the convenience store a few minutes later, Nadiya and Elizabeth sat in an empty booth while Henry prepared three coffees. Before he could approach the cashier, Agent Flynt stepped in front of him and held a ten-dollar bill out to her. "I'll pay for his three coffees and my bottle of water." He turned to Henry. "You want a donut or something?"

Henry shook his head and joined Nadiya and Elizabeth in the booth. Nadiya had already used a handful of napkins to wipe its tabletop clean.

Agent Flynt placed his bottle of water on the tabletop and stood at the end of the booth. "I'm sure you're all interested in why I would approach you at a funeral. It's federal government business. The State Department has received a complaint from the Russian government that at the time of his death your grandfather was in possession of certain classified documents which belong to Russia. They want them back."

Nadiya folded her arms. "Grandfather died only a few days ago. How would Russia know about his death unless one of their own secret agents killed him?"

"Miss Bodnar, I don't have an answer to your question. All I know is that the State Department was contacted by Russia two days ago. Whoever called was very direct about what they are seeking and indicated there would be serious international repercussions if that paperwork is not returned immediately."

Henry jammed his finger into the top of the orange Formica tabletop. "Then why bother Nadiya? You should go to his motel and search through his belongings. He never came to our home, and she only saw him for less than one minute in the hospital the evening after his surgery."

Agent Flynt opened his palms. "Mr. Hawkes...may I call you Henry? We are simply attempting to recover the stolen documents and return them to their rightful owner, the Russian government."

"Mr. Flynt," Nadiya said, "Mr. Hawkes is telling you the truth. I saw my grandfather for less than one minute in the hospital, and he was totally unconscious."

"But the police report says you called 9-1-1 for an ambulance. So, you were in his motel room and had the opportunity to speak with him before the medics arrived. You were also there long enough to go through his things and take whatever you wanted."

Henry jammed his finger into the tabletop again. "Are you calling my wife a thief? She didn't take anything from that damn room except some of his blood on her fingers. Maybe the stuff you're looking for was taken by the person who shot Nadiya's grandfather."

"So, she was there too?"

Elizabeth placed her hand over Henry's. "Yes, Mr.—"

"It's Flynt. Special Agent Flynt."

"Yes, Agent Flynt. When Nadiya and I went to see her grandfather at the motel, his room door was open. We found him bleeding to death. We called 9-1-1, and they came to the room and took him to the hospital. We followed the ambulance. We didn't see any paperwork in the room, we didn't look in his luggage, and we didn't take anything. Not even his wallet."

Henry moved his hand from beneath Elizabeth's and pointed his finger at Flynt. "Are you aware somebody poisoned Nadiya's grandfather after his surgery? He was murdered in the hospital, not in his motel room. Whoever did that probably has those documents you are trying to find."

"So, you don't have the documents in your possession?"

"No," Henry said. "Neither of these ladies is in possession of those documents. You can come and search our home if you must, but you won't find them there."

Agent Flynt opened the screwcap on his bottle of water and took three swallows. "Russia is not going to be happy about this…"

"What about her grandfather's murder?" Henry asked. "Does Russia care about that? Do they care about the deaths of any Ukrainians?"

Agent Flynt shrugged his shoulders.

Henry pressed on. "And does the FBI care enough about Mr. Bodnar to find his killer? You're never going to find those documents until you find his killer."

Agent Flynt thanked Nadiya and the Hawkes for their time. They waited until he left the coffee shop before uttering a word to each other. Henry was the first to speak. "Thank you for not telling Agent Flynt that I have the documents."

"If both Russia and your FBI are interested in the documents, they must be very important," Nadiya said.

"Yes," Elizabeth nodded. "And more valuable than any of us ever imagined."

Chapter 16

"Caesar, this is Henry Hawkes."

"Hello, my friend. How can I help you? You want to play eighteen?"

"Not today, unfortunately. But I do have two questions for you. First, have you had any success with translating the German drawings?"

"Yes," Caesar lied. "I am expecting them to be delivered later today. I'll bring them right over to you."

"No, please. Let me come to you when you have them."

"Yes, of course. You've never seen my operation. I would be happy to show you around."

"Let's just discuss the drawings today and save the tour for another day."

"Yes, if you wish."

"My second question, though: Do you have any influence with the Federal Bureau of Investigation or the US State Department?"

"Not me, personally. But our mutual friend, Mr. Jones, has a special relationship with an FBI agent who works out of Washington, DC. Perhaps he can be of some help to you."

"Excellent. I'll call him today."

**** 

Henry Hawkes called me mid-afternoon and told me about his encounter with the FBI.

"They know about the drawings Nadiya's grandfather had in his possession and they want them. They say the drawings must be returned to Russia, the rightful owner."

Henry gave me the name of the agent who had interviewed him.

I called Mona Casola, an FBI Special Agent who helped me with the case of Baby X several years ago.

"Mona Casola."

She sounded all business this morning.

"Mona, it's Bart Jones from Willow Falls. Sorry to bother you so early."

"Hey, Bart. What can I do for you?"

"Can you get me some information on one of your agents? His name is Special Agent Walter Flynt."

Mona snorted into the receiver. "We're all special agents. It's nothing special. But I don't know him. What can you tell me?"

"He says he's on special assignment, working on behalf of the government of Russia. He's hassling the nanny of a nice couple here in town. He says Russia wants some drawings the nanny allegedly has, and he's trying to prevent an international incident."

"Gimme some time. Maybe a couple of hours. Can I call you back at this number?"

"Sure. That would be great."

\*\*\*\*

I left home at four to meet with Caesar and Henry Hawkes at Cabrillo Construction at four thirty. I had driven four blocks when my cell phone rang. I touched the screen on my dashboard and answered the call. It was Mona Casola. I pulled over so I could concentrate on what she had to say.

"Whatcha got for me?" I asked.

"Five years ago, your guy was booted out of the Bureau for committing fraud. He's not an agent, at least not one of ours. He may be working for the Russian government, but if he is, it's nothing official. He may be a hired gun."

"Son of a..." I replied. "This is getting interesting."

"That's all I've got, Bart. Call me again if you learn anything more about him. I've already reported his alleged actions to my boss. We probably ought to collar him if we can catch him in the act of impersonating a special agent."

Mona seemed anxious to go, so I avoided any small talk. After she hung up, I put my car into drive and found my way to Cabrillo Construction.

Laverne greeted me at the door as I entered. She had her purse in her arms and was wearing a red canvas three-quarter length coat, so I knew she was headed out.

I walked through the door to the back hallway and knocked on Caesar's office door.

"Come in," he called out.

Henry Hawkes was with him, looking closely at paperwork Caesar had shared with him.

"It's good I have you both," I said. "I got some information on my way over here, and I think you'll find it interesting."

Henry looked up at me.

"You know that guy, Flynt? I need to know if he calls you again, and especially if he wants to meet with you another time, no matter where or when he wants to meet."

Henry lowered the papers he was holding. "This sounds ominous..."

"You have some concerns, my friend?" Caesar said.

"It's just that he's a liar. He's not with the FBI. He was drummed out for fraud five years ago."

Caesar's eyebrows touched each other. "So, he's running some kind of scam? Well, the drawings and instructions will take him nowhere, right? We're going to take care of that."

"What's your plan?"

"Henry and I have decided to get him off Nadiya's back by giving him what he wants, except they'll be fake plans. The drawings and their specifications will be altered... you know, different materials and different operating systems. If it flies at all, what we give them won't go anywhere."

"That may buy you some time, but you don't know who he's working for or what they'll do if they figure out the drawings are fakes." I nodded toward the paperwork Henry was holding. "Are you willing to share with me what you've learned?"

He looked at Caesar. Caesar nodded.

"You know I have a scientific and electrical engineering background. If this translation is accurate, it appears this device actually may alter how mankind reaches deep space. Certainly, liquid-fueled rockets will go the way of the horse and buggy."

"We plan to build a prototype," Caesar said. "Henry wants to use our Scentless trash facility to build and test-fly a prototype. If it works, Cabrillo Construction will build him a hangar out in Altamont and develop the full-scale model out there."

"Where will you find the expertise to build the prototype?"

"Henry and I spoke with La Araña this afternoon. He will get us the expertise we need—a small team of scientists who formerly worked at Area 51."

So, it was all coming together for Caesar. La Araña was his counterpart in the southwest. With his involvement, Los Equis was now in full partnership with Henry Hawkes in the development of the anti-gravity machine that Adolf Hitler had hoped to build to win World War II. He might have achieved victory if Maria Orsic hadn't disappeared with those plans. No wonder Russia wanted to get their hands on them.

Chapter 17

"Juaquin, this is El Escondido. Give me a call when you wake up. I have need of your skills."

Caesar French put the office phone back on its receiver. Less than a minute later, it rang.

"Yes, Laverne?"

"Mr. Juaquin Fajardo is on the line. He says you called."

"Put him through, sweetheart."

Several static clicks caused Caesar to pull the phone away from his ear. "This is Juaquin. Do you have need of me, El Escondido?"

"Juaquin, thank you for returning my call so quickly."

"Si, El Escondido. How can I help you?"

"I need you to modify those documents you translated for me."

"When do you need the work done?"

"As soon as you can begin. The work needs to be accomplished here in my office."

****

Caesar and I met with Juaquin Fajardo the next day. He was dressed in jeans and a "Let's go, Brandon" tee shirt when he came into Caesar's office.

"Are you a Conservative?" I asked.

"No, not really. But the current administration's ban on new oil rigs has left me without work. This is the only tee shirt I could find that points to my frustration with the change in leadership in Washington."

I felt some sympathy for Juaquin. Although the administration's turn away from fossil fuels didn't directly affect my employment, I wasn't happy with the "Defund the Police" movement because when it swept into Willow Falls, it cost me my job. The current federal administration rode into power on that movement. Well, that was part of it, anyway.

"Come sit, my friend," Caesar said. "El Gringo and I have additional need of your skills."

Juaquin sat in the green plastic chair I had used when Caesar and I met with Henry the day before.

Caesar spun his pointer finger in the air. "The plans you translated for us…are they on your computer?"

"No, El Escondido. I erased all traces of them in case my computer should fall into the wrong hands, you know…like Los Cuernos."

I flipped him the thumbs-up sign. "Good thinking."

"Yes," Caesar said, "but it means more work for you, Juaquin. Work you have already done."

"This is the work you mentioned last night?" Juaquin asked.

"Yes, I need you to draw the plans for a machine, any machine that appears as though it might fly by some unknown power."

Juaquin tilted his head. "Any flying machine?"

"Yes, but it must look like a real spaceship so people who see the drawing will believe it can fly."

Juaquin's expression signaled to us that meeting Caesar's needs would challenge him.

"The internet is full of pictures of Nazi flying

disks," I said. "I think you could use any of them as a model. And you might search web sites for bizarre alternative power sources...you know, the way-out stuff...something which actually might work, but never has been tried. Include one of those power systems in your fake machine."

Juaquin still had questions. "But what if the alternative system I select actually works?"

"Make certain it doesn't," Caesar said. "Change the specifications and materials which are presented with the machine you select." Caesar looked at me. "Are you free today to help Juaquin select an appropriate machine and write fake specifications?"

I had nothing on the burner except finding Kuzma Bodnar's killer. Given my recent vacation to Vieques, I hadn't spent much time on the investigation. So, I had no leads at the moment, and this little project with Juaquin would be a nice diversion until something broke. Meanwhile, by creating fake drawings, Juaquin and I would help Henry Hawkes' problem with the fake FBI agent, and it would help Caesar protect the secrecy of the Los Equis' "Cartel in Space" initiative. And anything which would benefit Caesar would benefit me. Let's get real—Caesar signed my paychecks. "Yes, sure," I said.

Juaquin and I set up a table in an adjoining office which was wired for Wi-Fi service and offered twice the elbow room of Caesar's office. I went to the main office, poured two cups of extra dark roast Colombian coffee, and then sat down beside Juaquin to begin work.

He was already ahead of the starting point. Once I was back in the room, he flipped through three web pages he had saved for consideration. "What do you think of these saucers?"

The first was a traditional Nazi Bell, which looked a lot like the Liberty Bell. "Nope. It looks like an antique. You got anything more modern?"

The second was the Haunebu, which resembled a kid's snow disk, turned upside down, with a turret mounted on top. Three machine guns were mounted beneath it. "That might work," I said, "but machine guns are old technology. If you're going to mount weapons, they should be lasers or missiles."

"Yeah, you're probably right about that."

The third was a Schriever Disc, which was like the traditional flying saucers of sci-fi movies. Its turret rose only a foot or two above the saucer and appeared much more aerodynamic and likely to manage high speed flights than the first two models. "There you go," I said. "Let's use this one as a model."

Juaquin used special software to cut the image of the saucer from the picture on the internet. Then he pasted it on a separate screen and increased the image size so we could carefully inspect it for telltale markings which would easily expose it as a fake. Next, he outlined it and pasted the outline on a third screen. "The outline will give us the basic form for the mechanical rendering."

"Sure," I said. I wasn't up to speed on the terminology he was using, but I understood the gist of it.

While Juaquin continued working on the drawing, I used my cell phone to search the internet for alternative power sources. I was intrigued by the WEAV motor, which uses magnetohydrodynamics to propel an object, until I saw that it didn't work in a vacuum. Space, of course, essentially is a vacuum.

Then I saw information about a plasma drive system, in which a vehicle is covered in electrodes which drive positive electrons away from surrounding gases, causing lift. Again, space is essentially a vacuum where gasses do not exist in quantities large enough to generate the necessary lift. But, since gasses surround the earth, perhaps the drive could propel a vehicle into space where friction wouldn't slow it down. I thought this system maybe had some possibilities.

Finally, I learned about an alien spacecraft, purportedly captured by the United States, which operated on Element 115, an anti-matter element which exists for only milliseconds in controlled laboratory experiments. I sent the article to Juaquin's computer and asked him to print it.

"You seem excited about this article," Juaquin said.

"The propulsion system it describes sounds realistic enough to be believed, but nobody has the technology to create a stable form of the anti-matter element. Let's design a mock anti-matter generator and let the USA and Argentina try to make it work. Ha!"

"No wonder El Escondido likes you. You can be funny when excited."

At eleven, I took a break and drove to the Burger Shack, where I bought three lunches to go. I knew Caesar liked their double cheeseburgers, so I got one and an order of fries for each of us. When I returned, Caesar was sitting with Juaquin in our workroom. In front of them was an open box of pizza and three plastic cups of soda.

I placed the bag of burgers on the table. Then I looked at Caesar. "Great minds."

Caesar pulled out his cell phone and hit speed dial. "Miguel, have you and your crew eaten yet?" He nodded. "Come to the team room. I have some burgers for you."

A few minutes later, someone knocked on the door. "Enter," Caesar shouted.

Three men entered, dressed in green work clothes which were spotted with oil or grease. Caesar pointed at the bag I had brought into the room. "El Gringo thought you might like an early lunch."

All three men bowed respectfully and then one picked up the bag of burgers. "Thank you, señor. Thank you."

They backed out the door and closed it as they left.

"It was a kind gesture you made toward my men, Jones. Thank you for thinking of them."

"And thank you for ordering us a pizza." I stuffed a piece in my mouth. I would have preferred the burger, but a couple of slices of room temperature pepperoni pizza would hold me over until I was home with Roxanne.

I pointed at the drawing on Juaquin's computer monitor. "What do you think so far, Caesar?"

"So far, so good. The devil is in the details. You know...the thickness of the materials, the assembly instructions, and the terms we use. But I have confidence in the two of you."

Juaquin put down his slice of pizza. "We will do our best, El Escondido. We think borrowing thickness and overall measurements from several examples will keep the American and Russian scientists busy." He moved his mouse and clicked it several times. A cutaway image appeared on his monitor. "You'll be interested in this, too, El Gringo. I found it while you were getting us lunch."

I looked closely at the monitor. The drawing looked like a cutaway of the human skin. "What are all those dots?"

"This is a cutaway drawing of the shell of a flying saucer supposedly captured by the Russians. Each dot represents an electrical conduit."

"Okay," Caesar said, "you're already using terms beyond my comprehension, Juaquin. Tell me in simpler terms."

"Si, El Escondido." Juaquin held up a pencil. "If I cut through this pencil and then make a drawing of what it looks like, I would make a round dot for the lead, a round circle for the wood, and a thin round line for the paint on its exterior. See?"

Caesar pointed at the cutaway. "So, each of those dots represents a wire?"

"Yes. But notice that some wires look like tiny targets."

"Can you increase the size of the image?" I asked.

"Si, El Gringo."

Juaquin touched a couple of keys, and the image appeared magnified. "Do you see the targets now?"

The targets Juaquin was describing looked like bullseyes...five concentric circles. "Yes. What are they?"

Juaquin straightened his back. "The targets are superconductor wires. The center dot is a thin copper wire. The next line represents an insulator of some kind. The next layer is a superconductor material. The fourth layer is a hollow tube for liquid nitrogen. The fifth layer is another layer of insulator material, and the final line is a covering of some kind. Probably synthetic rubber."

I shook my head. "It's so tiny."

"Yeah," Juaquin replied.

Caesar stared at the image for a few seconds. "So, I don't understand that term 'superconductor.' What does it do?"

"Have you ever touched an electric wire and felt heat?"

"Yes, of course."

"That heat is caused by friction, like the heat you make when you rub your hands together. As the electrons of electricity pass through a wire, they rub against the molecules in the metal wire and generate the same kind of heat from friction. The heat is lost power. A superconductor is a special material which, when frozen, conducts electricity without generating heat. There is no friction and no loss of energy."

"You freeze the wire?" Caesar asked.

"Yes. The fourth layer is hollow and liquid nitrogen is pumped through it to freeze the superconductor material."

"So, is the entire shell of the flying saucer frozen?" I asked.

"Maybe, but I don't think so. Here's the interesting thing. There are so many superconductor wires in the shell that the entire vehicle could be an electromagnet. It could be flying entirely on magnetism, using our planet's magnetic fields as the fuel for propulsion."

"Where did you learn all this stuff, Juaquin?" I asked.

"From the newspaper. There's a company in Schenectady which manufactures superconductor wire, but probably not as tiny as these wires. These are microscopic."

Caesar's phone rang. He pulled it from his pocket and looked at its screen. Then, he rose from his chair. "Well, gentlemen, business calls. I think you should use that superconductor stuff in the fake plans. It'll lend them more credibility." He put his phone to his ear and walked out the door. "Ola, Miguel. ¿Qué pasa?"

Juaquin and I went back to work. While he made several detailed drawings of the flying saucer and its various components and systems, I worked on the instructions and information pages, using the original documents as a model. It was tedious work, especially when we needed to confer with each other to be certain the information paralleled the drawings. When we were certain we had finished the project, I found Caesar in his office and asked him to join us.

"How can you be finished already?" he asked. "It's only five o'clock."

Caesar followed me into the room where we had been working. Juaquin handed him a printed set of drawings and a short stack of descriptive papers.

"We may want to sleep on these overnight," I cautioned. "Let's review them again tomorrow. We might find a mistake or two, or maybe something will need additional clarification."

"Good idea, Jones. We should be as thorough as possible." Caesar looked at Juaquin. "Can you give us another few hours tomorrow?"

"Si, El Escondido, at your pleasure."

"Tomorrow, we must make sure the paperwork is translated into German. When have finished the work, we will give it to the Hawkes and their nanny can give it to the fake FBI man, so he can pass it along to the Russians."

\*\*\*\*

Two days later, Caesar called Henry Hawkes and asked him to pick up the fake plans in case he needed to pass them along to Walter Flynt. As misfortune would have it, when Henry arrived home, Flynt was waiting for him at the gate to his estate. Flynt was leaning against the rear hatch of a black SUV, smoking a cigarette. Five butts were ground into the pea stones at his feet.

Henry pulled his car to a stop and rolled down his window. "You should have called me first and you wouldn't have had to wait out here, Agent Flynt. Civilized people make appointments and don't show up at someone's home without an invitation or an appointment."

"Cut the crap, Hawkes. You and I both know if I'd called first, you'd have left town with the plans I want."

Henry opened his mouth to say something, but Flynt pulled a large pistol from the belt behind his back. "You haven't left me much choice, Hawkes. I want those drawings your Ukrainian maid received from her deceased grandfather. It's a matter of national security."

Henry held both palms up toward Flynt. "This is not the way an FBI agent should conduct business, Agent Flynt."

"Sometimes, we have to motivate the people we do business with." He waved his pistol back and forth. "Now, let's drive up to your home together so you can give me what I want."

Henry spoke nervously. "Wha...wha...what you want is in the trunk of my car. Put the g...g...gun down, and I'll get it for you."

"Stay in your car, asshole. Just flip the little button under your dash and pop the trunk lid. I'll get it myself."

Henry did as ordered. When the lid popped open, Flynt walked to the back of Henry's car and pulled out the rolled tube of papers which had been rubber-banded together. He unrolled them. As Flynt stood looking at the drawings, Henry dropped his car into reverse and quickly backed up five feet. Flynt fell to the gravel driveway and yelled something obscene. Henry dropped the car into drive and smashed through the chain-link door to his sliding fence, bringing it tumbling down and scratching his car as he madly wound up the driveway to his home. When he reached the front door, he stopped and looked behind him. Flynt was on his feet. Henry watched as Flynt limped to his SUV, slowly climbed in and drove away. Henry called the New York State Police and reported his encounter with supposed Agent Flynt.

Chapter 18

Pyotr Berezovsky's driver spoke into the kiosk at the entrance to the Hawkes estate. The recently repaired massive steel gate slid to the left permitting him to deliver his passengers to the front of the stone mansion. From his position in the back seat, Berezovsky could see a man and a woman watching their car's arrival from the well-lit second floor balcony.

A minute later, the front door opened. Henry Hawkes stepped out, greeted his guests, and invited them into his home to meet his family. Elizabeth and Cooper waited cordially as the three guests stood and stretched. Henry reached for Elizabeth's arm. "Permit me to introduce my wife, Elizabeth, and my son, Cooper."

"Pleased to meet you all," Berezovsky said. "Where is your lovely daughter? Our intelligence says you have a daughter?"

"Charity is staying overnight with a friend in Marshfield. She's only twelve and much too young to enjoy an adult dinner."

"Ah, yes, of course. We will meet your Charity some other time." He turned to his wife. "This is my wife, Taisiya." And then he turned to a young woman. "And this is our house guest, Mariya. She will be with us for a few months as a graduate exchange student. We thought you wouldn't mind if we brought her along, especially since Mariya and your Cooper are almost the same age."

"No, we don't mind at all," Elizabeth said. "There's plenty of food, and I'm sure the young people will have much to talk about."

There was a knock on the front door. Henry opened it. Berezovsky's driver pushed a two-liter bottle of vodka into his chest. "Uh," Henry stammered. "Oh, thank you."

The driver nodded and then returned to his black stretch limousine.

"Oh, I forgot to bring that with me from the car," Berezovsky explained. "Boris doesn't speak much English, and he can seem gruff, but his heart is in the right place. The vodka is for our enjoyment after we eat. It is very special, made in Russia from Siberian potatoes. It is very rare and hard to come by. Of course, men like us...we can acquire anything we want, no?" He laughed.

Henry and Elizabeth escorted their guests into the great room, where a selection of wines and a charcuterie board stacked with cheeses and olives awaited. "Please," Henry said, "no formalities here. Help yourselves to whatever you would like. Dinner will be served in half an hour."

The six adults poured themselves a variety of wines and placed cheeses onto small plates Elizabeth had provided. Then they sat and chatted.

"How is construction coming along?" Henry asked.

"You know how contractors can be," Pyotr said. "They promise a certain date, and they always take longer. Our shelter should be finished next week. We'll move there until the renovations to our home can be completed."

"Shelter?" Henry asked.

"Yes, a bomb shelter. Weren't they all the rage in your country a few years ago?" Taisiya said.

"Really?" Elizabeth asked. "We have no need of such things here."

"Oh, perhaps you think not, but that North Korean crazy man seems intent on dropping a long-range missile or two onto your country, does he not? We Russians are always prepared for the unforeseen acts of a madman."

Henry changed the subject. "What will you do to stay busy here in the States?"

"Oh, that's easy," Pyotr said, "I will manage my investments during the day, drink vodka and make love to Taisiya during the evening." He laughed again.

While the women listened to Pyotr and Henry chat about business and boring world affairs, Elizabeth noticed Cooper and Mariya were engaged in a quiet conversation of their own, punctuated by her cheerful laughter whenever Cooper said something witty. Mariya was a beautiful blonde woman, with bright blue eyes and an engaging smile. Elizabeth silently feared Cooper would fall head over heels for her. And she was so right. He couldn't take his eyes off Mariya.

At seven thirty, the chef's bell announced dinner was served. "Permit us to present our daughter's nanny and this evening's chef," Elizabeth said. "Nadiya?"

Nadiya walked nervously into the great room from the kitchen. "The Hawkes asked me to prepare something a Russian family would enjoy," she said. "So, I have prepared Ukrainian borsch, chicken Kiev, *varenyky*, and *gombovtsi* for dessert. I hope you will enjoy."

"Ah, excellent," Pyotr exclaimed. "Where did you find such an amazing chef who knows Russia's newest delicacies? We must hire her to cater for us." He laughed again and patted Henry firmly on his shoulder.

Nadiya forced a smile and returned to the kitchen. Once the guests were seated, she served the meal, but instead of serving each person individually, she placed a soup tureen and large platters of each course on the table. Immediately, the guests busied themselves passing platters of food back and forth in traditional American "family style."

After dinner, Cooper rose and addressed Berezovsky. "Sir, would you mind if I escorted Mariya to a club in Albany? I promise to have her back home by midnight."

Pyotr looked at Taisiya. "Do you object, my little pigeon?"

"Let the young do what the young will do," she replied. "She is an adult. If she wants to go with this young man, is her mother here to stop her?"

Pyotr laughed. "So, there you have it, young Mr. Hawkes. Enjoy the evening with our ward. Have her home before dawn." He turned to Henry. "What have you done with the vodka?"

\*\*\*\*

Cooper took Mariya to Albany in his convertible SUV with its top down. Springtime bugs splattered against his windshield in the mild night air. Mariya squealed in delight when he drove through the frigid air which hovered over low spots and small bridges.

When they reached Dante's Inferno, he parked a block away. She straightened her windblown hair, and they walked together to the entrance. He held the door for her and walked inside behind her. In the dim light, they could see a few empty spaces. Cooper asked for a table for two, and the couple was escorted to one along the wall by the Asian hostess.

A waitress appeared shortly after they were seated. "What time does the band play?" Cooper asked.

"They should be arriving any time now. They usually begin at nine thirty."

"Excellent." He returned his gaze to Mariya. "What would you like to drink?"

She tossed her hair back and ran her fingers through it. "A Black Russian, of course."

"Make that two," he told the waitress. "We won't be needing a dinner menu."

"Very well, sir." The waitress returned to the bar.

After their drinks arrived, Cooper and Mariya chatted for a few minutes and then watched the five-member band set up for its performance.

"What style do they play?" Mariya asked.

"They vary every night. Sometimes they play popular music, sometimes country or bluegrass, sometimes big band songs from the fifties."

Mariya inspected the band members. "That's why they still play small venues—they haven't settled into a genre and made it their own."

"You're probably right, but I love their versatility and musicianship. Each guy can play any type of music on any instrument. And I think maybe they get bored with a single genre."

The band played an entire album before taking a break. "Had enough?" Cooper asked.

"Yes," Mariya replied. "Let's find someplace quiet.

I would enjoy learning more about you and your interesting family."

Cooper drove her back into the Helderbergs to an overlook where they could enjoy the view of the distant city lights and the stars above, and where they could chat, as she had asked. He backed into a parking space close to the guardrail and the young couple relocated to his rear-facing back seat. Talk soon gave way to kisses, gentle at first, and then more passionate.

Chapter 19

La Cabra did as he promised and sent four aerospace engineers to Willow Falls to build the antigravity machine detailed in the plans given to Nadiya Bodnar by her grandfather, Kuzma. I wasn't aware of their arrival until almost a week later when Caesar called and asked me to come to his office at Cabrillo Construction.

When I arrived, Caesar was standing in the sun outside the main building, wearing a straw cowboy hat and sunglasses. He held a green container of ice water in his left hand.

"Come with me, Jones. They should meet you, anyway."

I followed Caesar across the street and into a small one-story house owned by Cabrillo Construction. It was the three-bedroom Craftsman where I once was stationed to stake out Cabrillo's main office during the "garbage war" with Onondaga Trash Company.

We entered the side door and walked from the kitchen into the living room. "Good morning, gentlemen," Caesar announced.

Three men looked up from a worktable which had been set up for them. A fourth man came up the hallway from the bedroom area. "We're glad you could make it so quickly, Mr. French," he said.

Caesar shook his hand and then turned to the

others. "Gentlemen, I would like you to meet Bart Jones. He is my security specialist."

The four welcomed me with "hellos" and handshakes. They were dressed similarly in slacks and short-sleeved shirts with geeky prints, most likely from the discount racks at K-Mart.

The spokesperson was a muscular man, possibly in his early sixties. His salt and pepper hair was shaved into a nineteen-fifties' flat top. He wore a single gold wedding band on his left ring finger.

"Mr. French, we have a suggestion for you to consider. We are not altogether convinced the aerodynamics of this vehicle make it flightworthy. The electromagnetic engine holds promise, but before we invest your cash in building the full-scale machine, we would like permission to build a small prototype to test its functionality. Something perhaps less than eight feet in diameter. Would you agree to that?"

Caesar stroked his chin. "I am on a tight timeline, gentlemen. How much delay would such a diversion add to the construction of the full-scale machine?"

"Sir, we think we could have a small prototype ready to launch within two weeks if we begin today," a stout man with grey hair said.

The spokesman held up his hand to silence his associate. "Would you have us invest a quarter of a billion dollars into something that does not fly, or would you rather we constructed a million-dollar prototype that eliminates any doubt about the machine's capabilities?"

Caesar looked at me. "What do you think?"

"Caesar, you've employed four aeronautical experts to construct the only known Munich Device.

Why would you question their suggestion?"

Caesar grunted. "There you have it, gentlemen. El Gringo thinks you should build your prototype. Can you have it ready in ten days?"

"The engine's materials are all here," the spokesperson said. "We just need to fabricate the downsized hull components. Hopefully, you will join us to watch our first test flight a week from this coming Sunday."

"Yes, gentlemen. I look forward to that. Construct your prototype in Building C. Feel free to use any tools that you need."

****

Construction of the prototype Munich Device consumed four weeks, mostly because the engineers could not decide whether to utilize MIT's new polyaramid material or a combination of titanium and nickel called nitinol for the device's exterior. In the end, the conductive qualities of nitinol, as well as it's "memory metal" quality, gave it the edge. The problem was having enough of it manufactured in time for construction of the prototype. The engineers contacted the manufacturer and were able to special order sheets of nitinol and learned from the manufacturer how to bond it together to create a solid surface. That alone took a week and several conference calls. To compound things, the manufacturer had to make the product according to the engineers' specifications and ship it to Cabrillo Construction via special handling. The costs far exceeded anyone's expectations.

Finally, a month later than anticipated, Caesar called me at seven o'clock in the morning. It was a Monday, my phone was recharging, and I was sleeping in. So, he left me a message.

Roxanne was enjoying her third day off. The next morning, she would go back on twelve-hour days at the hospital for seven days straight. Some of those days would stretch into fifteen or eighteen hours. I don't know how health professionals tolerate the stress of such brutal schedules.

She was first to wake. When she rolled over, she unintentionally pulled the covers off me, drawing me into consciousness. "What are you doing up so early?" I moaned.

"It's already nine o'clock, sleepyhead. I have some errands to run. Didn't you say something about wishing I'd make you an egg and olive sandwich with that special garlic dressing from the co-op grocery? Got to shower and run if I'm going to deliver your sandwich by lunchtime."

Within moments, I heard the shower go on in the bathroom. Roxanne would wait thirty seconds for the hot water to reach the upstairs before she climbed into the shower. Just time enough to empty her tanks. I, on the other hand, pulled the puffy satin comforter back over my body and fought for a few more minutes of sleep.

Ten minutes later, the soft patter of bare feet told me Roxanne was out of the shower and moving about the bedroom. Additional sleep was hopeless, so I rose, put on my robe, and let her have the bedroom so she could dress without worrying about disturbing me.

Downstairs, I made a cup of coffee, and then sat in the kitchen looking out the window at Roxanne's back yard, where purple finches were flitting between the ground and a bird feeder she had hung from the branch of a hydrangea tree. Beneath the feeder, the granite patio block was covered with specks of guano. I was certain Roxanne would be asking me to hose it away before the weekend.

My phone pinged. I found it on the counter beside the chrome toaster oven and unplugged it from its charging cable. I had received three messages, the most recent from a news service informing me I could upgrade my subscription to premium status for only six dollars more per month. No thank you. More importantly, however, Caesar had left me a voicemail: "Good morning, Jones. The eggheads think they're ready to launch the prototype. It's scheduled for noon at the parking lot beside building E."

Lunch with Roxanne would have to wait. I climbed the stairs to our bedroom and found Roxanne working with her hair in the bathroom mirror. "Hey, babe, I have to go to work. Caesar has an important project set for noon. I think we'll have to postpone the egg and olive sandwich."

"Oh, do I have to whine and beg, Barty? Can't Caesar do this without you?"

"I'm afraid not. Sorry about lunch. How about I cook us some steaks for dinner, then we can romp in the hot tub before bed?"

Roxanne pouted like a spoiled child. Through the bedroom window behind her I could see the trees were motionless. It was a good day to launch the prototype saucer. "I feel really bad about leaving you in the middle of the day, Roxanne. It's not like I planned it. But I have to jump when Caesar tells me to. He's my paycheck."

"Oh, I know Barty, and I understand. It's just that I

don't get many days off, and when I do, I like to spend them with you. This is the last one for seven days."

"I'll try to make this evening memorable, hon."

"Oh all right, I'll quit acting like a schoolgirl. But you'd better treat me better than ever tonight."

"Or what?"

"Or I'll call in sick tomorrow and make you sand the callouses off my feet."

I winked at her. "I promise I'll be a tiger tonight."

She grunted and went back to primping her hair.

****

I arrived at Cabrillo Construction at eleven thirty and drove around the main building so I could park close to Building E. Six cars and a pickup truck were already waiting for their owners to return from the launch. I parked my car beside Henry Hawkes' black sedan and then walked around the building to the parking lot on the west side. A small crowd of men had gathered around a polished metal object, and three of the engineers were explaining the operation of the prototype.

"Following the design drawings, we installed three landing struts," an engineer explained, "but once the machine is activated, the struts are no longer necessary, except for when in storage. At all other times, the machine simply hovers in place, less than two feet above the ground."

"Amazing," Caesar said. "And the swirling mercury provides the lift? You don't need thrusters like NASA's rocket ships?"

"Yes, the two vats of mercury swirl in opposite directions. When a small electrical current is applied, the effects of gravity are eliminated, and the machine simply rises. Its speed of ascent depends upon the volume of mercury above and below the center point. Internal pumps move the mercury between the upper and lower chambers."

"And, no," a second engineer said. "Thrusters are absolutely unnecessary and would diminish the machine's total payload capacity."

"How many pounds can this little prototype carry, and how many pounds does that mean for a full-sized machine?" Henry Hawkes asked.

The third engineer stepped forward. The noonday sun exposed fingerprints on his eyeglasses. "This prototype should be able to lift almost half a ton. A full-size machine should be able to lift one hundred tons, less the weight of the crew and its food and supplies."

"Remarkable," Caesar said. His eyes met mine and he nodded at me.

"Well, should we begin the beta test?" the first engineer asked. He pointed at a row of steel plates which stood erect between Building E and the prototype. "Gentlemen, for your own protection, please stand behind the steel barriers we have constructed."

I recognized two men in the group as men who had attended the Los Equis meeting on Vieques. Two others may have been their bodyguards.

I stood to Caesar's left and watched the prototype. It looked like a traditional flying saucer, about eight feet in diameter with a small mound located in the center of its top. Its polished aluminum finish did not reflect the sun.

The three engineers stepped backward toward us. One held a metal box which sported several buttons and a single control bar, like you would have found in an old biplane. All three men put on goggles and then stooped onto one knee. The man holding the box conferred for a moment with another engineer and then touched a button. The prototype rose six inches into the air and hovered, almost motionless, the way a hummingbird hovers in front of a flower.

The engineer with the box turned his head toward those of us behind the steel barriers and nodded. He turned back toward the prototype and gently pushed the control bar forward. The prototype instantly shot upward like a bullet and then stopped quickly at one hundred feet in the air. In unison, Caesar and the men beside him broke into cheers and patted each other on the back.

Caesar turned to me with a huge grin. "It works, Jones. We're gonna be in business in space!"

The three engineers were equally ecstatic, shaking hands and dancing for joy. Unexpectedly hugged by another, the engineer holding the control box dropped it to the ground. The control lever broke away from the lid of the box.

"Remarkable," Hawkes exclaimed as he pointed toward the sky. "There she goes!"

I looked up again. The prototype accelerated toward the heavens like it had been shot out of a cannon, except its sudden ascent was absolutely silent. In a few seconds, its aluminum exterior faded into the blue of the sky and the machine was completely out of sight.

"Bring it back, gentlemen," Caesar exclaimed.

"We can't," one of the engineers cried. "We broke the control box."

"Where is the saucer?" one of Caesar's associates

asked.

"On its way to the moon," a second engineer said.

We all searched the skies. I could see nothing but baby blue with wisps of thin clouds. Then a bright flash of red and orange lit the sky above us. Immediately, black smoke appeared like a ball of soot which soon became a line in the sky. At the front of the line was a passenger jet. Then the sound of the explosion reached the ground like the low rumble of an earthquake passing through the mountains.

"¡*Joder!* Caesar, we shot down an aeroplane!" one of Caesar's associates shouted.

\*\*\*\*

NBC, CBS, ABC, Fox, and Newsmax all carried the same story at the top of the evening news:

American Airlines Flight 646 out of Philadelphia lost one of its four engines over Albany, New York, at noon today, when the large passenger jet was struck by a drone of unknown origin during its approach to Albany International Airport. Fortunately, Captain Samuel Longworth saved the day when he and his co-pilot negotiated the plane and its three hundred forty passengers to safety on the airport's busy tarmac. According to an unnamed source, residue on the plane's wing appears to be mercury. The FAA and local authorities are at a loss to explain what a drone was doing at twenty-four thousand feet. Anyone with information about the drone should contact the airport authorities immediately. American Airlines is offering a one-million-dollar reward for information leading to the arrest and conviction of the drone operator. Once again, aviation officials have called for increased restrictions and penalties for drone flights within five miles of any airport.

Chapter 20

Henry Hawkes arrived home at five o'clock in the afternoon. When he pulled up to his front door, a large black vulture launched skyward from beside a ground floor window and flew into the tall sugar maple trees which stood nearby. He wearily climbed out of his car. It was then he noticed a brown lump lying beneath the short row of boxwoods which trimmed his home. He moved closer to inspect it, then gasped in horror. "Marcello!"

Henry hurried to his front door. It was ajar. In his foyer lay Pablo, his other prized mastiff, its throat slit into a gaping smile. Blood had pooled into a four-foot oval on the Italian marble floor. A swarm of flies had congregated above the corpse.

"Elizabeth," he shouted, "why's the door open? Who has done this to our pups?"

Elizabeth did not answer him.

He strode into the kitchen. "Betsy?"

He opened the door to the basement. "Elizabeth? You down there?"

He put his right hand on the end of the hallway banister and called up the stairs. "Elizabeth?...Nadiya? Is anyone home?"

Before Henry could mount the stairs, the telephone rang. He marched to the foyer's side table and picked up the receiver.

It was Elizabeth. "Henry, I—

He heard the sound of cloth being swept across the telephone receiver.

"Elizabeth...are you okay?"

A man's gruff voice greeted him. "Yeah, she's okay. We've just stuffed a washcloth into her mouth."

"What?" Henry couldn't make sense of what he was hearing. "Put Elizabeth back on."

"Here's the deal, asshole. Your pretty little wife and her maid servant won't be home to cook your hamburgers tonight. In fact, they won't be home at all unless you give us those drawings the Ukrainian woman's grandfather sent to her."

"Please don't hurt my wife. I've already given the drawings to the FBI."

"You gave them fake drawings. We want the real ones. And no photocopies. I'll call you again in two days. Same time. I'll tell you where to bring the drawings. If we get what we want, you'll get your wife and the Ukrainian back. If we don't get what we want, you'll just get their heads mailed to you in a cardboard box."

"But wait..."

"Two days. Same time."

The receiver went dead. Then just a dial tone.

\*\*\*\*

When French called me, I was slopping some steak sauce onto a mediocre piece of New York strip steak I had overcooked on Roxanne's gas grill. I had forgotten to time the cooking of each side and chewing the steak's dry, sinewy flesh was my penalty for being imprecise.

"Jones, we got a problem."

"Hi, Caesar. What's up? Did the FAA trace the unknown drone to you?"

"Nothing so simple. Henry Hawkes is in a panic. Elizabeth and Nadiya have been kidnapped. Some guy called him and wanted to trade the women for the original drawings of the antigravity machine. Henry has two days to deliver them, or his wife and nanny will lose their heads."

"Does he have any idea who the kidnapper is? Did he hear anything in the guy's voice that could give his identity away? Did he hear anything in the background during the call which could help us determine her location?"

"I didn't think to ask those questions. Henry is beside himself, and you've got to find his women before the kidnapper does something bad to them. I've already alerted my professional network and offered a twenty-five-thousand-dollar reward for information leading to their safe return."

When Caesar and I hung up, I drove to the Hawkes' home. Henry was wearing out the hardwood floors in front of his picture windows. When he saw me pull up, he stopped his pacing and waited for me to join him upstairs. I entered his foyer and took the elevator to his living area.

"Henry," I said, "Caesar told me about Elizabeth and Nadiya. I'm going to need your help to find them. What can you remember about the caller and what he said?"

We sat on the great room's sofas while he carefully reviewed everything he could remember. I asked the same questions several times, each time trying to pull little bits of information from his subconscious memory. In the end, all I could pull from him was the caller knew the drawings Flynt had been given were fakes, he had spoken to Henry in English, and he had called him "asshole," the same term Flynt had called him several times.

"Do you think it was Flynt?" I asked.

"Maybe, but I can't be sure."

After milking Henry's memory, I drove to Van Rensselaer Drive to see my old friend Pedro "Mescal" Herrera. He and his gang of ne'er-do-wells lived in a neighborhood which had been upper middle class back in the fifties, but which had slowly morphed into an urban slum.

As usual, he was in when I knocked on the plywood door of his headquarters, formerly a sewing machine repair shop. The black death's head painted on the door was peeling.

Mescal was happy to see me. His three gold teeth shone in the glare of the streetlamp above him. His eyes were uncharacteristically sharp, their whites displaying no sign of their usual doping. "Hey, muchacho, long time no see." He slapped my bicep like were old friends. "Wha's happenin'?"

"I could use your help, Mescal. I'm looking for two women, one young and one middle-aged. They're Nadiya Bodnar and Elizabeth Hawkes. They were kidnapped from Mrs. Hawkes' home sometime today."

"So I heard. Is it true that El Escondido is offering a reward for their return?"

"Their safe return, yes. Even for less than that. Twenty-five thousand dollars. If the information he receives leads to her safe return, he'll reward the guy who gave him the information. Have you heard anything about who might have taken her?"

"Hawkes is doing business with El Escondido, isn't he? Maybe somebody at Onondaga Trash. I heard they're still angry about their warehouse being blown to smithereens by Scentless."

Scentless Waste Management was one of Caesar's two legitimate operations. Well, maybe it was legit on the surface. At least it was licensed by the State of New York. "I don't think Onondaga is the culprit this time. Whoever it is, they want a specific set of mechanical drawings that her husband doesn't have. They've given him two days before they cap their victims."

Mescal nodded thoughtfully. "I'll check around. I could use a nice payday. Maybe go to the cockfights tonight. Somebody there might know something."

"Can I come along?"

Mescal broke into a hearty laugh. "You like the cockfights, don't you, hombre? Bet you wish you weren't no gringo so's you could go without an escort. But, no, not tonight. Gonna do this by myself. Don't wanna split no reward with nobody."

****

After I drove away from Mescal's headquarters, I called Helen and didn't even give her my name before asking her an important question: "Did anybody report that Elizabeth Hawkes and Nadiya Bognar have been kidnapped?"

"Hey. Jonesy. Can't you even say 'Hello' before you get down to business? I've been missing you. No straight brown hairs in my shower drain. Everything is dark and kinky."

"Have you even heard a word I've said, Helen? Has anyone reported that Henry Hawkes' wife and nanny have been kidnapped?"

"Yeah, we know, but the chief wants to give it twenty-four hours before we call in the FBI."

"For what reason? Those women are in mortal danger. They have less than twenty-four hours to live."

"You know how the Bureau works...they take over. They treat us lower than dog poop. Even if the Department finds the ladies, the Bureau's going to take all the credit. Chief's hoping something's gonna break before we need to bother the Bureau."

"Yeah, and the chief's hoping when the ladies are laid out in the morgue, he can pin their untimely deaths upon tardy arrival of the FBI."

I hung up on Helen without saying goodbye.

Chapter 21

The Albany Cockfighting Arena was owned and operated by Julio Prognostico. His silent partner was Caesar French. Julio had stolen a kilo of his godfather's cocaine three years ago. Sale of the kilo to street gangs netted Prognostico almost $25,000, which was enough to purchase an abandoned warehouse from the City of Albany and renovate it into a Puerto Rican-style cockfighting arena. Normally, his godfather would have liberated Prognostico from life for stealing from him, but because Prognostico was his wife's godson, he survived. However, a twenty percent share of each evening's receipts was given to Los Equis in perpetuity to keep the grim reaper at bay.

Mescal and two of his gangbangers paid five dollars each at the door and entered the arena fifteen minutes before the Friday night fights began. Mescal and his lieutenant, "Gonzo" Goins, were flying gang colors and their presence sent a murmur through the crowd. Each man carried two pictures, one of Nadiya and one of Elizabeth Hawkes.

At Mescal's direction, the men split up and moved through the crowd, showing pictures of the women to each attendee at the evening's event. "Do you know who these women are? Have you seen these women? Do you know where they are?" Less important to Mescal was the verbal response from each man they questioned. More important was body language and eyes. "Read their eyes carefully," Mescal told his men. "The eyes never lie."

Mescal had queried his seventh attendee when a man's voice on the loudspeaker announced that the first fight was ready to begin. A young buxom woman moved through the aisle. She was wearing tight, low-cut shorts and a red "Fighting Cock Pilsner" tee shirt. In her left hand she held a fistful of one-dollar bills. In her right were yellow and white pieces of paper and a pen. She prodded Mescal. "Which bird you betting on, señor?"

"Not betting this fight. Maybe the next one."

"Please move so I can get by. I have some eager customers."

Mescal and his men collected at the side of the grandstands. "Study the crowd carefully, muchachos. Look for eyes which are on us and not on the cocks fighting in the ring."

The first match paired a large red rooster against a larger brown rooster. Each bird was wearing chrome spurs, and the birds pecked violently at each other when taunted by their handlers. At the referee's command, the bird handlers dropped their birds onto the sawdust floor. The birds circled each other slowly and then charged with wings spread, rising three feet into the air and swinging their spurred legs at the other's head. The crowd erupted into cheers; hands waved wildly.

The first match lasted almost nine minutes and included three one-minute breaks, probably a record for the Albany arena. It ended when the brown rooster jabbed a spur into his opponent's eye and pinned his head to the floor. The red rooster's handler threw in a towel, but too late to save his bird's life.

Mescal shook his head. "Glad I didn't bet. That one's in the frying pan *mañana*."

"Si," Gonzo said. "I guess we got to get back to finding *las mujeres*."

Mescal nodded. The three men separated and returned to the aisles to question more attendees.

Seven fights later, Mescal questioned two men who seemed suspiciously nervous at the sight of the two women in the pictures he held before them. Both denied knowing anything. However, when pulled aside by the three gangbangers as they exited the arena before the end of the evening's last match, they sniveled fearfully.

"Please don't hurt us, señors," both men pleaded. "We have done nothing to those *mujeres*."

Gonzo pressed the point of his stiletto into the throat of the most vocal man.

"Please don't hurt Pepe," the other begged. "We aren't for certain they are there, but we heard women's voices crying for assistance when we delivered food to a *casa* near Albany. We work as delivery drivers for a deli."

Mescal pressed his hand into the man's throat. "And you didn't report the fearful cries of women to the *policía*?"

The man's eyes widened in fear. "The hombres at the casa are large and made us fearful for ourselves, señor. They had guns. And we are *ilegales*."

"You will show us the *casa*."

"Tonight?"

"Si, tonight."

\*\*\*\*

I heard motorcycles arrive outside Roxanne's home

at half past midnight. Her doorbell rang a few moments later.

"Who could that be, Barty?" she asked wearily. "I have to work tomorrow."

"It's probably for me," I replied. "I'll try to keep them quiet."

I grabbed a robe from a hook on the closet door and hurried downstairs. The doorbell rang a second time before I opened the door.

Five men straddled their motorcycles at the roadside, engines still idling. Two were standing at the door. "I figured it was you, Mescal." I nodded to Gonzo.

"I got some news for you, gringo. I got an address in South Colonie." He handed me a piece of paper. "It's on a dead-end street near that recycling place. Those two women you're looking for...I think they are being held there."

"How did you find them?"

"I got my ways...you know that. Just you can't go there by yourself. There's more than four hombres, and they all got guns."

"Thanks, Mescal. I'll get on it right away."

"If it's them...I didn' see no women. My sources heard women's voices calling for help."

I nodded.

"Don' forget who gets the finder's fee."

"You can count on it."

Mescal pointed at my robe. "You look nice in pink, gringo."

****

I found my cell phone charging beside the toaster oven in the kitchen and punched in Helen's number.

"Whaaa..? Whooo....?"

I could tell I had awakened her from a deep sleep. "Helen, it's me...Bart. Who else would call you at this time of night?"

"What do you want, Jonesy? I was having lunch with a handsome movie star in Barbados..."

"You were dreaming, sweetheart. Back to reality...I have a lead on the whereabouts of those two kidnapped women."

"What?"

"I think I know where Elizabeth Hawkes and Nadiya Bodnar are being held captive."

"Chief doesn't want us to move on their kidnapping until the day after tomorrow."

"They'll be cadavers by then. We can go get them first thing tomorrow morning."

"Better we strike at night. Tomorrow night."

"No telling if they'll still be at this location...or if they'll be alive tomorrow night."

"We need a search warrant."

"Not if there's credible evidence they're being held captive."

"Aw, Jones," Helen complained, "why'd you wake me up? Are you certain about their whereabouts?"

"I have an address. Women's voices were heard coming from inside, calling for help."

"Okay, okay...Where do you want to meet?"

"The recycling center in South Colonie. No berries or cherries. Wear Kevlar. Bring semiautomatics and ARs. The guys holding them hostage are heavily armed."

"Give me a couple of hours. I got to round up an assault team. Everybody's home in bed."

"Call me when you're assembled, and I'll meet you at the recycling center."

"Okay."

"Oh, and Helen…don't put your head back down on your pillow."

## Chapter 22

Helen texted me at 4:00 a.m. She and four other officers were in tactical assault gear and leaving the department in two vehicles. She expected to arrive at the South Colonie Town Recycling Center at 4:20 a.m. We would confer briefly about the target house and then launch our rescue mission at 4:30 a.m, give or take five minutes.

I got to the recycling center at 4:22 a.m. Helen and her team weren't there yet. Soon, however, two black SUVs pulled into the parking lot. Helen and the four officers stepped out of their vehicles and approached me. Helen flipped her thumb in the general direction of the four men. "I think you know these guys, Jonesy: Bergen, Roselli, Sosnowski, and Johnston.

I nodded. They were the same team who had helped me rescue Helen eighteen months ago when she was kidnapped by a sanguinarian cult intent on killing her so they could drink her rare O-negative blood. They were a good team, meaning they knew what to do, were quick about it, and didn't let personal bullshit get in the way of performance.

I handed out the photos of Elizabeth and Nadiya. "We're looking for these two women. We suspect they're under heavily armed guard. We've been told there may be as many as seven men inside. Maybe some are outside."

"This could be a small war," Roselli said. "Especially if they have any outside cameras or digital early warning devices."

Roselli was right about that. We could have been walking into a major firefight. And we did.

We traveled to the "hostage house" in Helen's two vehicles. No sooner had we pulled up to the curb in front of the 1950s Craftsman than shots rang out from the house's side porch. The bursts of bright light from the muzzle of an AR or AK blinded us, and we all hit the ground. Nobody was hurt, but the side windows of both vehicles were shot out. Excited but unintelligible shouts from several males spilled out of the house. The lights came on and then quickly went out again.

Helen and Johnston moved left, to the yard of an abandoned house with overgrown hedges which separated it from the hostage house. Sosnowski and Roselli moved right. Bergen and I stayed front and center and returned fire to draw attention away from our team members who were moving to the sides. Intentionally, we fired high so as not to wound the captives, if they were truly inside.

Helen heard a window break at the rear of the house, but she couldn't reach the backyard in time to see if anyone escaped from our onslaught. When she appeared through the bushes, the back door swung open, and a man fired a burst of rounds at her. Two hit her in the leg, but she returned fire and the man went down, hanging limp across the porch's black steel banister. She fell to the ground and pulled her radio from her belt. "Officer down. Back yard. Officer down."

Bergen heard Helen's call for help and shouted at

me. "Someone's down out back. I think it's Martin."

Helen! Instinctively I shouted, "Cover me."

Bergen let fly with six rounds, spaced half a second apart. It was all I needed. I took off to the left of the house, following in the direction Helen and Johnston had gone when we first began our assault. In a few seconds I met Johnston, crouched in the bushes and watching the side porch and windows of the house. "Is that Helen?" he asked. "Is she down?"

"I think so. Stay here. I'm going to see if I can help her."

I found my way through the bushes and peered into the back yard. Helen was sitting on the dew-soaked grass, applying pressure to her right leg. I started toward her. She turned and fired a round at me. Thankfully, she missed. I heard the bullet hit the clapboard exterior of the vacant house next door. Helen uses a nine-millimeter semiautomatic, so I knew the round went through several walls before it settled into one. We'd find it later. "Helen, it's me," I shouted.

"I know that, you dumb ass. Next time, warn a woman before you sneak up on her from behind."

The back door opened again, but the rail rider wouldn't let it open all the way. A large foot thrust outward and pushed at the dead guy. The foot wasn't attached to a uniformed leg, so I fired three quick rounds. The guy went down, but he was trapped inside. I saw his left hand reach for his calf and pull it back inside the door.

Six or seven shots rang out from inside the house. Bullets smacked through the back and side walls of the house and ripped through the leaves of nearby bushes. I heard men shouting, some in English, some in something else. Maybe Polish or Russian. The shooting stopped. Then I heard men giving captives their Miranda Rights.

"Looks like the fight's over," Helen said. "Sounds like our side won."

The back door slammed against the rail rider again. His body slid onto the ground in a heap. A large man limped out the door. He saw us on the ground and fired a shot from a pistol in his left hand. I returned fire with my last two rounds. He went down, and I heard his pistol bounce on concrete.

I turned to comfort Helen, but she was on her back. The look on her face was one of surprise. Blood was streaming from her right arm. The shot fired by the guy I killed had hit her in the right shoulder.

I pulled my cell phone from my pants pocket and punched in 9-1-1. "Police officer down. Three bullet wounds. Small caliber." I gave the address.

The back light came on, and the back door opened again. I was out of ammo, so I was a sitting duck if it was another gunman. I saw Roselli's profile. "You two okay?" he asked. "We're good in here. We got two in cuffs."

"Detective Martin has been hit. I've already called for emergency medical."

Roselli hopped over the bodies outside and hurried to Helen. "How are you doing, Detective? We've got two alive inside. Everyone else bit the big one."

Helen nodded at him. "How about the women? Were there any women inside?"

"Yessir...I mean, ma'am. We have both of them. They were tied and blindfolded in the basement. They're okay now and very thankful for being rescued.

We're going to take them in for debriefing and call their next of kin."

"Why don't you give them the phone and let them call their next of kin. I think Mr. Hawkes would appreciate hearing from his wife and their nanny. Then you get on the phone and tell him you'll call him when they're able to come home."

Roselli nodded. "Yes, ma'am." He turned to me. "Would you mind staying with the detective until the ambulance arrives?"

"It'll be my pleasure."

Roselli went back inside to do what was needed.

"Well, Jonesy," Helen said, "looks like I'm going to the hospital again. How come that happens to me whenever I go out with you?"

"I don't know. I guess you're lucky. Some people go to the morgue."

****

Roselli met with Nadiya and Elizabeth in the same room. Both had been given bottles of spring water. And both shared the same story.

"It was midday," Elizabeth told him. "Henry was away at a business meeting with Caesar French in Willow Falls. Nadiya and I were at home, watching the latest news report on the Russian invasion of Ukraine."

"The Russians are being pushed back from the northeastern cities they captured earlier in the conflict," Nadiya added. "I cheered at that development."

"The dogs were outside and started barking loudly," Elizabeth said. "At first, I thought nothing of it, but then I heard one yelp. Then I heard the front door open. I got up to go see who was there...if Henry was already home. Then I heard another brief yelp."

"I heard Mrs. Hawkes cry out," Nadiya said. "I went to the front door to help her. A large Russian man was tying her wrists together with those plastic straps you can buy at the hardware store. There was blood all over the foyer floor."

"How do you know he was Russian?" Roselli asked, hurriedly taking notes.

"He was wearing Russian military boots, and he spoke to Mrs. Hawkes in Russian."

"You're certain it was Russian and not Czech or some other Slovakian language?"

"I am Ukrainian. I know his tongue. It was Russian."

"Then what happened?" Roselli asked. "Did you try to help Mrs. Hawkes?"

"She didn't have time to help me," Elizabeth said. "My dog was dead. He murdered my dog. Another man came in the door. Nadiya screamed and ran into the kitchen."

Nadiya nodded. "I ran to get a butcher knife to protect myself. Maybe to kill the men and to cut Mrs. Hawkes free. But he was on me before I could get to the knives. He pushed me down onto the kitchen island and tied my wrists with those same plastic straps."

"Yes. When Nadiya was pulled back into the foyer, her hands were tied and she had a black sack over her head," Elizabeth added. "I was still struggling with my captor, but then he covered my head with a sack, too. That's when I knew it was over."

"It?" Roselli asked.

"I knew I couldn't escape, and if I continued to struggle against him, I might get hurt."

"They led us outside," Nadiya said, "and put us in

a large vehicle. I had to sit on my hands. It hurt my wrists to do that. The plastic straps dug into my skin."

Elizabeth sipped from her bottle of spring water and then continued. "They drove us down our driveway and turned left on the main road. I think we drove for almost half an hour and took too many turns to count before they stopped and took us from the vehicle."

"You said the vehicle was large?" Roselli asked.

"Yes," Nadiya said. "Like a big SUV. We weren't in a small car. We had to step up into it."

"Could it have been a bus?" Roselli asked.

"No," Elizabeth said, "Nadiya is correct. It had fake leather bench seats. It could have been a minivan, but it was more like a large SUV or something that size. It was quiet on the road, too...not like a delivery truck."

"Then what happened?" Roselli asked.

"They moved us into the house where you found us. We knew we were in a basement because they took us down steep wooden stairs. The air was damp and cool."

"They made us sit on mattresses of some type," Nadiya said. "Mine felt like a day bed."

"They always had a guard on us," Elizabeth said. "We weren't allowed to talk to each other. They brought us food twice a day, but someone always held it near our mouths. We had to eat it from Styrofoam or paper plates like dogs."

"Yes," Nadiya said. "And when we had to go to the bathroom, we were taken upstairs to a smelly bathroom. A woman stood in the room with us while we eliminated."

"How do you know it was a woman?" Roselli asked.

"She spoke to us…at least to me," Elizabeth said. "She reassured me that we would not be hurt and that no man would see my privates. Strange, isn't it? Those men could have done any number of horrible things to us, but they didn't."

Nadiya nodded. "Yes. She seemed to care about our modesty."

"Did you recognize her voice? Did she have an accent?"

Nadiya shook her head. "No."

Roselli looked at Mrs. Hawkes, seeking an answer.

"No, nothing discernible. It was sort of like Russian or German…maybe a little like Nadiya's voice. I may have heard something like it before, but I'm not sure."

"There was no woman at the house when we rescued you," Roselli said. "Did you hear or see anything else?"

Elizabeth raised her hands to her temples. "Once I tried to use the mattress to pull the sack above my eyes. But when I did, someone pulled it back down and pushed me into a sitting position. He made it clear I wasn't to do that."

"I know a little Russian, but not enough to know everything that was said," Nadiya said. "Two of the men were talking about the woman. They called her 'Printsessa Orsic' and 'the ancient one.' 'Printsessa' means 'Princess.'" She paused for a moment and took a sip from her water bottle. "I think they meant 'Princess Orsic' in a demeaning manner, as though they didn't like taking orders from an older woman. It was like she was in charge."

"Yes," Elizabeth added. "I heard that phrase when

they were speaking, too…'Printsessa Orsic.' But the woman's voice I heard in the bathroom was not the voice of an older woman. She was no older than thirty."

Nadiya placed her palms onto the black Formica tabletop. "Please be sure Mr. Jones knows this information, Officer Roselli. It is very important."

"I'm sure you'll get to see Mr. Jones sometime soon. Maybe later tonight, after you get home." He thought for a moment. "What's so important about this 'Printsessa Orsic'?"

Nadiya sat upright on her steel chair and placed both hands palms down on the tabletop. "Are you aware my grandfather was recently a patient in the Schenectady hospital…and that he was murdered there?"

"Yes, Detective Martin told us that. But I don't get the connection."

"The last thing my grandfather told me was 'Beware of Maria Orsic.'"

Chapter 23

I visited Helen at Willow Falls General, a small hospital located a few blocks east of the police department. I found her on the second floor, lying in a bed with fluids being pumped into her left arm. Her hair was pressed to one side, as though she had been sleeping on it and her face showed wrinkles I had never seen before. "You look great," I lied.

"I saw myself in my cousin's compact this morning. I know I look like shit."

"Given what you've been through, I still say you look great."

"Bergen and Roselli stopped by to see me this morning. They say we got them all, except maybe for an old woman. Any clue who that might be?"

"Not yet. I'd be interested in hearing what the two captured guys said under interrogation."

"Nothing yet. They were Russian, and nobody can understand them. Roselli is planning to contact Albany PD to see if they have a vetted interpreter, maybe somebody from the university."

"Will he contact me to pass along what he learns?"

"Probably not." Helen shifted her weight onto her left hip. "But I'll give you any goodies he tells me. I'm irked those commie bastards put me out of commission for a few weeks. It would tickle me pink to see you find out what's going on and cap a couple other commies for me."

**\*\*\*\***

Once Henry and Elizabeth Hawkes were reunited, Henry gave Caesar French the "go ahead" to begin construction of an aircraft hangar on his property in the Helderbergs, on the condition it be located at least one hundred yards from his home and situated so it would not be visible from his large picture windows. French had his engineers out the next day, surveying and staking out the site, designing water drainage away from the main residence, and chalking the path of a new vehicular driveway from the hangar to the estate's electronic gate.

A day later, French walked the planned area with Henry, explaining the layout and drainage strategy. Henry liked what he saw. So, the very next day, large flatbed trucks bearing the Cabrillo Construction insignia delivered a bulldozer and a large backhoe to the property. The bulldozer carved the new roadway into the mountainside. Then dump trucks delivered fifty tons of rubble followed by #2 gravel, which the bulldozer spread evenly along the roadway. Next, the bulldozer leveled a space large enough to hold the hangar and parking for a dozen vehicles. Once the bulldozer was parked and its motor shut down, the backhoe growled to life and followed the roadway to the flat area where the hangar was to be. The backhoe driver dug the trenches to hold footings for the new building. At the end of the day, concrete trucks delivered enough product to fill the trenches.

"Your men move fast," Hawkes told French. "I thought the heavy equipment work would take at least a week."

"That's the way we work. Besides, we're behind schedule for completion of the antigravity machine. My men have been told to skip breaks and get this job done pronto."

Two days later, dump trucks arrived again and dumped tons and tons of gravel into the space inside the new footings. The bulldozer leveled the stone. At midday, concrete trucks arrived and emptied their contents on top of the gravel. Half a dozen men in rubber boots sloshed through the concrete, using two by fours to level the mud, remove imperfections and eliminate bubbles.

"The foundation is done," French said. "Now we wait for it to dry."

At 7 p.m, Cooper Hawkes and his new girlfriend Mariya arrived home from a drive in the mountains. "What is going on here?" Mariya asked.

"My dad and a friend are working on a secret project. Let's go see what it looks like."

They drove Cooper's 4X4 along the new stone driveway and parked beside the huge wet concrete slab.

"This is enormous," Mariya said. "Are you certain you don't know what it will be used for?"

"No idea. Dad and I don't talk much about his little projects. Maybe he's going to start collecting antique cars or something like that. You never know."

"When you find out, promise me you'll tell me what it is. It's so intriguing."

Five days later, a large crew of men from Cabrillo Construction arrived with a crane and several flatbed trailers of steel girders. Within a day's time, half of the building's vertical skeleton had been erected. At the end of the second day, the skeleton was completed, and the first sheet of steel roofing had been installed. Two days later, the roof and all the walls were in place and electric wiring had been installed. Finally, on the fifth day, the building's large doors and an electric winch system were installed and tested. On Saturday, the four aerospace engineers set up their workstations and oversaw the placement of tools and heavy equipment. Everything was ready, and assembly of the full-scale antigravity machine would begin after materials arrived at the site on Monday.

****

Six weeks passed before Mariya prodded Cooper to look inside the large steel building on the Hawkes' property. They had been out to dinner and then drinking and dancing to live country music outdoors at the Regional Performing Arts Center. It was almost two in the morning before they neared the Berezovskys' property.

"Please don't take me to the Berezovskys' yet," Mariya complained. "We've been living in a bomb shelter. There are no windows, the air is stale, and Mrs. Berezovsky insists on keeping the thermostat at eighty degrees."

"Well, I can't take you home with me because my parents would object to finding you in my bed."

"Can we just drive a little while longer? Maybe drive through Thatcher Park?"

"It's getting late for me, Mariya. My dad wants some assistance outside the hangar first thing in the morning."

"Will he make you mow the grass like some kind of peasant?"

"No, it has something to do with his project. He

wasn't explicit."

"Then take me to the hangar. Let me see what this project might be."

Cooper thought about her request. His father had not forbidden him from going inside the hangar, yet he had not ventured inside of his own volition. What could it hurt? He turned into his own driveway instead of the Berezovskys' and followed the gravel roadway to the hangar.

They climbed out of his truck and quietly opened the hangar's side door. Something large was situated in the middle of the fieldhouse-sized structure, but they couldn't determine what it was in the dark. Cooper found the switches and flicked on the overhead lights.

Mariya gasped.

Cooper looked up, and his jaw dropped. The frame of the circular device was large, disk-shaped, and at least ninety feet in diameter. Its top stood thirty feet in the air. Approximately a third of the device's top was covered in a shell of thin, dull metal, possibly aluminum. The remainder of the device consisted of a maze of framing and wires, all awaiting application of the thin metal shell. The bottom of the device stood seven feet off the floor, supported by three wooden platforms. Beneath the device stood ladders, stepstools, and wheeled toolboxes. Wires hung to the floor in at least half a dozen places.

"What the heck is this?" Cooper asked.

"Look at its shape, Cooper. It looks like a flying saucer. Do you think it could be?"

"My father has some experience in the aerospace industry, but I don't think he's ever worked with rockets or space capsules."

"This is no capsule, silly. Your dad is working with new technology. Do you suppose he invented it himself, or does he have partners?"

"As far as I know, his only partner is Caesar French of Cabrillo Construction. Mr. French built this hangar in a single week."

"He sounds like an ambitious man, this Mr. French."

An inside door opened and slammed shut, startling the young couple. A man's voice called out, "All right, who's in here? Show yourselves."

"It's me. I'm Cooper Hawkes. I live here. Mr. Hawkes is my father."

The man turned in the direction of Cooper and Mariya. He was dressed in desert camo and was wearing a Kevlar vest. He pointed his AK-47 at them. "So, show me some identification. Do you have permission to be here? The vetted employee's list has only eleven names on it, and yours isn't one of them."

Cooper handed the man his wallet. "Call my father, Mr. Hawkes, and tell him you have me at gunpoint. I'm sure he'll be right down."

The guard quickly found Cooper's driver's license, then lowered the muzzle of his weapon. He returned Cooper's wallet. "Your dad isn't going to be happy that you've brought a stranger in here, Mr. Hawkes."

"She's no stranger. She's my girlfriend and our next-door neighbor. Besides all that, my dad isn't going to be happy when he learns while you were on guard duty two people gained entry to his special project area through an unlocked side door."

The guard frowned, pulled a paper from his vest pocket, and waved it in the air in a sweeping motion.

"Why don't you two get out of here and don't come back without first getting your names on this list of authorized employees and visitors."

Cooper held the side door so Mariya could exit the building, then he pulled it shut. He took two steps and then heard the door's deadbolt lock click shut behind him.

"Will that man get into trouble for letting us in?" Mariya asked. "In Romania, he would be written up for dereliction of duty and perhaps lose his job."

"I don't think this project has anything to do with top-secret governmental stuff. I won't report him if you won't."

Mariya slid her arm under Cooper's and pressed her head against his shoulder. "This has been a wonderful evening, Mr. Hawkes. I hope I didn't get you in trouble by asking you to show me the new building."

"Don't worry about me, Mariya. My dad isn't a bad guy or a strict authoritarian. I'll be fine."

"Will you tell him about our encounter with the guard?"

"Probably not. I don't want to get the guard in trouble."

Chapter 24

Caesar French was at home roughhousing on his family room carpet with his twin children, Carmen and Emiliano, when his private cell phone rang. "Alas, you monsters, I have business to attend to. Why don't you watch television or play on your electronic tablets until Mama is home from the market."

The two middle-schoolers hurried upstairs to their bedrooms and closed their doors.

French answered his phone on its eighth ring. "Hello?"

An excited voice answered him in English. French recognized the voice as belonging to Luis Salazar, a gopher who worked directly for La Cabra. "El Escondido, El Escondido, you must come to Sinaloa. La Cabra has been kidnapped."

"When? Who? Have they made ransom demands?"

"No, nothing as yet, señor. But El Escorpión wants all regional leaders to come to Sinaloa immediately. Bring three bad hombres with you. When we find where they're keeping La Cabra, we going to come down on them like Pancho Villa's marauders."

"When and where are we supposed to meet?"

"In two days, at noon, in the back room at Mariana's."

"Tell El Escorpión that New York will be there."

French wasn't happy that El Escorpión had

assumed leadership in La Cabra's absence. He saw El Escorpión as a power-hungry hothead who might even have arranged El Cabra's kidnapping and probable death so he could take over the Los Equis cartel.

****

Cooper drifted through the Hawkes' great room and into the kitchen, where Elizabeth was pouring herself a cup of coffee. He sat on a high-backed wooden stool and rested his elbows on the white granite kitchen island. The morning sun streamed through the home's large windows, causing him to squint as he looked up at his mother.

"What's wrong, baby?" Elizabeth asked. "I hate it when you mope around and look dejected. Can I pour you a cup of coffee?"

Cooper shrugged his shoulders.

Elizabeth lifted a mug from a wall rack, filled it with coffee, and set it in front of him. "Why the long face?"

"I'm bored. There's nothing to do around here."

"Why don't you go visit Mariya? You seem to like her, don't you?"

"She's gone away for a week."

"Oh, that's the problem…you're lovesick. Where's your lovely friend gone?"

"Her parents have rented a condo in Mazatlán, and she's gone to be with them."

"Mazatlán, Mexico? That's a beautiful city. Maybe you should have gone with her."

"Her parents don't know about me yet, so she thought it best if I stay behind this time. She isn't sure how they'd feel about her dating an American."

"What's her nationality, again? I don't think we

learned that when she came to dinner with the Berezovskys."

"She's of German extraction, but her family has been living in Romania since the end of World War II."

"That's interesting." Elizabeth buttered a piece of a saltine cracker and popped it into her mouth. "World War II changed a lot of things for families in Europe. It had to be difficult for her family to relocate...you know, to leave their home and start from scratch somewhere else. I'm certainly glad we've never had to do that."

Cooper opened a drawer and took a slice of wheat bread from a loaf in a plastic container. He then opened a cabinet, retrieved a jar of peanut butter, and lathered the slice of bread with a thick layer of creamy brown paste.

"You have other friends, don't you, honey? Why not rekindle your relationships with them while your sweetheart is away?"

Elizabeth turned at the sound of shuffling feet.

Henry drifted into the kitchen in his summertime pajamas—a white tee shirt and black boxer briefs. His hair was askew, and he needed to shave. "Good morning, all. What's up with you two this morning?"

Elizabeth flicked her eyes toward Cooper. "Our young bachelor is lovesick. His Mariya has gone to visit her parents for a week."

Henry poured himself a mug of coffee and sat across from Cooper. "You know, son, she's only going to be at the university for the fall semester. Eventually she's going to head home to wherever and—"

The house phone rang. Elizabeth answered it and held it out toward Henry. "It's your friend who built the steel fieldhouse in our side yard."

Henry took the receiver from Elizabeth. "Hello?"

"Good morning, Henry. Sorry to bother you. I have to go out of town for a few days on business. You need to keep a sharp eye on those aerospace eggheads who are working on the machine. Keep them in line and on task."

Henry snorted. "I'll do what I can. They're into stuff I know nothing about. Where are you going?"

"Out of town. Listen, if they need anything, you try and get it for them. Money is no object. Just charge it to Cabrillo Construction. If you have to buy something with your own money, save the receipt and I'll settle up with you when I get back."

"What if they ask for you?"

"Just tell them you're acting on my behalf until I return. You're a full partner, and they know it."

"How long will you be gone? Can I call you if I need to?"

"I hope only for one or two days. I may be in Hell, and it's probably better if you don't call me. I'm not sure what I'm getting into down there. If things go really bad, I may not get back at all."

Henry had heard rumors about the questionable activities in which Caesar was engaged and caught the gist of what he was saying between the lines. "Listen, my friend, if anything happens to prevent your return, I'll ensure that legal documents are drawn up giving one fourth of the proceeds of our enterprise to your wife and children. Another one fourth will go to my heirs, and a full half will go to Nadiya, as we discussed."

"Excellent, my friend. Hope to see you in a few days."

\*\*\*\*

"You have a passport?" Caesar asked. He sounded stressed over the phone.

"Yes. I think it's still valid. Where are we going?"

Roxanne rolled on top of me and whispered in my ear. "Please don't commit to anything. I've got two more days off, and I want to spend them with you."

I rolled my eyes at her, pointed at the receiver, and mouthed the name "Caesar."

She rolled off me in a huff and got out of bed. I knew she was going to be upset with me because I always ran to Caesar when he snapped his fingers. That was our deal, and he signed my paycheck.

"Mexico, Jones. La Cabra has been kidnapped. We're going to help find him and liberate him from his captors."

This didn't sound like any kind of picnic to me. At its best, Mexico is a tough place to live and do business. All the cartels were constantly battling with each other over territory and product rights and all the police were on the take with one cartel or another. On top of that, nobody cared much for gringos, except for Americans with a wallet full of cash and a habit to feed. I was going to stick out like a lamb at a wolf convention. I wondered if I could learn to growl in Spanish in eighteen hours.

"We're flying out of JFK at 2 p.m. tomorrow," Caesar said. "There's a layover in Dallas, and then a second leg into Culiacán. From there we will drive to Navolato. Pack light, and don't bring any weapons that can be picked up by airport scanners. El Escorpión will provide us with the weapons we need. He buys them at the border from the CIA."

"El Escorpión?"

"Yes. He's in command until La Cabra returns. You better hope he does."

"Why's that?"

"El Escorpión takes nothing off nobody. No attitude, no jokes, no dissent, no nothing but strict obedience. If he says a rose is a daisy, it's a damn daisy."

"I got the picture. What time do we depart?"

"We're taking a shuttle from Albany to JFK. Leaves at 10 a.m. We leave from Cabrillo Construction at 7:30 a.m. We'll be traveling with two others, Galtero and Gijuante."

The names of our traveling companions signaled the mission we were on was going to be deadly. I knew Galtero had peeled a man alive and wasn't above such cruelty to anyone he considered an enemy. And Gijuante was the pet name of the largest of Caesar's men, a name created by Caesar from the man's real name, Juan, and the word *gigante* which translates to "giant" in English. Gijuante stood almost seven feet tall, and his body was close to three hundred pounds of solid muscle.

Chapter 25

El Escorpión had reserved rooms for forty-four men at Hotel San Francisco in Navolato, half an hour west of the airport which serves the State of Sinaloa, Mexico. The men represented the eleven regions of Los Equis' international business districts and were attending a meeting to discuss the recent abduction of El Cabra, the cartel's ultimate leader. The cartel's regional directors sat in the first two rows, up front. A badly wounded man sat in a wheelchair beside El Escorpión.

"I welcome you to Navolato," El Escorpión said in a deep voice. He was dressed in green army fatigues, and he had not shaved in several days. "I am sorry to bring you here on such bad business. This hombre beside me is Jose De Leon, on loan from the hospital for an hour. He has been a loyal and trusted soldier in Los Equis since the beginning. He is also the sole survivor of an attack on our headquarters by unknown and unprovoked assailants, who killed seven of our men and kidnapped La Cabra." He turned to the man in the wheelchair. "Tell our amigos what happened, Jose..."

Jose spoke slowly. His face and body language disclosed pain in his abdomen. "Me...I was coming back to La Cabra's meeting place. He had sent me to purchase refreshments for the soldiers who were meeting with him to discuss a peace treaty offered by

Las Sinistas cartel here in Sinaloa. I had just left the cantina with an armload of coffees and breads when I heard shooting. I looked up and counted ten hombres leaving the building with automatic weapons." He held his hand to his forehead. "No, there were nine hombres and one *mujer*, probably a *señorita*."

"What were they driving?" French asked.

"Outside the building were two vehicles...dark green minivans with rental plates. Three men had La Cabra. His hands were bound behind him, but he fought with them as they forced him into the first van. One hit him in the head with the butt of a *pistola*. I yelled at them, and threw my tray of coffees at the windshield of the first van as the hombres pulled away with La Cabra. When the second van passed me, the *señorita* in the open back window shot me in the belly three times with an AK. She was a blonde."

La Araña headed the cartel's West Coast operation. He raised his hand but began asking his question before being recognized to speak. "Who were these hombres?"

"I have never seen them before, Señor. They were not Mexicanos and not Americanos. I think those gringos maybe were Russians. One man wore a jacket with their sickle sign on his shoulder. Most wore the boots of the Russian military."

"Good observation, Jose," French said. "You are to be commended."

"Have they demanded ransom?" the regional director from Baha asked. "We must be prepared to deliver millions of dollars if they do."

The forty-four men in the room broke into loud murmurs.

El Escorpión raised his hand to silence the group.

"I took a call from a woman last night. Maybe the same blonde woman. She wants the plans for the antigravity machine that El Escondido is building for us. We have two days to produce them. She will call me again tomorrow night to set a time and place for the exchange."

"I can have copies of the plans here by then, El Escorpión," French said.

"Do that." El Escorpión turned to one of his soldiers. "Have you discovered who rented the vans?"

"Not yet. They were not rented in Sinaloa. My source is checking across all of Mexico for the rental of two green minivans from the same place of business. We should have something soon."

El Escorpión closed his eyes, took a deep breath, and exhaled forcefully. "We cannot tolerate such an attack. Our vengeance must be swift and devastating."

****

The group broke up and agreed to meet again in two hours. Galtero and Gijuante roomed together across from Caesar and me. We checked both rooms to be sure they were safe, and then settled in. Back in our room, Caesar dialed Juaquin Fajardo's cell phone number.

"Ola, El Escondido," Juaquin said before French greeted him on the phone.

"Hello, my friend. I need your immediate assistance."

"Would you like me to come to your office?"

"No, that won't be necessary. Did you save the second set of drawings for the antigravity machine...the fake ones?"

"Yes. I saved them on a flash drive."

"Excellent. I need you to send them to me as soon

as possible. Within the next two hours, if possible. Can that be done by email?"

"Yes. I can do that within the next half hour. Where would you like me to send them?"

French gave Juaquin the email address used by Los Equis for secret business. "Stay by your computer until you hear from me that I have received the documents."

"Yes, of course, El Escondido. Can I do anything else for you?"

"What you are doing is of utmost importance, Juaquin. I will reward you well when I return to Willow Falls."

\*\*\*\*

Two hours later, El Escorpión met again with our group of forty-four men. An aura of dread filled the room. Some remained hopeful that La Cabra would be rescued unharmed. Others assumed the worst and feared the aftermath of such an outcome. Caesar told me that lines of succession are not always clear in a cartel because nobody is exactly sure on whose head the crown would ultimately land, and bad blood between some members meant execution of those who had earlier done a disservice or dishonored the new leader.

"Through anonymous contacts," El Escorpión began, "we have learned the two vans were rented in Reynosa and driven here. We also have learned La Cabra is being held in Santa Rosa. Because of its proximity to Reynosa, where the vans were leased, we believe it is Santa Rosa, Texas."

"In the USA?" La Araña asked. "Those hombres would have had to carry him across the border, through federales and border *policía*. That would take some cojones."

"Or, like us, they paid somebody at the border to look the other way," Caesar said.

Eleven cell phones went off in unison, some silently vibrating while others ringing loudly in their peculiar ringtones. Men began pulling them from their pockets and off their belts to see what had interrupted the meeting.

"What is this?" El Escorpión shouted.

"It is a video of La Cabra," La Araña replied excitedly.

El Escorpión pulled his own cell phone from his pocket and looked at the video message he and the other eleven leaders had received. It was indeed La Cabra, face bruised and swollen, blood trickling from his mouth. His eyes appeared unfocused and moved in circles, as though he were drugged. A woman's voice said, "Smile." La Cabra painfully did. One front tooth was missing, the other broken. A feminine hand and arm pressed a stun baton against his chest. La Cabra's torso heaved violently as a million volts of electricity leapt into it. His head fell to his chest. The woman's voice ordered, "You have less than thirty hours to give me the plans for the antigravity machine. If you fail to do so, this hombre's head will fly at the top of a flagpole in Sinaloa."

Angry shouts burst from men throughout the room. "Vengeance!" "Death to his captors!" "Kill the *mujer*!"

El Escorpión shouted over the outcries. "We gonna find this puta and spread her body parts all over Mexico."

The shouting and outcries continued.

El Escorpión swept his arm from the middle of the

room and to his right. "This side of the room will go to Santa Rosa, Texas. You will find and free La Cabra. Once you do, you will burn the town to the ground because it welcomed the bastardos who harmed La Cabra."

A man on the left side of the room shouted, "And what about this side? What will we do?"

"You will stay here with me, and we will prepare Los Equis for war."

Caesar, Galtero, Gijuante, and I were among those selected by a sweep of El Escorpión's hand to go to Santa Rosa, Texas, to find and free La Cabra. "We have no choice except to go," Caesar said. "As long as El Escorpión is in command, we do as he wishes. All of us."

****

Someone knocked on our room door. I looked through the peep hole and saw a short woman of Aztec descent waiting for me to open the door. I did. Her hair was jet black, her cheekbones high, her nose hooked, and she stood no more than four feet tall. She was the perfect model for an Aztec doll or perhaps a cultural sculpture. In her hands, she held a large manilla envelope addressed to El Escondido. I took the envelope from her, handed her a couple of dollar bills, and closed the door. "Caesar, it's for you."

Caesar opened the sealed envelope and poured its contents onto his bed. "Juaquin came through. These are the technical drawings and descriptive pages I promised to get for El Escorpión."

"Good," I said, trying to be supportive.

Caesar excused himself from the room, taking the paperwork with him. I assumed he was going to find El

Escorpión and deliver the goods.

Caesar came back fifteen minutes later. He looked uneasy, but I didn't ask him about it. He poured himself a glass of whiskey and sat against the headboard of his bed. After a few minutes, he turned on the room's television, and we watched two black and white rerun episodes of *The Cisco Kid*, dubbed in Spanish.

As evening approached, we dressed in black outfits and Kevlar vests which were delivered to our rooms by maids who were dressed in hotel uniforms. Each of us was given an AK-47 with two fully loaded clips. At the appropriate time, we collected Galtero and Gijuante and found our way to the hotel's garden entrance, where we met two more women in hotel garb. They escorted us to two open-top tactical cargo trucks. Caesar said something to the drivers, and then we boarded.

We were driven to the northern edge of Navolato, where the drivers proceeded in single file onto a narrow trail through acres and acres of tall marijuana plants. The moon was rising over the desert in the east, and I could tell it would be full, or almost full, when it was high. I hoped it wouldn't affect our operation, especially since our helicopters would be easy targets against a brightly illuminated night sky.

When the trucks stopped, I could see four large black helicopters waiting for us in an oval clearing. When ordered, we disembarked and were directed into specific helicopters. The bays we climbed into reeked of marijuana, probably because they were used to smuggle the crop into the United States. I climbed in after Galtero and offered my hand to Caesar. He took it, and we sat side by side on the webbed seating which lined the cabin's walls.

The doors to the choppers remained open. Caesar motioned to a man nearest the door. The man turned and pounded three times on the metal wall separating us from the pilot. The pilot started the motors, and the chopper's rotors began spinning, slowly at first and then faster and faster. The noise was deafening. Dust filled the air outside. In moments, we lifted off and joined the other helicopters. We flew in a diamond formation toward the northeast and the unsuspecting town of Santa Rosa. Night air swirled inside the bay and cooled my sweaty neck.

Once we were in the air, I pulled my cell phone from my vest pocket and opened Google. I typed in "Santa Rosa, Texas." I learned it was a small town bordered by the Rio Grande and situated twenty miles west of the Gulf of Mexico. Home to only two thousand six hundred people, it was an impoverished village with high unemployment and inexpensive housing. Its police force was part-time, and their primary responsibility was to set up radar traps on the main road where speeders could be ticketed and pay their fines directly to the policeman by sliding a credit card through a small square device which plugged into a cell phone. So, it seemed like a great place to hide an abducted cartel leader. But God only knew where we'd find La Cabra.

I shouted to Caesar over the roar of the beating blades. "Hey, how are we going to know where La Cabra is being held? We can't just bust into every home and demand he be freed."

"You're right, Jones. El Escorpión has sent a small contingent of hombres ahead of us to scope out the town and identify the likely location."

Chapter 26

When we reached Santa Rosa, all four helicopters circled the town and then landed on an empty field behind its only elementary school where an X was burning in the grass. I wasn't sure if the X marked our landing spot or if it stood for Los Equis...or maybe both.

It was after eleven at night and only a few of the homes displayed lights indicating someone might still be awake. We disembarked. Almost immediately, a set of headlights came toward the field from beside the school. The vehicle leapt over a six-inch concrete barrier. Its high beams bounced off the tops of nearby trees and then off the ground as it did. It quickly came to a halt near us, covering us in dry dust. The passenger side door swung open, and a man hopped out. "Where is El Escondido?"

I pressed my hand against Caesar's chest and stepped forward. "What do you want with me?"

"El Escorpión sent you a message. He held up a piece of paper and read from it. "Cucaracha, you must scrub the mission. The target is in Mexico. Return to the departure point. We will refuel and double the force."

"*Gracias*, señor," I said. I turned to Caesar. "Do you think this man is lying to us?"

"No, Jones. He began the message with the signal

184

given to me by El Escorpión. He called me 'cockroach.' Nobody else would dare do that."

I snickered. "Back to Navolato?"

"Yes." Caesar turned to the twenty-one other men in our swat team. "El Escorpión was given the wrong location for this mission. We must go back to Navolato to get more men and to refuel. Then we take another ride."

Some of the men grumbled in aggravation. But they climbed back into the helicopters, and we returned to Mexico. As we passed over the Rio Grande, three US fighter jets blew by us perilously close. The wind behind them shook us violently. I think it was a warning not to come back across the border. Hell, we looked like drug runners, didn't we?

"Where will we be going next, Caesar?" I asked.

"Most likely to the Yucatán Peninsula, to the other Santa Rosa...the one in Mexico."

"Are there others?"

"Yes, one in Argentina. It's too far away and probably doesn't have internet access. The video of La Cabra came to our cell phones by internet, did it not?"

I nodded my head. Sometimes Caesar was better at deducing clues than I am. I wondered how he would have handled La Cabra's kidnapping if he had been left in charge of Los Equis instead of El Escorpión. It was something I could only imagine, and something I doubted I would ever know. Certainly, it wasn't a question I could ask him at the moment.

The trip back to Navolato took two hours. All of us were tired and let down from the adrenaline high of expecting a fire fight in Santa Rosa. From the air and in the light of the full moon, I could see an additional three helicopters waiting on the ground, along with a fuel truck to refill the tanks of the four helicopters we had taken to Texas and back.

Word came quickly that we had half an hour to empty our tanks in the marijuana fields and then get back on board our assigned choppers for the flight to the Yucatán Peninsula. As I stood peeing on a marijuana bush that was taller than I was, I wondered if the person who ultimately purchased this bush on the street in the USA would notice the difference in taste between this bush and others he had consumed over the years. I guessed not.

Caesar's cell phone rang. "Hey?" he said. He nodded and put his cell phone back into his vest pocket. "Okay, muchachos, our pilots have been given location coordinates. Let's go rescue La Cabra."

A barrage of cheers rose from forty men, who quickly moved to their assigned helicopters and climbed aboard. When we had approached Santa Rosa, Texas, we had been a raiding party invading an unsuspecting, almost uninhabited desert barrio, but now we were a small army advancing upon an unsuspecting city. I pulled out my cell phone and did the Google thing again. Santa Rosa, Mexico, was only a crossroad with five residents. Yes, only five. Our arrival jumped the population by 800 percent! Certainly, El Cabra wasn't being held there. I switched to Google Maps. The closest city was Guadalajara, with a population of one and a half million. If La Cabra was being held anywhere, it would be there, where the arrival of a couple of green minivans and a captive cartel leader wouldn't be noticed by anybody.

I held my phone so Caesar could see the map of

Santa Rosa. I leaned close to his ear. "La Cabra isn't being held in Santa Rosa. He's probably in Guadalajara."

"Probably on the outskirts of Guadalajara. Or maybe another small town. Santa Rosa is the target for our drop-off. The pilots know where to land."

I hoped Caesar was right about that. I had sensed tension between Caesar and El Escorpión and wondered if we weren't being sent on a mission where those men who might oppose El Escorpión's possible ascent to supreme leadership of Los Equis would be eliminated. I silently wished the pilots would drop me off a few miles from our destination so I could thumb a ride to Tijuana and find my way across the border.

After a few minutes, one of the other men in our chopper pointed out the west bay door. The full moon was like a dazzling spotlight brightening everything below us. I could see the ocean in the distance. Then I realized what he was pointing out to me. We weren't headed west at all but were actually heading east. I turned to Caesar. He nodded. I leaned toward his ear. "All right, would you mind telling me what's going on?"

Caesar turned and spoke into my ear over the beating of the rotors above us. "El Escorpión didn't want anyone to know where we were going, just in case someone in the group is on the kidnappers' payroll."

I nodded. Now it all made sense.

We flew in formation for an hour and then the choppers began circling and descending at the north end of another small town. I pulled out my cell phone and punched in a location app. We were directly above the small city of General Cepeda, about thirty miles west of

Monterrey. According to Google, the popular places to visit included a dozen restaurants, two dozen bars, a bird museum, a Mexican Revolution museum, an elementary school named after Dr. Jesus Ramos and, across the street from it, the Hotel Santa Rosa. Bingo!

Like they had before, the pilots set our choppers down on the large playground of the elementary school. Once the choppers had settled, we piled out. Caesar huddled the men together and quickly shouted orders to each group over the beating roar of the rotors above our heads. One of the men handed out dayglow yellow bandanas which we tied above our left biceps. We were more than forty men, all carrying automatic weapons. It was important that we didn't fire at each other, and the bandanas were the only sign of friend versus foe.

I was afraid our delay in entering the hotel would give La Cabra's kidnappers enough time to counter our assault. Hell, the noise of seven helicopters landing next door should have awakened everyone in the city from the deepest sleep. I was right on all fronts. We split into four groups to approach the hotel from all sides. I was assigned to one group. Caesar, Galtero, and Gijuante joined others.

My group hurried around the school and began to cross a narrow cobblestone street to enter the left side of the hotel building. Immediately, gunmen on the hotel's rooftop opened fire. Dozens of rapid-fire shots rang out. *Pop! Pop! Pop!* Each "pop" was accompanied by a burst of bright light from a gun's muzzle. Sparks flew as bullets ricocheted off rocks, and the sounds of breaking windshield glass erupted in the quiet of the night. Lights came on in a dozen nearby homes.

Two men in our squad were hit and went down,

bleeding on the street. Several others were pinned down behind a brick façade in front of the elementary school. I zigzagged across the street and found safety as I pressed unscathed against the hotel's stucco exterior. Four other men joined me. We slid sideways toward a window in the hotel's wall. I was third in line. The window ahead of us opened with a squeak and a quick burst of rounds took out the man in front of our group. The two men in front of me returned fire. Our attacker was hit. His weapon dropped to the ground in front of us.

Continuing against the wall, the four of us stepped over our dead comrade and proceeded to the window. The first guy in line dropped onto all fours. The second stood on his back and peered into the window. He turned to us and nodded, then he pulled himself into the window. I followed suit, stepping onto the back of the first guy and pulling myself into the window. The guy behind me did the same. Then he held his hand out the window and assisted our human stepstool into the building. The four of us were now inside the ground floor kitchen of the three-story hotel.

On the floor beside the open window a dead man lay face-up in a pool of blood. Several wounds oozed red liquid from his neck and face. Clearly, he didn't appear to be Hispanic, and the red star patch on his left shoulder hinted he was probably Russian.

Two long rows of stainless-steel worktables were set in the middle of the kitchen. Equally interspersed were several sinks. To the left were four stoves and three ovens. To the right stood freezers, refrigerators, and storage cabinets. Directly in front of us was a swinging door. I assumed it opened to the dining room.

One of the men waved his hand toward the swinging door. "La Cabra."

I nodded. We needed to find La Cabra and get him to the helicopters for a ride home to safety. The presence of the dead Russian confirmed we were at the correct Santa Rosa. The primary question was which way to go? Was he being held captive upstairs or in the basement? Given where the Russians recently had held Elizabeth Hawkes, I touched the sleeve of one of the other men and pointed to the floor, opting for the basement. He nodded and signaled to the other two that they should head upstairs where the popping sounds of semiautomatic weapons meant the Russians were continuing to spray lead at our friends on the street. Then he touched my forearm to draw my attention and tapped twice on his chest. "Juan."

I pressed my fist against my chest. "Jones."

Juan nodded, then pointed toward the kitchen door. We both approached it. Juan peered through the swinging door, and then on his signal we exited the kitchen and entered an anteroom where two elevators sat with open doors. I stepped inside one, pushed the down button, and then stepped back outside. The door closed and the elevator traveled to the basement. We waited twenty seconds. Rapid fire sounded below us. Unintelligible shouts rang out. If we had been in that elevator as its door opened in the basement, we would have been cut down by the enemy below.

Deciding against taking the second elevator down was a no-brainer. Instead, we carefully followed the beige stucco walls and searched for a stairwell. As I turned a corner, I saw a door close and pointed to it. Juan nodded and motioned that we should investigate that door. He ensured the small room was vacant and then waved me forward. I hurried to the door. Shots rang out below. I pressed against the wall beside the door and then slowly opened it. More shots rang out. Louder. Then shouting.

"Go, gringo," Juan said. He pointed down the stairs. "El Escondido's there."

I bolted into the doorway and waved my AK-47 back and forth. The stairwell was empty, but shouts and firing continued below. I looked over the handrail and down the divide between the concrete stairs. The stairwell looked clear. Juan and I descended quickly, but carefully, weapons pointed forward as we descended.

At the bottom of the stairwell, Juan pressed his ear against the steel door and listened to the commotion on the other side. "El Escondido," he said. He stood erect and opened the door. Six men on the other side of the door turned and pointed their weapons at us. We raised our hands, our AKs held above our heads.

The men saw our arm bands and lowered their weapons.

"El Escondido?" I asked.

The group of men parted. Caesar was sitting against a concrete column. Blood was trickling from his forehead into his left eye and onto his cheek. He seemed dazed.

I rushed to him and bent down on a knee. "Caesar, are you wounded?"

Caesar looked up at me. "Only my pride." He pointed at a dead man across the room. "I didn't see the Russian until he was on me. He hit me in the head with the butt of his rifle. It was my good fortune that

Gijuante shot him before he struck me a second time."

I turned to Gijuante, who was standing to my left. His AK-47 hung from his left hand. "Thank you, my friend, for saving El Escondido. If you ever need my help with anything, it will be my honor to assist you."

Gijuante nodded, kissed his thumb, and pushed it in my direction.

"What about La Cabra?" Caesar asked. "Has he been found and freed?"

"He's upstairs," a man behind me said. "*Muerto*."

Caesar thrashed his arms in front of himself and tried to get up. I grasped an arm and helped him to his feet. He wavered a bit, unstable from the blow to his head. "This is not good, Jones."

"Yeah, I know."

"Take me to him. I must see for myself."

One of the men pressed his palms against my shoulders. He was my height and had a tattoo of a pinecone below his left eye. "Gringo, we will go up first. You wait here with El Escondido until the elevator bell rings three times. That will be the signal that all is safe. Then you bring him to the third floor."

"Si," I said. I don't know why I answered in Spanish. The guy seemed to know as much English as I did.

Caesar wanted to go up in the first elevator, but he did as the guy suggested. Three men climbed into each elevator. One ascended. The other paused for five seconds and then headed up. I think the delay in arrival would let the guys in the second elevator prepare for fireworks if the first elevator opened to unexpected gunfire.

The elevator bell rang three times. Then one of the

elevators began its downward journey to the basement where Caesar and I waited. When the door opened, the elevator was empty. We climbed in, and I hit the button for the third floor.

I leaned against the chrome elevator wall. "How's your head, Caesar? It looks like you've lost a lot of blood."

"My physical head is going to be painful for a few days. But what really hurts is my brain. If La Cabra is truly dead, many wheels will be set in motion as men with ambition seek to fill his shoes."

"You're afraid of an aftermath like the one which followed El Chapo's arrest?"

"Yes. We could be in a horrendous war in only a few days."

"Who do you fear the most?"

"All of them. Some may request alliance with other cartels. If that happens, Mexico will not be a safe place for any of us."

The door to the elevator opened. We had arrived at the penthouse—the third floor. A dozen men were assembled in front of the elevator. They backed away to give Caesar room to pass. He said something in Spanish to one of the men. The man lowered his head and pointed to the right. I assumed that was the way to La Cabra's body.

Caesar led the way. The hallway was full of men, all fully armed and all muttering in conversation. When we reached room 304, men in the hallway moved aside and we entered.

Inside, the room was a basic square with tan low-pile carpeting. Its stucco walls were adorned with cheap paintings of bullfighters and bulls in black vinyl frames.

Shiny minerals in the stucco walls reflected the light from a single bulb in a lamp on a built-in dresser. A double bed mattress stood on end against the window to the outside. The air was stale.

A wooden armchair was positioned a few feet from the wall to our right. In it was strapped the body of the man I had met when Caesar and I visited the island of Vieques. His fingers had been stripped of their nails. His arms showed evidence of cigar burns and his chest of branding, perhaps by a hot fork. His head was propped backwards, his throat sliced into a gaping cavern. The carpet below him was saturated with blood.

Caesar crossed himself. "Madre de Dios," he whispered.

"What is your command, El Escondido?" Gijuante asked.

"Have these men find bedsheets and prepare La Cabra's body for flight back to Navolato. Tell them to treat his body with ultimate respect, as they would their own fathers."

Gijuante said something in Spanish to a group of men. They laid down their weapons and began gathering what they would need to wrap the body.

Caesar spoke to the remaining men in Spanish. Two responded to him. He gave them orders and then followed them out of the room. I followed the small group. We entered another room, where a large man with short blond hair was hanging by his bound wrists from the bathroom door jamb. His legs were bent at the knees, and his feet sprawled behind him on the tiled bathroom floor. Caesar said something else in Spanish. Three men spoke in unison to him. He prodded the captive with the toe of his boot. The man looked up at him and grimaced. His face had been battered, his eyes swollen almost shut. He was missing three teeth.

Caesar looked at me. "Do you speak any Russian?"

"I only know 'nyet,' 'vodka,' and 'Sputnik.'"

"Then we have a problem. Nobody here speaks Russian, and this *bastardo* doesn't speak English or Spanish. I want to know how many of them were here, who led this group, and where the leader is now."

"How about the proprietor? He might know something."

"Good idea, Jones. That's why I brought you along."

Caesar gave orders to the men standing beside me. Two of them left the room.

A few minutes later they returned with a short man who was dressed in dungarees and a grey suit coat. Held on his tiptoes by larger men, his eyes telegraphed the fear he was experiencing.

Caesar asked him several questions in Spanish. Words poured out of the man's mouth faster than a tape recorder could capture them. I caught a few "no's" and "si's" and "señor's" and then I heard him say "Orsic."

"Orsic?" Caesar repeated.

"Si, Señorita Maria Orsic."

\*\*\*\*

We gathered our dead and wounded and returned to the choppers which waited for us behind Dr. Jesus Ramos Elementary School. Caesar, Galtero, Gijuante, and I rode with La Cabra's body in the second chopper to leave the ground. The first carried seven dead Los Equis soldiers. The others carried the remaining survivors, several of them with minor wounds.

Our trip home was somber. Not only had we not

been able to save La Cabra, but we had lost fifteen percent of our strike force. And the mystery woman, Maria Orsic, had eluded capture again.

Caesar gave me the details. "The proprietor told me that a German woman named Maria Orsic arranged for and paid for the rooms in cash, upfront."

"Did he describe her?"

"Yes. Young, blonde, and assertive. She was in charge."

"The same thing Elizabeth Hawkes said about her captors."

"Yes. He also said the hotel's Russian visitors had been gruff and disrespectful and none of them spoke a word of Spanish. Miss Orsic had developed a menu for each day's meals and had given it to the proprietor when she arranged for the men's lodging. The Russians didn't like her menu selections."

"What about the Russian we captured?" I asked.

"He killed two of our soldiers from the Guadalajara chapter. Since the hotel was so close to Guadalajara, I left him for their disposal. I imagine he will pray for death long before it arrives."

Chapter 27

It was a Saturday afternoon four days after our return to Albany, and we were in Caesar's office. "We meet again on Vieques in two days," he said.

"How should I dress?"

"You won't be going with me this time, Jones. Our colonels are meeting to determine who will become our organization's new generalissimo, our supreme leader. There will be much bartering on the side, hombres buying loyalty from others until the final ballot is cast."

"Who do you support? I assume it will be El Escorpión. I mean, he assumed leadership when La Cabra was kidnapped, and you deferred decisions to him."

"I knew from experience that deferring to him was better than challenging him, especially when one is on his home turf. His name means what is sounds like, 'the scorpion.' He earned that name for his quick and vicious reaction to anyone who threatens him."

"From experience?"

"No, not exactly. I was there when one hombre asked El Escorpión's woman to dance at a social event in Navolato. The woman consented. After the event, the man was found dead in a wooden barrel with one hundred scorpions on his body. He was buried in the barrel along with the remaining scorpions."

I shuddered. "Death by scorpion stings must have

been terrible."

"I think he was dead long before he was stuffed onto the barrel. The scorpions were probably poured in afterwards. You know, like a message to all the hombres who might want to dance with his woman."

I changed the grisly subject. "You know, Caesar, I've been thinking about the situation you and the other Los Equis leaders are facing."

Caesar bent over and pulled two bottles of cerveza from a mini-refrigerator on the floor near his desk. He popped the caps with an old-fashioned church key and handed me a bottle. "Go on. I'm all ears."

"How much money is enough?"

"Huh?"

"How much money does any one leader need? One hundred million? Two hundred million?"

I took several large swallows from my bottle of beer. Caesar waved me on.

"They say Al Capone earned ten million dollars per week. In half a year, he amassed 260 million. Couldn't he have retired after six months or a year at most? Why did he keep going? What drives the need for more money when it's almost impossible to spend what you already have, especially when it's untaxed?"

Caesar leaned back in his chair and put his right foot on his desktop. His cordovan boots were scuffed along the insole. "The money is a side benefit. I think it's more about the power."

I held my bottle with two hands at my waist. "I think you should suggest the Cartel consider succession planning."

"What? Never heard of it. Is it some kind of American thing?"

"It ought to be, but only a few organizations use it."

"'Splain it to me."

I chuckled at Caesar's imitation of Ricky Ricardo. "Well, think about the fate of leaders in the Mafia or in other cartels in general. You once explained it to me. Hungry men are always envious of the leader's power and prestige. Eventually, somebody always knocks off the leader and takes over."

"Yes, that's why I have never aspired to be supreme leader of Los Equis."

"If Los Equis created a designated line of succession, where each man knew when it would be his turn to lead, the leader would not have to be so concerned about those below him. Each man could wait his turn to be cartel leader. When it was his turn, he could be leader for a year or two and then retire with the fortune he has amassed—more money than anyone needs to live like a king for the rest of his life."

"What would be the glory for those who step down? They would have lost power."

"Not necessarily. They could become 'Generalissimo Emeriti,' and could serve as a board of advisors to the current leader. Their knowledge and connections could be put to good use for the benefit of the entire cartel. They would be like godfathers to the next generation of leaders."

Caesar smiled. "I am intrigued by the concept, but I don't think others will think the same way. I may suggest it at the meeting, depending upon the direction the discussions go. But I think your suggestion only transfers the fear of death to those lower in the pecking order. What if the hombre in position number three wishes to be the next leader? Wouldn't he simply cause hombre number two to have an accident?"

I nodded. Caesar had discovered an obvious flaw in my suggestion. I suppose there's nothing worse than an impatient man with a thirst for power.

****

"Mariya is coming for dinner tonight," Cooper announced to his mom. "She's home from visiting with her parents in Mazatlán."

"How nice. What will you be cooking for her?" Elizabeth asked. "Your father and I are meeting with the new Vice President of the School of Sciences at SUNY Oneonta. It's another dinner at a country club. They're either seeking a donation, or they have need of your father's scientific expertise. Either way, we won't be home until midnight."

Joy left Cooper's face. "Will Nadiya be home? Maybe I can wrangle her into cooking us something Ukrainian."

"You're out of luck on that front, too. Nadiya will be taking your sister to the theater to see that new kid's musical as a reward for creating her first personal website. You should ask Charity to show it to you. You'll be proud of her."

"I guess I'll just have to take Mariya out to eat."

"Why don't you do something special with her...maybe cook hotdogs over an open fire? I used to love it when your father did primitive manly things like that."

"That's maybe not too bad an idea, mom." Cooper walked into the kitchen, pulled open the bottom drawer of the refrigerator and rummaged through the assorted meats until he found two frozen filet mignons. "These will be perfect."

Mariya arrived at seven. Henry and Elizabeth had already departed for Oneonta, and Nadiya and Charity were busy eating burgers and fries at Jack 'n' Jill's, a popular outdoor venue in Scotia, less than five minutes from Proctor's Theater.

Cooper opened the front door, took Mariya into his arms, and gave her a passionate kiss. "God, it's great to see you. I dreamed about you every night while you were away."

"I missed you, too," Mariya replied. "Are your parents home? They left the garage door open, and their car isn't there."

"No. They have a dinner meeting in Oneonta tonight. I think the state university wants Dad to teach a course or maybe lead a seminar. The place is ours until midnight."

"I thought maybe your father might be home because the lights are on in the warehouse where he is working on his special project."

"The guys he's hired started working twenty-four hours a day while you were gone. They even work weekends. Dad's partner has promised to bring in even more specialists. They're running at a record pace to meet some deadline his partner has established. That's all I know."

Cooper escorted Mariya into the kitchen and poured her a glass of red wine. "Speaking of parents, how were yours? Were you happy to see them?"

Mariya swirled the wine in her glass and then took a sip. "I'm always happy to see them." She perched on a stool with her left hip and rested her arms on the kitchen island's top. "Daddy seems preoccupied with the war. He's hoping it doesn't spill over into Romania. So far, the Ukrainians have done a good job of repelling the Russian invasion, but Daddy says if Ukraine falls, Romania may be next. On top of that, the refugees are pouring into our homeland and devouring our social services. Mom and some of her friends have been assisting with food distribution at one of the many tent cities which have popped up."

"How did the Berezovskys react to your parents' thoughts about the war?"

Mariya's eyes opened wide. "Oh, I wouldn't discuss anything like that with them. I wouldn't want to offend them. As far as they know, I support Russia's attempt to take back land that once belonged to them."

"You mean their leader's attempt to recreate the Soviet Union?"

"Yes. Mr. Berezovsky is close friends with him, so I never stray into politics with them."

"That's probably wise." Cooper grabbed the bottle of wine and took Mariya's hand. "Come with me. I want you to stray into the back yard with me."

Cooper led Mariya out the back door, across his home's large slate patio, and up a narrow pathway into the open field behind the family's mansion. At the top of the hill, where the undisturbed tree line began, he had set up a small campsite. A fire was smoldering in a ring of large native rocks. Two nylon camp chairs stood upwind of the fire. A cooler was stationed under a small folding table which stood to the right of the chairs. Behind the table and nestled beneath a maple tree, a green and yellow four-man tent sat waiting for occupants.

"What have we here?" Mariya asked. "You aren't

trying to seduce me, are you, Cooper?"

He dodged her question. "Look in the coals. You'll see two lumps of aluminum foil. Those are potatoes, baking for your dining pleasure." He opened the cooler and pulled out two defrosted beef filets and a round bundle of asparagus. "Your chef will be busy for a few minutes." He pointed at the folding chairs. "Sit back in one of the thrones he has provided and watch culinary mastery in action."

"You still haven't answered my question, Cooper. Are you trying to seduce me?"

Cooper grinned at her, shrugged his shoulders, and poured more wine into her glass. Then he busied himself preparing the items he had gathered for their reunion dinner.

Mariya watched as Cooper placed the wire top from an old charcoal grill on the circle of stones and across the fire. Then he pulled a cast iron skillet from a canvas bag and set it on the grill top. He plopped a spoonful of butter into the pan and, when the butter had melted, he sprinkled the filets with a generic steak spice and laid them carefully in the pan. After four minutes, he flipped the filets and placed a handful of asparagus spears into the bubbling butter beside them. Four minutes later, he removed the pan from the fire and served dinner on large wooden plates his mother had purchased during a visit to Puerto Rico.

The young couple faced east, away from the glare of the setting sun. The sky above them turned crimson and then it darkened. Tiny dots of light—stars and planets—began to fill the void. In the distance, the lights of Albany reflected off the towers of the Empire State Plaza.

Cooper threw a few more pieces of hardwood onto the fire and emptied the last of the wine into their glasses. A loud "clang" came from the right of the home below. They both turned toward the sound. "I think someone dropped a heavy piece of steel onto the concrete floor," Cooper said.

"Don't let those men spoil this moment, Cooper," Mariya said. "I'm happy to be home from Mexico and to be with you again." She gently pulled his chin to turn his face toward hers. "I want you to kiss me."

Cooper did.

The kisses became more passionate. She led him to the tent and onto the air mattress inside. They hastily undressed and explored each other's bodies in the darkness until he erupted for a second time. Then they slept.

Several hours later, Mariya awoke at the sound of car tires on a gravel driveway. Then she heard car doors close and a man and woman talking. The Hawkes were home.

She shook Cooper, but he wouldn't wake. She dressed and crept quietly downhill to the fieldhouse where the team of men was working on Henry Hawkes' project. She squatted in the low brush for twenty minutes, watching and listening.

Finally, the men took a break from their work and gathered at the front of the building to enjoy something caffeinated and, perhaps, a candy bar or a cigarette. That was all she needed.

Mariya found her way to the back of the building. The steel door was unlocked. She carefully opened it. No alarm went off. She peered inside and inspected the interior corners. She saw no cameras or motion detectors. So, she slid inside the building.

The antigravity device appeared to be nearly complete. At least, its exterior seemed totally intact. She raised her cell phone and shot three quick pictures. Then she set the phone on "video" and slowly panned the complex.

The ramp to the device's interior was down. The urge to scale the ramp and see the interior was strong, but she knew the men would soon be returning from their break. She turned to leave but stopped short when she saw a schematic drawing on a workbench near the door. She quickly rolled it up and carried it with her when she exited the building.

She was halfway back to Cooper's love nest when the men below her re-entered the building. She was glad she hadn't entered the craft, or she would have been immediately discovered.

Mariya entered the tent. Cooper was snoring lightly. She found her nylon jacket and slid the schematics into one of its sleeves. Then she lay beside Cooper and whispered into his ear. "Cooper. Cooper?"

He groaned and rolled toward her. "Hey, baby." His breath was horrible.

"Your parents are home. What time is it?"

Cooper moved his hand around the tent floor near his head until he found his jeans. He removed his cell phone and clicked it to life. "Jesus, it's two in the morning," he blurted.

"Will your parents be upset if they find me up here with you in the morning?"

"How would they ever know you spent the night here?"

"My car is parked outside your front door, silly."

Cooper put his hand on his forehead. "I guess there's only one thing to do—tell them the truth. They've probably already figured it out anyway."

"It's a little embarrassing for me, Cooper. How will I ever face them?"

\*\*\*\*

The sun woke them at six in the morning, but Cooper and Mariya didn't leave their tent until almost seven thirty. Mariya had found some mints in her purse and had shared a few with him. Then, they had made love again, this time with her on top.

At seven forty-five, they entered the Hawkes mansion through the sliding glass doors at the patio. The air smelled of bacon and coffee. Elizabeth was at the stove, holding the handle of a frying pan in her left hand and a spatula in her right. She turned when she heard them. "Oh, there you two are. I thought you might have been upstairs in Cooper's room."

It wasn't the greeting Cooper had expected. He felt like a naughty little boy, but Elizabeth treated both him and Mariya as the adults they were.

"We took a walk up the hill, Mom. This time of day the birds really sing. I thought we might see some deer, but we didn't."

"Don't try to bullshit an old bullshitter, Cooper. What you two have been doing is written all over your faces. It's a perfectly natural expression of affection, and your father and I are accepting of it. We were young once, too."

"Where is Dad?"

"Over in the hangar, checking how things are going. You know, he's been so secretive about it. I've never even seen what he's doing."

As if on cue, Henry strode into the kitchen. "Good morning, everybody." He smiled at Cooper and Mariya. "I trust you two had a pleasurable evening."

Mariya blushed and pressed her shoulder into Cooper's chest.

Elizabeth waved her spatula toward the breakfast bar. "Sit down, Henry. Your eggs are getting cold, and these young folks are hungry."

Elizabeth divided the eggs into four equal portions and slid them onto ceramic sandwich plates. Next, she pulled a pizza pan from the oven and shoveled pre-buttered toast onto each plate. And finally, she moved a platter of bacon from the kitchen counter to the breakfast bar. "Who wants juice? Who wants coffee? Who wants both?"

They ate in silence for a few minutes, then Cooper broke the tension. "You seem preoccupied today, Dad. Is everything okay?"

Henry swallowed a bite of bacon. "Oh, it's just that somebody misplaced the drawings for an Alcubierre Warp Drive. I have to print another copy and take it over to the engineers. I don't like the idea of missing plans, especially on a top-secret project."

"Never heard of it. But I know what a warp drive is. So does everyone else whoever watched Star Trek," Mariya giggled. "Are you making a science fiction movie over there?"

Henry finished his glass of orange juice. "It's more science than fiction, and when it works, NASA will be out of the rocket business."

"That sounds incredible, Pop. Will you let Mom and me see what you're up to?"

"Maybe someday. I couldn't do it without first

getting permission from my business partner, Caesar French. He's very sensitive about sharing too much information with others."

Elizabeth clanked her fork on her plate. "We're not exactly 'others,' Henry. We're family. It's not like we'd steal your idea and sell it to someone else. Hell, between the two of us, Cooper and I don't know enough science to pass a ninth grade Earth Science test."

"Mom's right, Dad. I was never very good at math and science. I was always best with English."

Henry laughed. "Got any more coffee, Lizzy?"

Elizabeth rose and filled his mug again.

Henry turned to Cooper. "You were always best with English because that's the language we taught you when you were growing up. I wish to God I had spent more time tutoring you in the sciences. That's where the future is. There will never be a loss of jobs for good scientists."

Elizabeth patted her mouth with a paper napkin and turned to Mariya. "How was your trip to Mazatlán, darling?"

"I enjoyed seeing my parents, thank you, but Mexico isn't a good place to visit anymore. There's too much crime—you know, the cartels run everything, and a young woman needs to be very concerned for her personal safety. I stayed very close to my parents, and we never left the resort."

"Trapped in a resort?" Elizabeth laughed. "It sounds heavenly."

Cooper changed the topic. "So, tell us about your warp drive, Dad. What does it do?"

Henry put down his coffee mug. "It's only a

theory, mind you, but a warp drive propels a craft in space at speeds exceeding light. The concept is for an interstellar vehicle to contract space in front of it and expand space behind it. It's based on Einstein's concept of space/time. Normally, an object could not travel faster than light. An Alcubierre system utilizes positive energy waves to change space/time around an object and, thus, permits it to attain fantastic speeds."

"It sounds incredible, Mr. Hawkes," Mariya said. "And you have such a device?"

"Only in theory. We've developed plans for such a device, but we won't know if it works until we field test it. We're a little behind schedule, but in a few weeks, we should be able to test our device as the engine of a machine we've almost completed building."

Elizabeth leaned back in her barstool and smirked. "Have you hired Captain Kirk to pilot your machine, Henry?"

"Better than that, sweetheart. We've hired real astronauts. Men who have flown similar machines while stationed at Area 51. You've heard of that, haven't you?"

Mariya stood. "Would you excuse me? I need to use the *baie*."

Elizabeth dropped her fork onto the floor. "Oh, excuse me. I'm such a klutz."

Henry nodded at Mariya and pointed toward the hallway. "Sure thing. I'm sure you know where it is by now."

Elizabeth's eyes followed Mariya as she left the room, and then she turned to Cooper. "Where did you say she is from?"

"Romania, Mom. Her parents are Romanian."

Chapter 28

Caesar had flown from Newark to San Juan, but instead of hopping a single-engine plane to Vieques, he opted to travel by ferry to Isabel Segunda from Fajardo, a small city in the northeastern portion of the main island. The trip took four hours, and the ride was rough because the wind was blowing out of the west at fifteen miles per hour. He fought nausea for the last hour on the ferry; however, arriving by ferry was unexpected, and if anyone hoped to eliminate him as competition for the position of supreme leader of Los Equis, his arrival at the small pier at Isabel Segunda would be unanticipated.

The heat and humidity were oppressive when Caesar arrived at Isabel Segunda. His silk shirt clung to his chest and the small of his back. Beads of sweat covered his forehead, and occasionally he needed to wipe perspiration from his sunglasses.

Once the ferry was moored, with suitcase in hand, he stepped from its ramp onto the concrete pier which jutted fifty yards out into the water. He raised his hand into the air and waved a twenty-dollar bill. A silver Honda Civic pulled up and stopped beside him. The front passenger window opened, and the young man inside leaned toward the door so he could speak. "Where you going, hombre?"

Caesar removed his sunglasses and squinted at the

driver, whose upper lip bore a thin-line moustache. The yellow and white plumeria flowers on his island shirt belonged in Hawaii, not Puerto Rico. "Casa del Sol."

"Hop in. I'll get you there pronto."

Caesar opened the back door, placed his suitcase on the seat and climbed in beside it. The driver accelerated and weaved through backstreets until he reached the narrow strip of asphalt which headed southeast from town.

"You here for the festival at Media Luna?"

"Haven't heard about it. Should I go?"

"Lots of cerveza and langosta, *arroz con gandules*, and steel drum music. Plenty of women, too."

"When is it?"

"Starts Friday around dinner. Ends Saturday around Sunday."

"If I find the time, maybe I'll drop in for a while."

"You want a woman, señor? Maybe two?"

"No, amigo. I'm here on business. No time for *mujeres*."

"Too bad for you. They grow nice ones on Vieques. Need any weed? I got three varieties."

"I only need a ride to Casa Del Sol."

The driver turned left and followed a single lane highway over a small rise. Casa Del Sol appeared in the distance.

"Señor, they got armed guards at the entrance today." The driver's expression showed concern. "You sure you want me to drive in, or would you like to go someplace else?"

"Just drive in. I assure you, no harm will come to you."

The driver pulled into the driveway and stopped

when a man with an AK-47 waved it at his car. "I don't want no trouble," he said to the guard. "I'm just delivering an hombre who wants to come here."

The guard motioned for the driver to wind down the back window. The driver pushed a button on his door and the window automatically descended. The guard stooped over and looked into the back seat. "Buenos días, El Escondido. They are waiting for you."

Caesar nodded and tapped on the driver's seat. "*Continúas*, amigo."

"You are El Escondido?" the driver asked. "The El Escondido?"

"It seems that way," Caesar replied.

The driver pulled up to the front of Casa Del Sol, hopped out, and opened the back door for Caesar. "I did not know who you were, señor. I hope I have not offended you in any manner."

Caesar handed the driver a fifty-dollar bill. "I thank you for exhibiting good driving skills. I am happy to have arrived safely."

"Can I carry your bag for you, señor?"

"No, *gracias*. I can manage from here." Caesar picked up his four-wheeled suitcase and climbed the four steps which led to the hotel lobby.

He checked in at the registration desk.

"Your accommodations have already been paid for, señor," the desk clerk said, "compliments of your friend and colleague, El Escorpión."

*Probably an attempt to buy my vote*, Caesar thought.

He took his room key from the desk clerk and climbed the stairs to the second floor. His room was decorated in the same grassy wallpaper which had adorned his room on his last visit, and the floors were polished in the same deep mahogany finish. This time, however, his window included an expansive view of Sun Bay, the finest crescent beach on the island. On the dresser were four six-ounce glasses and a bottle of 151 rum.

Caesar changed into island clothes—tan Bermuda shorts, a baby blue moisture-wicking polo shirt, and matching blue slip-on canvas loafers—and then he walked downstairs to the outdoor pool.

Sitting by himself at the end of the pool, El Escorpión waved Caesar to his side and patted on the seat of a reclining sun chair. Caesar folded his bath towel and hung it over the head rest before sitting. *By sitting beside him, I am sending a message to observers that I support his aspirations to lead Los Equis*, Caesar thought. *But I cannot offend him. If I do and he is successful, I will be a dead man.*

"Thank you for your generosity, El Escorpión. It was not necessary to pay for my room, but I greatly appreciate the gesture."

"How about the rum, Caesar? It is your favorite, no?"

"Si, amigo. You thought of everything. Perhaps you know me too well."

El Escorpión laughed and waved for a pool attendant to come. The young man hurried to his side.

"Bring my friend whatever he likes and refill my glass, amigo."

The young man turned to Caesar.

"It is too early for rum. It goes to my head quickly in the heat. Please bring me a cold light beer."

"Si, señor. I'll be right back. You would like a

glass, no?"

"No. The bottle is fine. But open it in front of me."

"Keeping your wits for tonight's meeting, Caesar. You are a wise man."

"There is much riding on tonight's discussions and the deals which will be struck. A clear head will be necessary." He searched the concrete patio around the pool. "The guard at the front led me to believe I was the last to arrive. Where are the others?"

"Probably in their rooms striking deals, amigo. You know how the game is played. And you...you still have no interest in leading Los Equis?"

Caesar knew that El Escorpión was searching for another supporter. "I am happily situated with my family in New York. I hope to continue serving Los Equis and our new leader from that location. I have many irons in the fire across the Rio Grande where there is much dinero to be made."

The young pool attendant arrived with Caesar's beer. He opened it with a large antique bottle opener bearing a full color picture of Orlando Cepeda, the famous Puerto Rican first baseman for the San Francisco Giants. The young man handed French his beer and placed the bottle cap on a round server's tray. Then he handed El Escorpión his second glass of Pitarro on the rocks.

"Tell me, Caesar, how is our space project going?"

"You'll be pleased to know we are still on track for launching the machine by the end of November."

"If I am elected to leadership, I will expect you to launch the machine by the end of summer, my friend. Such a feat will signal a new era for Los Equis and its new commander."

"That timeline may be impossible, El Escorpión. The machine has many intricate parts, and its engine is still only theoretical."

"Call me by my Christian name, Caesar. We are friends, no?"

"If you wish it, I will, Alejandro. But if you are elected to be our leader, I will continue to call you El Escorpión out of respect."

"Only when others are present, amigo. We are close friends, no? When we are together, you should only call me Alejandro."

Caesar nodded. "Your request is indeed an honor, Alejandro."

"Yes, it is. And your launch should be scheduled for the end of summer."

****

At six o'clock Caesar joined the other Los Equis leaders for dinner on the terrace, a new feature only recently opened by Casa del Sol. Surrounded by ceiba trees and red hibiscus bushes, the terrace was a rectangular platform raised two steps above the ground and paved like a checkerboard in pink marble slabs which alternated with translucent smoked glass panels. The raised platform permitted the ceiba trees' large sprawling root systems to find their way to water and nutrients in the soil beneath.

The twelve Los Equis regional leaders sat at a single banquet table where they were served roasted goat and grilled langosta with yellow rice, plantains, and a mixed greens salad. When the main course had been devoured, after-dinner drinks and Cuban cigars were shared by all.

"How we going to begin the election?" the leader

from Veracruz asked loudly. "We should have hired a moderator."

"One with a *pistola*," the leader from Puebla laughed.

"I think El Escondido should serve as moderator," the leader from Yucatan suggested. "He don't want to be no supreme leader."

All the heads around the table nodded. "Go on, El Escondido," the leader from Yucatan said. "Help us choose our generalissimo."

Caesar didn't want the role which had been thrust upon him. But he had no choice. He rose from his seat and moved to the head of the table.

"Amigos, what we are about to undertake this evening is both a sad and a happy occasion. First, I ask you to raise your glasses."

The men all held their glasses in the air.

"To La Cabra, the first and only generalissimo of Los Equis until his recent untimely death at the hands of our Russian enemies."

"Si! And to finding and decapitating their leader!" El Escorpión shouted.

The men cheered in agreement and drank from their glasses.

Caesar set his glass down. "Now, do I hear a nomination for our new generalissimo?"

A single hand rose into the air.

"I call upon the gentleman from Chiapas."

"I nominate our highly qualified amigo El Escorpión. Who could possibly be better to lead us into this unclear future which we face?"

"Do I hear a second?" Caesar asked.

Five hands shot into the air.

Caesar could see that the fix was already in. Five hands in the air plus the nominator and nominee made a total of seven. That left only four other votes and his own. "Are there any other nominations?"

Nobody said anything.

The leader from Nuevo Leon raised his hand.

"I call upon the gentleman from Nuevo Leon."

"I move that the nominations be closed."

"Is there a second to this motion?"

The same five hands shot into the air.

"All in favor of closing the nominations please raise your hands."

Every hand around the table went up.

"Then we have made our decision, gentlemen. Our new generalissimo is El Escorpión."

The leader from Chiapas stood. "Let us raise our glasses to El Escorpión."

The men all raised their glasses and cheered.

El Escorpión moved to the head of the table and shook Caesar's hand. Then he leaned toward Caesar's shoulder and spoke into his ear in an authoritative voice. "Launch that machine by the end of the summer, amigo."

Chapter 29

I returned from Mexico to an empty house. Roxanne's sink was full of dirty dishes and the dryer was full of clothes needing to be folded. I added the clothes from my suitcase to the pile of dirty clothes on the floor of the laundry room and then folded the clothes I found in the dryer, stacking them neatly on the Formica table which stood next to the dryer. Then I emptied the dishwasher, reloaded it with dirty dishes, and started its "heavy clean" cycle.

A quick inspection of the refrigerator let me know that Roxanne hadn't been grocery shopping in the past few days either. I had no idea what to fix us for dinner.

I texted her:

—*I'm home. What time will I see you? Got any special requests for dinner?*—

She wasn't quick to reply, so I took a shower to get the Mexican dirt and dried sweat out of the pores of my skin. After I shaved, I checked my phone. Roxanne had replied:

—*Home around midnight. Work is crazy. Fix me something nice. I deserve it.*—

I checked the time. It was now six o'clock. So, I drove to the grocery store and bought a basketful of the stuff Roxanne usually buys. I also threw in a couple of ribeye steaks, two baking potatoes, and a handful of fresh asparagus. Then I stopped at her favorite liquor store and bought a couple of bottles of Australian wine. Red, the way Roxanne likes it.

As if on cue, Roxanne arrived home at midnight and found me out back. The moment I saw her, I plopped the steaks and asparagus on the hot grill. The potatoes already had been baking for an hour.

We kissed like spouses do. Then I popped the cork on a bottle of wine and poured her a glass.

She took a sip and, still wearing her uniform, sat on a chaise lounge. "Oh, how I've missed you," she said. "You're absolutely my savior tonight."

"What's going on, Roxanne? COVID on the rise again?"

"It's been hell the past few days. The night you left, the news broke that officials at the Catholic diocese have mismanaged their retirement accounts."

"So, what does that mean...an extra collection on Sunday?"

Roxanne took another sip of wine and crossed her legs at her ankles. "Actually, it's waaay worse than that. All their employees who thought they had retirement accounts now have nothing. We're talking teachers, nurses, and all maintenance staff. Hundreds of people."

I took Roxanne's steak off the grill. Only one minute per side, as she prefers. "All those people have nothing?"

"Yes, and it affects all the Catholic hospitals and parochial schools. It means all the past retirees suddenly have no monthly checks coming in, and all the current employees who have been contributing to their retirement accounts with the expectation of a comfortable old age suddenly have nothing. Some were planning on retiring soon."

"How did this happen?"

Roxanne finished her first glass of wine and held her glass out for me to refill. I did.

"There's some scuttlebutt that almost two hundred men have sued the diocese for sexual abuse which happened to them as children at the hands of priests. The diocese can't afford to pay the claims."

"So, they paid the first battery of claims using the retirement monies, and now they are going into bankruptcy. And, so, they don't have to pay the others?"

"You're pretty quick for a private eye."

"So, how has that impacted you?"

"Most of the staff at the Catholic hospitals have walked out, and the hospitals can't serve the patients they have. They've transferred most of their patients to all the public hospitals. It's a mess for all of us. The sudden increase in workload has been awful."

I took my steak off the grill and shoveled asparagus and a potato onto each of our plates.

"You want to eat outside tonight?" she asked.

"You mean 'this morning.' It's after midnight, Roxanne. It's a new day. Let's eat and then romp so you can start the day fully charged."

We hurried through our small feast and then stripped and climbed into her hot tub, just long enough to remove the day's labors from her skin. With our clothes wrapped around us, we hurried upstairs. Making love was fast and heated, and we were both asleep before one in the morning. Well, one thirty.

\*\*\*\*

My cell phone woke me at nine o'clock in the morning. Roxanne was already out of bed and hard at work at the hospital. "Bart Jones here…"

"Bart, it's Elizabeth Hawkes. I need to speak with you about something."

"Sure. What's on your mind?"

"Not over the phone. Can you come to our place?"

"Yeah. I'll be there in an hour."

The skies above the Helderbergs were threatening rain as I drove up the Hawkes' driveway. I couldn't help noticing the hangar that Caesar had built next door. Cars and trucks were parked outside it, and there was no question people were hard at work on the antigravity machine project.

Elizabeth greeted me at the door when I pulled to a stop in front of her home. She was wearing a beige exercise suit. A young mastiff pulled at the short leash in her hand.

"Don't mind Enzo," she said. "He's in training, but I don't think he'll ever be as good as the two boys we lost when I was kidnapped."

"How are you?" I asked.

"Oh, I'm fine in general, except I'm unsettled about something, and I wanted to pass it by you."

She shoved Enzo into an office and shut the door. He pawed at it vigorously.

"Let's go into the kitchen, Bart."

I followed her. The light coming into the great room from her picture windows was grey. She poured herself a mug of coffee and then held the pot in the air. "Would you care for some? It's fresh."

"Thanks, but I've already had two cups." I sat in a white leather reclining chair. "Your call intrigued me."

Nadiya, the young tutor from Ukraine entered the room. I rose and greeted her.

"I've asked Nadiya to join us so she can hear what I have to say."

Nadiya poured herself a cup of coffee and sat across from me on a sofa. Her bare feet extended from faded jeans.

Elizabeth paused for a moment and then began. "This is going to sound motherly. I mean, what I'm going to say may sound like a mother who is trying to protect her son from a young woman whom he loves and about whom his mother is very unsure."

I nodded and motioned for her to go on.

"The other morning our son Cooper invited his new girlfriend into our home for brunch. She's a nice girl…attractive…intelligent. She's an exchange student from Romania."

She paused to sip from her coffee mug.

"We were having a nice time, Henry and me, with the two young people. Cooper has taken such a shine to her, and we wanted to learn more about her." Elizabeth took another sip from her mug. "Well, she had been sharing about her recent visit to Mexico with her parents. Then she asked if she could use our bathroom. She called it the 'baie.'"

Nadiya gasped.

Elizabeth nodded to her and then continued. "When we were being held captive by the Russians, a woman escorted us to the bathroom twice a day—"

"Yes," Nadiya said, interrupting Elizabeth. "The first time she asked us if we needed to use it, she said, 'Who wants to be first to use the baie?' Then she said, 'Oh yes, you call it the 'bathroom.'"

Elizabeth nodded. "Exactly. When I heard her use that word, I thought it was a Russian term, but then when I heard young Mariya use it, I checked online. The Russian term is—"

"*Vannaya komnata*," Nadiya blurted.

"Yes, exactly," Elizabeth said.

My interest definitely was piqued. "You said she has just returned from Mexico?"

"Yes," Elizabeth replied. "Her parents had flown to Mazatlán for a week's vacation, and she flew down to join them. Her father may have had some business there. She just returned the other day, and the first thing she did was come to be with Cooper."

"What else can you tell me about this young woman? Where does she live?"

"She is staying with our new neighbors, Pyotr and Taisiya Berezovsky."

"They are rich Russians," Nadiya slurred, as though something distasteful was in her mouth.

It was all too obvious to me. When Elizabeth and Nadiya were being held blindfolded by Russians, the woman who assisted them had used a Romanian word. And now the young Romanian who has been dating Cooper used the same word. And she had recently returned from Mexico, where La Cabra had been held captive and executed. I couldn't hang her for all that, but when added to the fact that she is living with Russians…well, it was all too much to ignore.

"What is this young woman's name?"

"Mariya."

"Spell it for me, please."

Elizabeth looked at Nadiya. Nadiya slowly gave me the letters, "M-a-r-i-y-a."

"And her last name?"

Elizabeth struggled with the pronunciation.

"Or…Ar…Auer…Sook…Sock…Such. Yes, Mariya Auersuch."

Again, Nadiya spelled it out for me, "A-u-e-r-s-u-c-h."

"This is a Romanian name?" I asked.

"No," Elizabeth replied, "Cooper says her family is of German extraction. They fled to Romania during World War II."

I'm not always the sharpest tack in the box, but if Mariya was of German descent, her name probably had morphed after relocation, like what happened to so many people who came to the United States though Ellis Island. I wondered if she could be a descendent of Maria Orsic's. The two names were almost identical. Who knows, maybe she was Maria Orsic, except if Maria Orsic were still alive, she would be over one hundred years old…unless she really did travel to the stars with the aliens who purportedly gave her the plans for the antigravity machine. My mind was spinning.

"What do you think, Bart?" Elizabeth asked.

"I'm so glad you shared this information with me. Many pieces of the puzzle seem to be falling into place. I'm suggesting you find a way to gently pull Cooper away from Mariya without alerting him to your suspicions."

"That's going to be nearly impossible," Elizabeth replied. "He has the worst infection…he's a lovesick puppy."

I thought about what Elizabeth had called love—an infection. Maybe Roxanne could help me separate young Cooper from Mariya long enough for me to get the goods on her.

Chapter 30

Cooper Hawkes answered his cell phone. "Hello?"

"This is Roxanne Windsor from Schenectady Hospital. Is Mr. Cooper Hawkes available?"

"Hello, Mrs. Windsor. This is Cooper Hawkes."

"Excellent, Mr. Hawkes. I am just calling to verify that you have an appointment for your annual physical with Doctor Hemmingway next Thursday at 10:30 a.m."

"Yes, it's on my calendar."

"The doctor has requested that you come to the hospital's lab for a routine blood test prior to your appointment."

"Really? Does he suspect something? Usually, he schedules the bloodwork for after the general physical."

"No, there's nothing to be upset about. It's just the new protocol. Because the Catholic hospitals have reduced their hours, his workload has increased. He'd like to have the analysis prior to seeing you in order to prevent your coming in for a second appointment if anything unusual appears in your blood."

"Are you asking me to schedule it now?"

"Yes, that would be helpful. We'd rather have you on the schedule than have you walk in unexpectedly."

"Do you have any openings tomorrow?"

"Ten fifteen or two thirty?"

"Ten fifteen works for me."

"Good, we'll see you then."

The next morning, Cooper showed up at ten fifteen for his scheduled blood draw. The young woman who was assigned to draw his blood appeared nervous. Her face and neck were splotchy, and her hands visibly shook.

"Is everything okay?" Cooper asked.

"This is only my first day as a phlebotomist. I've had five days of training. I had hoped you wouldn't notice."

"I'm sure you'll do fine. What did you do before you became a phlebotomist?"

"I worked in the cafeteria as a dishwasher. But the hospital needed lab workers, and the pay is a whole lot better...twenty dollars an hour. They only pay fifteen in the cafeteria."

Cooper shot out his arm and rolled up his sleeve. "Do it to me. I have places to go."

The young woman wrapped an elastic band around his bicep and swabbed a spot in the fold of his elbow. Then she poked his arm with a hypodermic needle. Cooper flinched.

"Sorry, sir. I was supposed to warn you about a slight pinch."

"It's okay. It didn't really hurt."

The woman drew a tube of blood, withdrew the needle, and taped a small gauze patch on Cooper's arm. She wiped her brow. "Thanks, Mister Hawkes. You've really been kind to me."

Cooper stood. "I think you're better at drawing blood than you give yourself credit for."

\*\*\*\*

Cooper's cell phone rang at four in the afternoon.

He dug it out of his pocket. It was the hospital. "Cooper Hawkes here."

"Mr. Hawkes?"

"Yes, that's what I said."

"Did you have blood drawn at Schenectady Hospital this morning?"

"Yes, I did."

"Was your phlebotomist an older man or a young woman?"

"A young woman."

"I'm afraid I have to ask you follow COVID protocols. The young woman who drew your blood tested positive for COVID at one o'clock this afternoon. You should remain in quarantine for ten days."

"You're shitting me!"

"No, sir. I'm sorry to give you this news, but I am obligated to ask you to follow COVID protocols, so we limit the spread of the disease. You shouldn't leave your home for ten days. Do you have anyone at home who can feed you and monitor your health?"

"Yes, damn it."

"Do you have at least four COVID quicktests on hand? If not, I'll have some delivered to your home."

"You'd better send me some. I'm not sure if we have any."

"I will do that. Thank you for understanding. This could have happened anywhere…at the grocery store, at an athletic event, even on a date. We regret that it happened at our medical facility—"

Cooper ended the call. He texted Mariya:

*—Have been exposed to COVID today. Can't see you tonight or for ten days. Sorry—*

Mariya texted back. Her text was accompanied by a frowning emoji.

*—I think I want to cry. Was looking forward to tonight. Call me later. Phone sex?—*

\*\*\*\*

Roxanne got home at midnight again. I had made stir fry, but she wasn't interested in eating because the hospital administration had ordered pizza and wings for every department.

"It was an unexpected treat, and we all were grateful." Roxanne placed her purse on the kitchen countertop. "At least we know they know we're busting our arses."

"Did you do it to Cooper?"

"Yes, he came in like a good little boy and when I called him later to instruct him to stay home for ten days, he wasn't a happy camper."

"Did you see him yourself?"

"No, I had a newbie draw his blood. I thought I should stay unidentifiable."

"That was probably a good idea."

"Yes, and I called from a desk phone in the maternity department. I spoke to him directly, so there shouldn't be a recording of my voice."

"Excellent."

I pulled a bottle of red wine from the wine rack, opened it, and poured us both a glass.

"Ah, you think I played a role as well as Cameron Diaz would have," Roxanne whispered. She kissed my neck.

"Maybe better. I now have ten days to get the goods on Cooper's girlfriend and solve the mysteries of who killed Kuzma Bodnar...and who executed La

Cabra in Mexico. I'm convinced it was the young Romanian woman, Mariya Auersuch, but I need to find absolute proof."

Roxanne slipped off her uniform and stood before me in her bra and panties. "Pour me some more wine, Barty."

I filled both our glasses and then she pulled me into her living room. We sat on her sofa, silent for more than a minute. Then Roxanne began exploring my case.

"Do you remember the night my girls performed the circle around you?"

"Yes. It was definitely memorable."

"I mean the outcomes of our labor. Do you remember what the girls had to say?"

"Some of it. I wish I had written it down."

"The old man, Kuzma. Several said he was killed at the hand of a young woman."

"Yes, I remember that. I think she was Cooper's girlfriend."

Roxanne sipped her wine. "Yes, I agree with you. Do you remember several of my ladies saw death hovering around a young woman?"

"Yes."

"Death may be accompanying her, not to kill her, but to capture others with whom she comes into contact."

I drank some wine and nodded thoughtfully. Much death had been accompanying a blonde woman in the Capital Region and in Mexico.

"Do you remember one of my ladies telling you she saw a foreign woman locked in a small room, sobbing. Could that have been the Hawkes' young nanny?"

"Possibly. But she wasn't locked away alone. Elizabeth Hawkes was with her."

"Perhaps it is something yet to come."

I slipped off my shoes and put my feet onto the coffee table. Moisture from my socks created a small patch of condensation on the waxy surface around my heels.

"Do you remember one lady seeing that 'descendants of the Conquistadors are working to steal something away'?"

"Yes. I assume she meant that Caesar is trying to steal the machine that Henry Hawkes is building."

"You told me that Caesar's cartel has just elected new leadership?"

"Yes, Caesar told me the new leader is a guy named 'El Escorpión.'"

"Perhaps Caesar isn't the thief. Maybe he's playing it straight with Henry Hawkes, but Caesar's new leader is the thief."

I hadn't thought of that. "That paints a new possibility. It's an entirely new perspective."

"Let's be honest, Barty. You haven't given much thought to what my ladies divulged to you."

I nodded. Roxanne was teaching me to be a better analyst by not neglecting avenues to be investigated. My police training would have pooh-poohed anything coming from a séance. But maybe the ladies had sensed some things which could be useful. They certainly had painted a scenario of possibilities.

"And one last thing. Do you remember some of my ladies telling you that a sister could help you solve this case?"

"Do you think they meant Helen Martin? She was

busted up pretty badly in the shootout in Albany when we freed Elizabeth Hawkes and Nadiya Bodnar. She took several rounds."

"Have you checked in with her lately?"

I dropped my chin to my chest. I'd been avoiding Helen since I'd hooked up with Roxanne.

"Don't worry, I won't be jealous if you and Helen work together on solving cases. When you've worked together, you solved everything you've been presented."

Roxanne was right about that. Helen and I were quite a team when we worked together as cops. My being a private detective had put a small glitch in our working relationship, and my reluctance to nurture that relationship had widened the glitch into a gulley. But I was pretty sure it wasn't anything insurmountable. I made myself a promise to call Helen in the morning.

Roxanne took me by the hand and led me around the downstairs shutting off all the lights and locking the doors. Then she pulled me upstairs, undressed me, and threw me down on the bed. She unhooked her bra and stepped out of her undies.

"I'm off tomorrow, so you'd better rack my bones tonight. And in the morning, you'd better let me sleep in."

When I finally looked at the clock on our bureau, it was a few minutes after three in the morning. Roxanne was snoring lightly. I closed my eyes and joined her.

Chapter 31

I called Helen at ten in the morning.

Her voice sounded raspy, as though she had a cold. "Where you been, Jonesy? Thought you didn't love me no more."

"I've got no excuse for not calling you or coming to see you, Helen."

"Well, at least you're honest. Hope you feel guilty."

"More important is how are you doing? Are you able to get around okay? When will you be able to go back to work?"

"I've been better, but I'm through the worst of it. The round I took in the leg has been the most difficult one to deal with. It's been painful to walk on, but I'm managing. I go back to work on Monday morning. Light duty only. Chief's been very generous to me."

"He could have called me back in to substitute for you, but I guess I'm too far down on the list for even a temporary re-hire."

"You got a reason for calling other than feeling bad for not coming to see me?"

"I've got a lot to tell you."

"Like what?"

"Like who I think killed Kuzma Bodnar and held those two women captive."

"Well, go on…"

"Not over the phone. How about you let me buy you lunch at Captain Mambo's?"

"You mean you just callin' me 'cause you got a hankerin' for Captain Mambo's and you got nobody else to take you into the establishment."

"Something like that…"

"How about today? Meet you there at 12:30?"

"I could pick you up if you'd like."

"I'd like to drive. I need the practice of driving with a weak leg."

"You sure? I'll open my car door for you and even snap you into your seatbelt."

"No way, Hondo. You just wanting to put your arms around me. See you there at 12:30, Jonesy. And don't be late."

****

I pulled into the parking lot at Captain Mambo's at 12:20 p.m. Helen hadn't arrived yet, which was her usual MO. If she was early for an appointment, she would drive around the block a few times so she could ring the doorbell precisely at the agreed-to time. I stayed in my car until she arrived because there was no way I was going into Captain Mambo's without an escort. It just wasn't done.

I saw Helen when she was half a block away. As she passed through the neighborhood, the hubcaps on her Japanese sedan reflected the noonday sun against the storefront façades like a battery of photographers flashing their cameras in sequence. When she pulled to a stop to let oncoming traffic pass before turning into the parking lot, her hubcaps kept spinning as if they were motor-driven.

When the path was clear, she parked, got out, and

walked in my direction with a slight limp in her right leg. She was dressed in blue cotton pants and a white cotton pullover top with gold-tone chains around her neck. She looked tired, but I didn't care. I was happy to see her.

I opened the door to my SUV and gave her a big hug. "You look like you're ready to go dancing."

"Don't be telling me I'm cute when I know I'm walking like a little old lady. Well, I am cute...but you know what I mean."

I laughed.

We went inside. As usual, the air smelled of hot oil and fish, and the clientele stared at me like I didn't belong. I ordered a shrimp platter and an iced tea. Helen surprised me when she ordered fish and chips—something she had never ordered before.

She saw my surprised expression. "Don't look at me that way, Jonesy. A girl can order anything she wants. I don't always order the seafood platter. Thought I'd try one of Chaquille's usuals and see if it's worth the money."

"Chaquille? Chaquille Bergen? Are you dating him?"

Helen looked over her shoulder, away from me. "We been seeing each other a little while."

"Even after he bit your big toe, and it got all infected?"

"Yup, even after. He's come around. Learned how to treat a lady. Knows I'll cut it off if he don't treat me the way I deserve."

We found a table for two near the window. Two men who were seated next to us relocated across the room.

"Brothers think you got something they don't want to catch."

"Nice, Helen. So much for cultural sensitivity."

Helen pulled the end off her fish plank and dipped it into a small cup of tartar sauce. "What you got to tell me?" She stuffed the fish into her mouth.

"There's a young woman living next door to the Hawkes."

"She's rooming with that Russian bigwig, isn't she? They ever finish that fortress they're building?"

"Yeah. The Berezovskys. And no, I don't think they've finished building. Anyway, the young woman's name is Mariya Auersuch...at least that's the name she's been using. She's dating Hawkes' son Cooper. Mrs. Cooper and their nanny Nadiya think Mariya is the woman who orchestrated their kidnapping by the Russians."

"I need real proof. You got anything else?"

"Nothing that will stand up in a court of law—at least at the moment. Didn't the Russian we captured say something about Maria Orsic being their leader?"

"Yeah, he called her 'the ancient one.'"

"She's not ancient." I peeled the fin off the tail of shrimp and plopped it into my basket. "But there's more. Down in Mexico a couple of weeks ago, a group of Russians kidnapped a cartel leader and slit his throat. They were led by a young blonde woman named Maria Orsic. She escaped."

"Interesting, but what's the connection?"

"Cooper Hawkes' girlfriend was in Mexico during the same time period. Her name is Mariya Auersuch. Mariya and Maria are the same name, just spelled differently. Her last name 'Auersuch' sounds almost the

same as 'Orsic.' I think there's more here than
coincidence. I think they're the same person. I think
Cooper's girlfriend kidnapped his mother and flew to
Mexico where she kidnapped and killed the cartel
leader."

"Why would she do that?"

"She's after a set of plans for a flying machine that
Hitler wanted to build. Nadiya Bodnar's grandfather
had those plans. I think she killed him for them."

"This is getting complicated."

"I think you need to find an excuse to take her in
for questioning. Maybe it's her connection with the
Russians. Maybe threaten to turn her over to the FBI."

"I'll talk to the chief about it on Monday, but I'm
supposed to be on light duty. He's not going to okay my
going all ballistic on this young woman, especially if all
I got is suspicion." Helen ate some more fish and a
handful of fries that she dipped in ketchup. I knew she
was mulling over my suspicions about Mariya
Auersuch. Finally, she asked me a question. "So, what's
this stuff about Hitler and a flying machine?"

"It's supposed to be an antigravity machine that
could revolutionize space travel. It's like a flying
saucer. Google the name Maria Orsic, and you'll find
everything there is to know about it."

Helen rolled her eyes at me. "If it could be done,
NASA would have done it already." She finished her
fish and wiped her mouth with the tan paper napkin
which accompanied her meal. "I'll look into this
Mariya Auersuch woman and see what I can learn
about her. Maybe see if she's in our database. Might
even bring her in to talk about the Russians...see what
she tells me."

"Good. Thanks, Helen."

"We still don't know who the Russians who shot me were working for. They dropped a name. Maybe it was to throw us off the trail of the real culprit." She plopped her napkin onto her paper plate. "In one sense, this could be a national security case that should involve the FBI, but I prefer to consider this case a local crime and solve it locally."

****

Mariya called Cooper at nine o'clock in the evening. Still locked in his room to prevent the spread of COVID, he was watching the Yankees lose to the Red Sox for the second time in two days. Mariya wasn't as upbeat as normal. Her voice was almost sulky.

"What's the matter, Mariya? You seem preoccupied."

"How do I say this, Cooper? I don't want to alarm you. I just need to know how you really feel about me. Like, am I a summertime fling, or do you feel it could be a long-term thing? If things between us continue to gel, would you ever consider marriage?"

"I love you, Mariya. You know that. I've told you that a hundred times."

"I wish I could see you, so I could look into your eyes when you tell me you love me."

"I wish I could be with you, too. But it won't be long. Just another week until I'm out of COVID quarantine."

"I have something important to tell you. Something you need to know…something that cannot wait seven days." Her breathing was heavy, probably upset. "I think I'm pregnant."

"Oh, oh God…"

"I knew this news would upset you."

"No, I'm not upset. I'm just a little floored by the news. Will you marry me? We can get married at the courthouse in Albany. It would take less than a week to arrange."

"Your parents will hate and distrust me. They will think I got pregnant so I could become an American citizen, or that I want to use the baby as a ploy to steal their fortune."

"My folks aren't that way. They'll let us live here in Altamont until I can support you, and we can find a home of our own."

"But I want my baby to be a citizen of Romania."

"We have time to figure that out. Maybe they permit dual citizenship. If you must have the baby in Romania, we can fly there before your due date." His head was spinning. "There's time to figure this out…all of it."

Chapter 32

Elizabeth was in the kitchen when Henry walked in briskly.

"Pyotr called," he said. "He wants to see me. He should be here in a few minutes."

"Is it a neighborly call or business?" Elizabeth asked. "Will Taisiya be coming with him?"

"I have no idea. But he's only been here once since they moved into their bomb shelter."

"The Berezovskys are strange people, Henry, with strange customs. Besides, they're pushy Russians, and I'm not altogether convinced he wasn't involved in my kidnapping."

The sound of large car tires on the gravel driveway interrupted their conversation. "That may be him now."

Henry looked out the second-floor picture window. The sky above was blue and sunny, but in the distance, gray skies and poor visibility indicated Albany was in the midst of an isolated thunderstorm.

Below, the Berezovsky's black limousine pulled to a stop in front of the stone mansion. The driver, a large man with a shaved head, exited the car and opened the back door. His hand seemed gargantuan as it gripped the chrome door handle. Pyotr Berezovsky scooted forward and used both hands on the door frame to pull himself from the black leather interior. He squinted in the sun and wiped his head with a handkerchief. Then he approached the front door and rang the bell.

Henry and Elizabeth took their small elevator to the first floor and opened the front door.

"Good afternoon, Hawkes," Pyotr bellowed. "And you, too, Elizabeth. Taisiya sends her regrets, but she is engaged in selecting clothes for an upcoming journey."

"Oh, you'll be traveling?" Elizabeth asked.

"Yes, it's just family business. Besides, she needs a break from living underground."

Elizabeth forced a smile. "May I offer you something to drink? Vodka?"

"Would you happen to have any Kentucky whiskey? It reminds me of good Irish whiskey, but it has better bite. I have grown fond of it while we wait in our little bunker for our new home to be completed. I shipped a case of it back to Vladimir, but he has yet to acknowledge my gift."

"Come," Henry said, ushering Pyotr with his right hand. "Let's go upstairs. Perhaps we can watch lightning strike the Corning Tower."

The trio entered the elevator and rode it to the second floor. Elizabeth hurried to the bar and returned with an eight-ounce glass half full of whiskey and a small, insulated container of ice cubes. She handed Henry a beer because she thought it was too early in the day for him to be drinking hard liquor.

"Ah, this is very nice. Thank you," Berezovsky said. "No ice for me, however. It dilutes the whiskey's essence."

They sat in the white leather reclining chairs and watched as an occasional lightning bolt hit the ground in the distance.

"Do you think the storm will be heading this way?"

Pyotr asked.

"It seems to have come from the northwest, so we should enjoy a pleasant afternoon," Henry replied.

"Doesn't it seem to you that all storms and strikes come from the West?"

Henry didn't fail to notice the subtle jab in Pyotr's words. "Bad storms come from many directions, Pyotr, not only from the west."

Pyotr held his glass in the air. "Well said, my friend."

Elizabeth sat down beside her husband. "Henry says that you've come to discuss something important. Do you need us to watch your property or work crew while you're away?"

"My business is with your husband, madam. I hope that does not offend you."

Elizabeth excused herself and walked into the kitchen.

Henry sipped from his bottle of beer. Condensation ran down its edge and dribbled onto his pants leg. He wiped it away. "How can I help you, Pyotr?"

"Well, my friend, I have come as a nosy neighbor. You have constructed a warehouse to the south of your home. Will you be using it as a barn? We are not partial to the aroma of cattle."

Henry chuckled. He was certain Pyotr already suspected what was happening in his steel hangar and came seeking verification. *Elizabeth's concerns may be well-founded*, he thought.

"Strange sounds may emanate from my warehouse from time to time, but the sounds will not come from livestock. I am working on a special scientific project. It's top secret. Not even the U.S. government knows about this project."

Pyotr raised his glass into the air as if saluting or toasting to Henry. "So, the mild inventor seeks to expand his fortune. This is a good thing, no?"

"I'll tell you this much: It will change the world of aviation."

"Are you working on a new safety device, perhaps something which allows aircraft to avoid collisions with other craft nearby?"

"No, it's a propulsion system based on the Vimana, and mechanical principles found in Hindu writings from 15,000 years ago. Are you familiar with the Vimana?"

"Are you certain that your government is unaware of your project? Could it be they are permitting you to fully develop it with your own dollars before they swoop down and seize it from you as a national security interest?"

Henry sat upright in his chair. "Why would you ask that?"

"Let me warn you to be careful, my friend. I have friends in the Federal Counterintelligence Service of Russia, the FSK. It is the organization that replaced the KGB. They are aware of your project and have asked me to spy on you...to learn what I can and to share that information with them."

"Really?"

"They are relentless. They may have orchestrated your wife's kidnapping. The men who took her were my countrymen, no?"

Henry leaned back against his chair.

Pyotr continued. "Have no fear of me. They were my countrymen, but they were not my employees."

Henry nodded, deep in thought.

"Keep the plans for your flying machine in a secure place, my friend, and keep your protective forces on high alert."

"Thank you for your concerns, Pyotr." Henry stood. "Come with me."

Henry led Pyotr into his study. He touched the cover of a book entitled Code Red and pulled it forward. The bookcase slid forward. Henry pushed it to his left, exposing the face of a large safe with a digital combination lock. "I keep the plans to my machine in here. This safe is impervious to fire and explosive devices. I believe it will keep out both the FSK and the CIA."

Pyotr swallowed the last of his whiskey. "Good, my friend. I think you are well prepared for anything they may send your way." He lifted his empty glass. "You have, perhaps, a little more for an aging ambassador of good will?"

Henry closed his bookcase. "Come, let's see where Elizabeth has hidden the bottle."

As they walked out of Henry's study, Pyotr put his arm around Henry's shoulder and laughed. "You have left me in an unenviable position. Now that you've shown it to me, if someone cracks your safe, you will think I had it done."

\*\*\*\*

Elizabeth Hawkes screamed at Cooper and threw the book she was reading at him. "She's what? You stupid idiot. How could you have…?"

Cooper held his hands out as he pleaded. "We took precautions, Mom. Honest. I don't know when it happened."

"When is she due?"

Cooper shrugged his shoulders. "I don't know, Mom. I haven't seen her since I was exposed to COVID. I'm not even sure she's seen a doctor yet."

"Does she plan to keep it or do the right thing and eliminate it?"

"Mom? How can you ask that? I know you oppose abortion except in certain circumstances."

"This may be one of those circumstances, son. She is possibly an evil person, a very evil person."

"Don't say that. You barely know her."

Cooper stormed out of the living room and slammed the door to his bedroom.

Five minutes later he returned. "I'm sorry I walked out on you, Mom. But, if Maryia's pregnant, I plan to do the appropriate thing and marry her."

"And I'm sorry, too, Cooper. But if she's pregnant, marriage absolutely is out of the question at the moment."

Chapter 33

Caesar and I were enjoying a cup of Columbian dark roast coffee when Laverne buzzed him.

"Si, Laverne?"

"The men from Fort Drum are here to see Mr. French."

"Excellent. Send them back."

A few moments later Caesar's door opened. Three muscular men in desert camo entered his office. I stood and pulled my chair aside to make enough room for five people in Caesar's small office. The men looked at me suspiciously.

Caesar stood and motioned in my direction. "Gentlemen, this is Bartholomew Jones. Mr. Jones is my security officer."

Their expressions eased, but they still seemed reluctant to state their business in my presence.

"I'll step outside, Mr. French," I said.

"That won't be necessary," one of the soldiers said. He was probably in his early thirties. His light brown hair was shaved on the sides with a short, pointed flattop. On his forearms were tattoos of green cobras, coiled and ready to strike. His black name tag was inscribed with the name "Krabb."

Caesar and I sat.

Krabb did the talking for the small group. "We've come to negotiate the price for more fenethylline. We want a bulk discount."

I looked at Caesar.

"Captagon," he told me.

I nodded.

Caesar leaned back in his chair and put his right foot on the open bottom drawer of his desk. "I take it your customers were satisfied with the quality of the last batch. How much more do you want, and what do you feel is an appropriate price?"

"They're getting it for thirty dollars per bottle at Pendleton. We want it for the same."

"How many pills in the bottles from Pendleton?" Caesar asked.

Krabb looked at the man behind him, a man whose nametag said, "Ramos." Ramos fumbled in the pocket of his cargo pants and pulled out a bottle of capsules. He handed it to Krabb. Krabb poured the capsules onto Caesar's tabletop and counted. "Sixty." He looked at Ramos. "Did you use any of these?"

"No. This is a new bottle I got from Garcia yesterday."

Krabb's expression displayed his confusion. "So, they're costing the guys at Pendleton fifty cents each." He looked at Caesar. "Your bottles have one hundred capsules, and you're charging us forty dollars. I think you're already giving us a better deal."

Ramos scooped up the sixty pills and carefully poured them back into the small green bottle.

"The guys from Pendleton should be buying them through us. We could sell them a bottle of one hundred pills for forty-five dollars and make five dollars per bottle."

Caesar removed his foot from his desk drawer and

set it squarely on the floor. "Gentlemen, if you're thinking of expanding your business into the west, perhaps we can reduce the price even more on a sliding scale by volume."

"What's that mean?" Krabb said.

"The more bottles you purchase, the lower the price per bottle. We can devise a sliding scale so you can see exactly how much profit will result from each shipment. Perhaps if you order thousands of bottles to sell to western military facilities, you can make thousands of dollars to split among yourselves to supplement your personal military retirement programs."

I shouldn't have been surprised by Caesar's suggestion. His deal to sell Captagon to La Araña had been agreed to under La Cabra's leadership. But La Cabra was now dead, and Caesar would push the envelope by continuing to sell Captagon to La Araña at a small profit, while undercutting La Araña's volume by selling directly to the military in the east who would, in turn, transfer it to the west at a lesser price than La Araña could afford to meet. It was genius.

"How many bottles you got for us today?" Krabb asked.

"I have only the one hundred bottles you ordered."

Krabbe pulled a brown envelope from his own cargo pants pocket and laid it on the desktop.

Caesar turned and pulled two cardboard boxes from the floor behind him. He handed them to Krabb, who handed one each to the men behind him.

Caesar reached into the opened desk drawer where his foot had rested earlier. He placed nine bottles of Captagon on his desk. "Of course, I have an extra three bottles for each of you men to take with you free of charge. Let's call it an incentive to consider my proposal to open a gateway to the west."

Krabb scooped up the nine bottles and divided them among his companions. "Thanks, Mr. French. Nice doing business with you, as always."

"Gentlemen, if we do agree to enter into an expanded sales partnership, nobody can know where you obtain your product. Is that understood? Nobody. Just refer to me generically as your 'source.'"

All three men nodded. "Yessir." They did not reply in unison, but it was clear they understood what Caesar expected.

\*\*\*\*

It was his last day of confinement, and Cooper was anxious to see Mariya. He had been away from her for ten days. For the last two, she had been non-communicative, not responding to his texts and not answering his calls. Her cell phone recording now responded, "The mailbox of the person you are calling is full. Please try again later."

"Mom, where are my car keys?" he asked at noon. He was dressed in workout sweats and his tennis shoes were draped over his shoulder.

"Your father locked them in his safe until tomorrow morning when you are ethically permitted to intermingle with people again."

"It's not fair. I need to go see Mariya."

"You know how I feel about that, Cooper. Stay away from that young woman until I give you permission to see her again."

"I'll walk there if I have to."

"And will Mr. Berezovsky's security guards let

you through their gate?"

Cooper threw his Reeboks into the back of the white leather sofa. They bounced into the air, spun like chain shot, then dropped to the floor.

At eight o'clock in the evening I arrived at their home. No dogs bayed at my arrival, but Elizabeth greeted me at the door and let me in. "Good to see you, Bart."

"You, too, Elizabeth."

We rode upstairs in the elevator. "Care for a drink?" Elizabeth asked as the door opened.

"Got a beer? I mean anything basic, like a ballpark might offer?"

"Would an IPA do?"

"That would hit the spot."

"Henry should be here momentarily. I've asked Cooper and Nadiya to join us."

Nadiya came into the room. She looked tired from a day's work entertaining the Hawkes' daughter. "Charity is busy building herself a new avatar, so I have a few minutes."

Cooper then came into the room. He seemed upset and sat as far away as he could without being totally unfriendly. I nodded to him.

We sat quiet for five long minutes looking at each other and out the window toward Albany. The sun was low in the sky and cast the shadow of the mountain behind us onto the mansion. Finally, Henry came out of the elevator. "Good, we're all here." He shook my hand. "Nice to see you, Bart." He sat beside his wife. "So, what have you learned?"

"I have enlisted the assistance of an old friend from the Willow Falls Police Department to look into the movements of Mariya Auersuch."

"I knew it! I knew it!" Cooper blurted. He leapt to his feet. "You two couldn't let me be happy without prying into the privacy of the woman I love."

"Sit down, Cooper," Henry ordered. "This has nothing to do with your love life. It has everything to do with an investigation into your mother's and Nadiya's kidnapping."

Cooper sat down with his arms across his chest. The bottoms of his feet were directed at his parents. If they had not been Americans, they would have been offended.

"Detective Martin was able to obtain fingerprints from the glasses and wine bottle you obtained."

Henry spoke directly to his son. "I gave them to Mr. Jones after your evening party in the tent on the hillside above us."

"Hrrummpff," Cooper grunted.

I gestured toward Elizabeth and Nadiya. "Her fingerprints match a set the Albany police lifted from several places in the house in Albany where you two were held captive by the Russians."

"Aha!" Elizabeth cried. "So, she was there!"

"And through friends in Mexico, I was able to obtain a matching set of fingerprints lifted by Mexican police at a hotel room where a man was savagely executed, also by Russian operatives. The hotel was near Mazatlán, where Mariya supposedly was vacationing at the time."

Cooper unfolded his arms and dropped his hands into his lap.

I continued. "I am still working on confirming her exact location in Mazatlán at the time of her vacation.

However, nobody with the last name of Auersuch or Orsic was registered at any hotel in Mazatlán during those dates."

"How about my grandfather, Mr. Jones?" Nadiya asked. "Did she kill him?"

"It appears the woman who killed him was a brunette. However, nobody on staff has been able recognize her from the video. The hospital security cameras still record in black and white, which has not helped this investigation."

"Too bad," Elizabeth said.

"Do you remember when we went to see your grandfather at the hospital, Nadiya?"

"Yes."

"Do you remember passing a young nurse as we entered the critical care unit? You said, 'Good afternoon,' and she responded, 'Yes, it is very good.' That young woman had dark brown hair, but her eyebrows were blonde. At the time, I thought it was strange, but I shrugged it off. Now I realize she was wearing a wig. I cannot prove it was Mariya, but I am convinced it was."

"So, you believe Mariya killed my grandfather?"

"Yes, I do. She was after the set of plans your grandfather sent you."

Henry cleared his throat and waved his arm toward the south end of his property. "For the machine we are constructing in the warehouse, Nadiya. If the project is successful, you will become a very rich woman."

"And what about me?" Cooper asked. "Mariya and I are in love."

"Maybe you both are, son," Henry replied, "or maybe just one of you is. The other perhaps has been using you to get to the plans she has been seeking."

Cooper folded his arms again. "Well, tomorrow I'm going to see her in person and ask her to marry me."

"The Willow Falls Police have issued an APB for her arrest, Cooper," I said. "I'm sorry, but her fingerprints implicate her in the kidnapping of two people—the two in this room with you—and the shooting of a police officer."

Henry stood and looked out the window. "What is that noise? It sounds like firecrackers." He saw nothing, so he sat down again. "It's probably something over at Berezovsky's."

"Are we done?" Cooper asked.

"Yes, I think so," Henry replied.

Cooper stood. "Goodnight, Mr. Jones. I can't say it's been nice seeing you again."

"It's sad news, Cooper," Elizabeth said, "but we all needed to hear it."

Cooper left the room.

"Cooper has been so lovesick," Elizabeth said. "I hope this news hasn't crushed him irreparably."

Nadiya slapped her hand on the cushion beside her. "Well, I hope the police are successful in finding that woman and bringing her to trial."

Cooper shouted from his bedroom. "Dad! Dad! Your warehouse. Your warehouse is on fire!"

Henry shot out of his chair. Cooper and I followed him into the elevator. It couldn't go down quickly enough. When it finally opened, we bolted from it and out the front door. I punched my security code into my cell phone and handed it to Cooper. "Call 9-1-1 and report the fire."

Henry and I hurried across his side yard, then to the gravel driveway and to the open delivery door of the warehouse. Smoke was billowing out, but the flames seemed to be contained deep inside. We rushed in. On the concrete floor, lying in a perfect row lay the bodies of six men. "Let's get them out of here," I shouted.

Henry and I each grabbed the feet of a man and pulled him toward the door. I got mine out first, then helped Henry pull his man fifteen feet from the door. We went back inside. I grabbed another man and began pulling him out. Cooper arrived. "Here, let me help you!" he shouted.

"Go help your father. He's not as strong as I am."

I pulled my second man out and headed in for a third. Henry and Cooper passed by me, each pulling on the leg of a large body. I grabbed the legs of a third man and pulled. Henry and Cooper passed by, going for the last man. They reached the drop-off point the same time as I did.

"Is that all?" I shouted.

"Should only be six," Henry replied breathlessly.

"Did you reach the emergency dispatcher?" I asked Cooper.

"Yes. They should be here soon."

"What about these men?" Henry asked.

"They've all been executed, Henry. Look at their heads."

Henry inspected two men. Both had holes in their foreheads made by a large caliber weapon. "Oh, Jesus," he moaned. "It had to be the Russians. You think it could have been the FSK?"

"Why would they kill these men? Wouldn't they be after the plans for the machine?"

"Yes, most likely. Why would they seek the plans here?"

"Your men are using them, aren't they?"

"Yes, but each man only has access to that portion of the plans which pertain to his skill. Nobody has the complete set, except for me and Caesar."

Three firetrucks arrived a few minutes later. We could hear their sirens for a full minute before they pulled into the Hawkes' estate. Behind them came the fire chief and two police cars—one from Albany and one driven by Helen Martin.

The fire chief hurried up to us. "Sir, are you the owner of the building?"

"Yes," Henry replied.

"Where is your pond or the nearest source of water?"

"The closest source is my well, up near the house. Otherwise, there's a small creek about two hundred yards up the main road."

"Your well won't do. We have 10,000 gallons of water in the tanker. The most we can hope to do is to contain the flames at this location until the fire burns itself out. Do you have someone who can man a garden hose up by your house, in case any flames should drift that way?"

Hawkes pulled his son over. "This is my son, Cooper. He can man the hose."

The fire chief gave Cooper explicit instructions, and Cooper ran back to the house to defend it from drifting ash. The chief left us and began giving instructions to his men.

Helen approached me. She was still limping. "Shit, this is a mess, Jonesy. Anybody hurt?"

I pointed at the bodies lying in a row on the gravel. "Got six dead. Executed, I think."

"Russians?"

"No, these are all scientists and technicians."

"No, butthole, I mean do you think the Russians did it?"

"We won't know until your guy does an autopsy and we get a reading on the caliber of the bullets. But from all appearances, the Russians would be a very good guess."

"Did they get what they were after?"

"No idea."

Helen called in the fatalities and had three ambulances dispatched from Willow Falls. "I want those bodies. Don't want to have to get them transferred from Albany."

"It's out of your jurisdiction, isn't it?"

"I'll work it out later. It'll give Chief Comstock something to yell at me about."

I looked toward the Hawkes' mansion. Small pieces of burning ash regularly broke away from the plumes of smoke and floated in that direction in the gentle breeze. But before they settled on the house, Cooper picked them off one by one with the garden hose.

Henry's cell phone rang. It was Elizabeth. He answered without a cordial "Hello." "Yeah, we're good here. Fire department has it under control. It's gonna have to burn to the ground. Coming down to watch?"

"No, Henry. You need to come up here. Your safe has been burglarized."

"We've got to go back up to the house. Somebody broke in. This fire may have been a diversion."

"Ride up with me," Helen said.

Henry and I climbed into Helen's car. I had to throw an empty pizza box into the back seat with Henry as I sat down. Helen backed onto the rocky hillside and then turned toward the gravel roadway. We followed it to the driveway and then turned toward the mansion.

Elizabeth was standing at the door. "I feel so violated," she said. "It must have happened while Nadiya and I were with Charity. We heard nothing— not a sound."

Henry led Helen and me into his study. The bookcase was open, and behind it, a safe door stood open. Papers were strewn on the floor.

"Yup, they took the plans," Henry said.

"You don't seem too upset, Mr. Hawkes," Helen said.

"I directed them to this safe," Henry said. "I always questioned my business partner's motives, but a few days ago I was visited by Pyotr Berezovsky. I showed him this safe and bragged about its security. He said if someone broke into it, I would blame him. He was right about that."

"But your drawings, the plans...they're gone," I said.

"No, they're not. The burglars took plans I had altered."

I smiled. Hawkes had done the same thing Caesar had done. He had created a bogus set of plans to buy himself time to build the real machine. Perhaps they were a perfectly suited set of partners.

Chapter 34

I arrived home at midnight. The lights in the kitchen were on, but Roxanne was out back and already halfway through a bottle of wine.

"Eeew, you smell like smoke, Barty."

"Yeah, I was at a barn fire tonight."

"Did you bring me any roast beef?"

"You're funny, Roxanne. Mind if I plunge into the hot tub?"

"I wish you would. Call me when you're sweet smelling again."

I walked over to the hot tub, stripped, and climbed in. Roxanne wasn't in her chair when I looked back towards her.

I took a breath and then slipped entirely beneath the warm water. It felt great to be submerged, and I knew the chlorine was doing its best to rid my hair and body of the acrid scent of melting plastic and electrical insulation which was clinging to every part of me.

I saw a form appear above me. I came out of the water and wiped my eyes.

"I brought you a towel and your robe, Barty...and your own glass of wine. You'd better hurry up. I'm already into my third glass."

She walked back toward her chaise lounge. She was wearing only a long see-through silk robe and the lamp post behind her let me see everything she owned.

Arousal comes quickly to a man my age. Well, to me at any age past fourteen.

I chugged my glass of wine and climbed out of the hot tub. Then I dried myself and threw on my robe. I walked quietly to Roxanne's side. A freshly opened bottle of wine stood on her favorite wrought-iron table. I poured myself a second glass.

Roxanne sighed. "Be a good boy, and go turn off the lamp post, would you."

I did. And when I turned to walk back to her, I saw that she had lighted the flame on a fat red candle. "It'll give you just enough light to see what you're doing."

I knelt on the grass beside her chaise lounge and kissed her. Her robe fell open. She didn't pull it back on to cover herself. That was the signal I was hoping for.

****

Helen called me at nine in the morning. "Going over to that Russian guy's house to see if he's home. Hoping to find Goldilocks. You want to come along?"

"Yeah, I sure do. What time?"

"Meet us at the gate at high noon."

Roxanne had already gone to work. She had left me a note, asking me to put her silk robe in the wash. I did. Then I fixed myself a bowl of raisin bran with a banana and a handful of blueberries. I turned on the television. The morning news was over, and only talk shows were on. I watched five minutes or less of three shows, and then hit the remote's kill button. Noon couldn't come quickly enough.

Then Caesar called me. "We've got an eleven o'clock meeting at Hawkes' house today, Jones. There was a fire at the warehouse. Heard you were there."

"Yeah, I was."

"You could have called me."

"Yeah, I could have, but I didn't want to wake you at three in the morning, and I slept in until you called me. It was a late night."

"How many dead?"

"Your entire second shift. You're going to need to replace them and restart the project."

"Hawkes seems to think we can start where we left off. Just gotta clean up the mess first and get some new tools."

"See you there at eleven, Caesar."

I had just enough time to bathe and dress before it was time to leave for the Helderbergs.

\*\*\*\*

The day was going to be hot. The sun was beating down on the Helderbergs like it was Arizona instead of upstate New York. I arrived a few minutes before eleven. Caesar was already standing outside the burned warehouse. With him were a dozen men, all the engineers and technicians from the first and third shifts. Dressed in Bermuda shorts, a white tee shirt and flip-flops, Henry Hawkes was walking across the field to greet them.

I parked behind a four-door pickup and joined the group of men. Caesar shook my hand.

Elizabeth Hawkes' voice roared toward us. "You're a numbskull, Henry! Take off your clothes before you come into the house. I don't want any ticks inside."

Henry joined us. He shook Caesar's hand and then mine.

"What was that about?" Caesar asked.

"Lizzy's got a thing about ticks. The dog brought

one into the house the other day, and she found it crawling up her leg. She's deathly afraid of Lyme disease."

"So, she didn't want you fishing for ticks by walking through the weeds?"

"Yeah, that's about the size of it."

Henry turned to the group of engineers and technicians. "Let's go inside and see what we can salvage, gentlemen."

He led us all into the large bay door of the warehouse. The air inside felt scratchy on my throat. Around the edges of the interior, workbenches and tools were in various stages of destruction. Most were blackened with soot. Electric wires hung from the walls, their rubber exteriors melted beyond repair. A 5-gallon plastic bottle dangled limp from the top of its cooler. Long sheets of steel had fallen from the roof and lay twisted here and there across the floor.

In the middle of the warehouse floor stood the machine. Its gray exterior sported a headdress of three sheets of steel and its upper body bore stains from the fire's heat. We walked under it and inspected its belly. Large electric wires hung from the craft's ports and were still connected to sockets beneath.

Henry pointed to the ports. "Is this what you were talking about, Falconer?"

"Yessir. The wires were protected from the heat by the exterior of the craft. Second shift was running the superconductor last night. If it's still on, the ultra-cold wires protected the hull and the machine's interior wires from heat damage."

Henry's face lit up. "Well, let's test it and see what we have."

Four of the eight men busied themselves for ten minutes. Caesar, Henry, and I just watched them work. The other men spread throughout the building looking for salvageable materials and tools. There was little to be found.

Two of the men came to us together. One was holding a steel engine part with a hole melted through it. "They used phosphorus grenades to start the fire," he said. "They probably added an accelerant before lighting the grenades."

"What is the significance?" Henry asked.

"They were probably military or paramilitary. They were hoping for complete destruction of the machine."

"So, it was either the Russians or our CIA," I said.

"It was Russians, Bart," Henry said. "Pyotr Berezovsky as much as told me so before they arrived."

A loud clatter of steel on concrete startled us. Falconer stepped down from the hull by ladder. "Sorry, I didn't mean to drop the wrench. But I have good news. All the machine's systems seem to be unharmed. I think we should be able to clean her up and continue assembly as soon as we replace the necessary tools."

"Excellent," Caesar said. "I'm still hoping we can launch by September."

"Maybe during September," Falconer replied. "Some of our more highly sophisticated test instruments may not be so easy to replace quickly."

Caesar nodded. "Make a detailed list of everything you need, and I'll have it to you faster than you can imagine."

"This certainly is good news," Henry said. "I'll have the list together by tomorrow. While we're waiting for the new equipment, the men and I can begin cleanup."

"You men focus on identifying the necessary tools and equipment. I'll have a large crew over here this afternoon. Reconstruction of the ceiling and wiring can begin as soon as tomorrow."

"You do work fast, Caesar," I said.

"I have to. El Escorpión has given me a deadline."

\*\*\*\*

I was standing beside him when Henry punched a number into his cell phone, and then he put his phone on speaker. It rang three times. Then we heard a fumbling noise before Pyotr's voice bellowed, "Good morning, Henry."

"Just like you suspected, Pyotr, someone broke into my safe last night."

"It wasn't me, my friend. Maybe your CIA."

"They also burned down my warehouse. They destroyed everything."

"Oh, I am so sorry to hear that. Surely, you'll be able to rebuild your device in no time."

"The thieves took my plans."

"I swear I took no part in such a mission. In fact, I am in Montreal as we speak, in the line boarding a flight to Moscow. Vladimir has asked to see me."

"Do you know who broke into my safe, Pyotr?"

"Of course not. Oh, look, I must give my boarding pass to the attendant. Talk to you soon."

The phone went dead, and then we heard the dial tone.

"What do you think?" Henry asked.

"Convenient time to be called to Moscow. He's transporting your plans and is going to hand them personally to Russian leaders. Maybe it will buy him some good will and get him back in good graces with the Kremlin."

"My thoughts exactly."

\*\*\*\*

I said goodbye to Caesar and Hawkes and drove half a mile to the Russian compound. It was five minutes past noon, and I was late for my appointment with Helen at the front of Berezovsky's home.

Berezovsky had spared no money on opulence. His new home was still incomplete, but already it bore colorful towers and spires reminiscent of Moscow in the heyday of the czars. The building itself spread over more than two acres of land and was set back in an alcove which had been hollowed from solid rock by huge machines.

Helen's car and three Willow Falls Police cruisers were parked outside. The massive front door to the mansion was wide open. Helen was standing in its arch, looking somewhat like a minnow being swallowed by a bass. She was in uniform and was wearing her official police cap. She waved at me and then tapped her wristwatch, which let me know she had expected me to be on time.

I exited my SUV and shouted up to her. "Sorry, Helen. I was involved with a client, and the time got away from me." I climbed the seven marble steps which led to the front porch.

"You weren't having sex, were you?" Helen asked. "You've done that to me before. You know, making me wait while you're making time."

"No, actually, I was listening to Berezovsky apologize for not being able to answer any questions. He was boarding a flight from Montreal to Moscow."

"That explains where he is, 'cause he sure ain't here."

She looked around the foyer. Its ceiling was open three stories high and was capped in stained glass. "You know, you could put my whole house in this space and still have room to park a couple of cars. Come to think of it, the front door is so large I could drive a truck right through it and not scratch a thing."

"Money makes that happen, and this clown has more money than we can imagine."

Helen got down to business. "The guys are searching the house, seeing if we can find anything incriminating. I want to pin Mrs. Hawkes' kidnapping on Berezovsky. And maybe the murder of Kuzma Bodnar, too."

"You've got to find his fallout shelter. He and the missus have been living there while this monstrosity is being built."

"What about their guest...you know, the girl who calls herself Mariya?"

"She's incommunicado, too. She may be sitting on Berezovsky's lap on the plane."

"So, they flew the coop before we could grasp them with the long arm of the law?"

"Maybe."

I looked for a doorway to the cellar. Helen followed me. When I found it, I hit the light switch and we both climbed down the stairs. Helen held her Sig in her hand, just in case. But I was certain we wouldn't bump into anything unexpected.

The cellar was huge. Its ceilings were fifteen feet high, and its concrete floors reminded me of photos I had seen of the interior of Cheyenne Mountain. A dozen or more separate footprints in the dust led from the stairway toward the left. "Something has been going on that way," I said.

"No kidding? You must have been an Indian Scout in your last life. I would never have known."

Helen was kidding with me. That was a good sign.

The footprints led to a steel door which was bolted into the concrete wall. "Maybe this is the bomb shelter," I said.

I pulled on the door, and it opened easily. Without warning a hundred fifty pounds of growling mastiff hit my chest, knocking me backwards and spraying my face with saliva.

Bang!

The dog fell limp on me. I rolled him off and stood up.

"You okay, Jonesy?"

I quickly scanned my body. I was shaken but not out of business.

"Your left hand is bleeding. We gotta treat that bite when we get back outside. No telling how many dead rats that dog has eaten today."

My left palm was, indeed, bleeding. Three toothmarks were obvious. In the excitement, I had never even felt the bite. "Damn," I complained as it began to hurt.

Helen holstered her Sig and gave me a handkerchief to wrap my hand.

Then we stepped into the bomb shelter. The light switch was mounted on the right. Helen flipped it on.

The shelter was constructed like a four-bedroom ranch house. The main door opened into the living room. From there, it was a short hop into a fully equipped kitchen and dining area. Dirty dishes and a couple of pans waited in the sink for someone to wash them. A hallway departed from the living room. The first door on the right was a bathroom. The first on the left was a small bedroom. The next two on the left were also bedrooms. And the last one on the right was another bedroom with its own small bathroom. Each room was modestly furnished with a bed and dresser, side table with lamp, and a small closet. The rooms evidenced recent occupancy, but they had been wiped clean and only needed a vacuuming to be rent-worthy.

As we searched each room, Helen looked for clues. In the smallest bedroom, she found a cell phone in the drawer of a nightstand. It was a cheap model anyone could buy at a discount store. She turned it on. Instantly it flashed messages from the same number. "This is interesting," she said. "Should we call this number?"

I suspected I knew who owned the phone.

"There's a string of texts, too." Helen opened a text. "It's from Cooper Hawkes."

"You'll be pleased to know you have in your hands the reason why Cooper hasn't been able to raise the love of his life," I said. "That's Mariya Auersuch's cell phone."

"I expect wherever she is, she isn't expecting to hear from Cooper anymore."

"I think she finally got what she came here for— the plans to Hawkes' machine."

Helen nodded. "Well, I'm going to have forensics download all the numbers that have been called and print us copies of the text and verbal messages." She paused a moment. "You want to give the bad news to Cooper, or would you like me to?"

"Hawkes is paying me, so I suppose it's my job. When you get the printout of all the calls she made, I'd like a heads-up in case there's anything incriminating involving Cooper."

"Roger on that, Jonesy. Let's go treat that bite and see if the guys have found anything."

Chapter 35

I delivered the bad news to Cooper as soon as Helen had field-dressed my hand. It was tough to see a young man cry. Most of us guys have experienced unrequited love, or we've had the hots for some girl who wouldn't give us the time of day. Sometimes we're simply out of their league, but other times we fall in love with some sweet thing who has the hots for some bad ass who ruins her or bruises her or otherwise doesn't give her the respect or affection she deserves. Didn't somebody write a song about how love stinks? In my own marriage, my lover stepped out on me and wound up owning everything I had. From my experience, I'd say that love doesn't stink. No, it actually sucks.

After I chatted with Cooper, I thought I should meet with his parents to let them know what Helen and I had discovered and what I had done as a result. I didn't want them to think I would hurt their child unnecessarily, but in this case, their son needed to grow up. Maybe I should have talked with Henry and Elizabeth first. Maybe.

After I told them about Cooper's lost love, Elizabeth sighed in relief. "So, I don't have to wonder anymore if my potential daughter-in-law actually kidnapped me? Woohoo." She mixed herself a strong drink, mostly bourbon, chugged it, and then mixed herself a second one.

I turned to Henry. "You don't seem too upset with the theft of your plans. Are you still going to be able to complete your machine without them?"

"Oh yes, and hopefully within Caesar's desired timeframe. The Russians got a nice set of plans, but they weren't the originals, and it will take them ten years to decipher what I did to them. Meanwhile, anything they build won't work—well, at least not for too long."

****

Caesar's team of ten men arrived at four in the afternoon and began cleaning the burned material out of the warehouse. By ten at night, they had created a large pile of wreckage outside the building.

The next morning a flatbed carrying a hydraulic excavator appeared in the gravel driveway. Four dump trucks bearing the Cabrillo Construction Company logo appeared several minutes later. Three men disconnected the excavator from the flatbed. One of the men drove it off the trailer and began using its claw-like arm to pile the damaged materials into the beds of the dump trucks. As each truck was filled, it was driven away and the next one in line moved forward to be filled. Material removal was completed by early afternoon, and the hydraulic excavator was reloaded onto the flatbed and driven away.

At noon, a team of four men attached camouflage netting beneath the steel beams which held the damaged roof. "To keep spying eyes from spotting our machine from the air," Caesar told me.

At three o'clock, a delivery truck brought new steel roofing and siding and rolls of electric wire. A team of eight electricians worked through the night to replace all the wires which had been damaged during the intense blaze. They were protected by a team of six armed sentries. A second team of electricians worked the next day installing new lighting and alarm systems.

Roofers appeared the second day, as well, replacing missing and damaged sheets of corrugated steel. Total replacement took two days.

The two teams of engineers evaluated their equipment needs for the remainder of the project and presented a list to Caesar, as he had asked. Included was a list of a dozen engineers and scientists who also had worked on top secret projects at Area 51 and Area 52 and who were now available for work. They were interviewed and prioritized for potential hiring by Henry and Caesar, who flew each person to Albany and personally made the final selections. By the time the replacement equipment arrived three weeks later, the new participants had been intermixed with the existing teams, introduced to the machine, and fully prepped on its systems.

Work to complete the machine commenced on August 1. Caesar was behind, and he hoped El Escorpión would forgive the delay. During a Facetime chat, Caesar noted, "The delays have all been because of the destruction caused by the Russians."

"Si, the same *bastardos* who killed La Cabra. Someday we will avenge his death."

"We believe the machine will be ready to fly by mid-November, Alejandro. Why don't you come to Albany for its first flight. Henry and Elizabeth Hawkes have a lovely guest room in their mansion, and I am certain they would welcome you with open arms."

"I have a better idea, Caesar. Have your men do the necessary test flights and work out any small problems with the machine. Then I will come to see this wonderful device and visit with you in the spring to discuss an idea I have. I think Los Equis should be waiting on the moon to welcome NASA when they begin work on their Artemis Base Camp. We can offer the astronauts champagne and cannabis and *mujeres*. You know, enlighten the astronauts to the pleasures of space flight."

"Ha! I like the way you think, amigo. No wonder you are our supreme leader!"

Chapter 36

Work on the machine began again, accelerated by the efforts of additional engineers and technicians. Armed guards stood at every entrance, and a radar unit searched the skies for possible air attack. Nothing so much as a visitor approached the warehouse beside the Hawkes' mansion.

Two weeks before Christmas, Elizabeth Hawkes called me. "I'm worried, Bart. Henry told me he was going out for a ride, and he hasn't returned."

I had never known her to express any concerns about her husband, except for his habit of helping the indigent. "How long has he been gone?"

"It's been four days now, and he didn't take his car."

This did seem like odd behavior. "Has he ever done this before…you know, gone away for more than a day without giving you advanced notice?"

Elizabeth sighed. "Only when he flew to Las Vegas to meet with an attorney about representing him in his patent infringement lawsuit."

"Well, maybe he's doing something like that again. He doesn't impress me as someone who intentionally wants to worry you."

I heard noise in the background over the phone.

"Well. There you are, you sorry bastard," Elizabeth shrieked. "I've been worried sick."

"Elizabeth?" I asked. "Elizabeth, is Henry home?"

"Yes, he just walked in the door and he's wearing the same clothes he was wearing the day he didn't come home. I'll get to the bottom of this…" She hung up.

Henry texted me an hour later:

—*Elizabeth told me she called you to initiate a search party. Let me assure you I'm fine. In fact, I've never been better.*—

I texted him back:

—*I guess you gave her quite a scare. I think she was worried that the Russians kidnapped you.*—

He replied:

—*If I told you where I've been, you wouldn't believe it. I'm keeping it a secret for now, but I'll let you know when the time is right.*—

What could I say to that? Henry was an adult, and he was my employer for the time being. There is no sense in trying to drag a secret out of your boss, especially one whose IQ runs circles around your own.

I still had no information to share about the whereabouts of Mariya Auersuch. Henry and I said a few pleasantries and promised to get together soon.

\*\*\*\*

At noon on January 5, all major news channels carried a live event from Russia. It was 7:00 p.m. in Moscow. Cameras and concert lighting had been set up in Red Square, where Dmitry Morosov, director of Russia's space agency, Roscosmos, greeted the world from a platform stage. Behind him stood a dozen special guests.

I was at the Hawkes home, invited by Henry to watch the special world telecast. Their son Cooper and Nadiya Bodnar were seated on a sofa across from me. I was on my second glass of New York vodka, the only beverage the Hawkes served that evening. "It's better than that Russian crap," Elizabeth said.

The commentator on NBC babbled on about the impending world expose of a new and secretive invention the Russians advertised as "miraculous." It was "a marvel that would change the world as we know it."

Live cameras panned the stage. "Look, there's Mariya!" Cooper exclaimed.

Standing to Morosov's left, Mariya was dressed in a red parka with a traditional Cossack-style fur hat. She looked cold and didn't appear happy.

"Yes, and Berezovsky is right beside her," Henry exclaimed. "Bastard…"

Berezovsky was wrapped in a floor length fur coat. A beaver fur trooper cap adorned his head. His teeth clenched a fat cigar, probably Cuban. He appeared to be inebriated. But he always appeared that way.

The camera zoomed in and focused upon Morosov. A dozen microphones were taped to his portable podium. "Comrades," he began, "our highly skilled Russian scientists and engineers have invented a machine that will change the face of aviation. Many of you have seen similar vehicles shoot across our skies at breakneck speeds, unstoppable by the fastest jets of militaries across the world. Today, however, our beloved Russian homeland joins those who venture to the stars and to distant galaxies."

The crowd applauded politely.

Morosov pointed his left hand toward a large black curtain which stood thirty yards from the speaker's platform. "Behold!"

The curtain dropped. The crowd burst into exclamations of awe and amazement. Standing on three spindly legs was a flying saucer. It was fatter than the one developed by Hawkes and French from Maria Orsic's plans, possible forty feet thick at its center. Around its edge spun white lights, circumventing the craft the way lights slowly revolve around a theatre marquis. The saucer's shell was shiny aluminum in color. Not the dull finish of Hawkes' saucer.

The announcer on NBC babbled on and on in excitement. "Do you think they captured it…you know, a crashed alien device?" he asked a guest commentator. "Do you think they'll share this technology with us, Martha, or will they simply use it to bury us economically?"

"What is this?" I asked.

"Just watch," Henry replied. "I knew they'd never test it before going public. They're just like the Chinese. They always trust our scientists and engineers to do the hard work of development, then they steal the work and put it into immediate use as something of their own."

"Hush, you two," Elizabeth chided. "What's his name is getting ready to speak again."

The television picture flicked from the saucer to the NBC commentator. "Look, Martha. Something spectacular is going on with the saucer."

The picture returned to the saucer.

Yes, something certainly was going on. The lights on the saucer's thin edge began spinning faster and faster until they became a blur and appeared to be a single neon light. Then the saucer lifted a few feet from the ground and its spindly legs retracted into its hull.

The saucer hovered, then quietly floated ten feet off the ground.

Dmitry Morosov spoke to the crowd again. "Watch now, as courageous Russian pilots ascend to the stars!"

The crowd broke into loud cheers and applause.

The saucer rose slowly to twenty and then thirty feet.

"I feel static electricity," the NBC announcer cried. "Look! It's climbing higher."

The saucer quickly moved to one hundred feet in the air. It wobbled slightly, then shot straight upward. When it reached five hundred feet, it paused. The white light on its edge turned bright red, and then flickered. Boom! A fireball lit the skies above the crowd. Balls of burning metal and chunks of shrapnel fell toward Earth.

The crowd screamed. Panic filled the square.

Nadiya Bodnar leapt to her feet and screamed with delight. "Justice! Justice for Ukraine!"

Television cameras followed the burning saucer. It plunged to the ground, falling directly upon the stage where Mariya Auersuch and Pyotr Berezovsky stood, frozen by the spectacle which descended upon them.

The NBC newscast turned to static. A moment later the picture returned. This time, however, its lead newscaster addressed the nation. "Ladies and gentlemen, we have just witnessed a tragic event of horrific proportions. I am left essentially speechless. It appears as though our correspondent in Russia has perished in the explosion. I don't know what else to say. We will await word from the Russian government as to the status of the crash of the flying device in Red Square."

The television went to advertisements.

"Jesus, Henry, I hope that doesn't happen to your precious little experiment," Elizabeth blurted. "The world will hate you."

"We've experienced no problems thus far, darling. Ours already has been test flown as far as Mars. Did you know there's more breathable atmosphere there than NASA admits? They've been lying to us for years."

Aha! That's where Henry was when he disappeared for four days: Mars! And it sounded as though Elizabeth was still unaware of his escapade.

Chapter 37

Roxanne helped everyone into her hot tub before she athletically hopped in herself. I handed her the glass of Bordeaux I had held for her.

"I'm so glad you've joined us," she said. "I'm sure we'll all become the best of friends."

Seated across from us, Helen and Chaquille Bergen raised their glasses. Well, Helen raised her glass of wine and Chaquille raised his brown bottle of IPA.

We touched glasses. "To friendship," Helen said.

"So, how is your Russian case going?" Roxanne asked.

"Well, we know who killed the old man," Helen replied. "The same perp kidnapped two women and probably killed a guy in Mexico. You know I'm not allowed to say more than that."

"The Russians took care of the perp for us," I said. "You saw the replay of her execution on the nightly news."

"It was certainly awful, wasn't it?" Roxanne said.

Helen sipped her wine. "It stands as a solved case with no American justice served. I hope she's dead, but you never know."

Chaquille tilted his head. "Wasn't that woman supposed to be dead in 1944, but she showed up in 2024 as young as she ever was? The guys in homicide are all talking about it."

"They've all got it wrong," I said. "The perp was just a distant relative who bore an uncanny resemblance to the German woman who supposedly flew to the stars."

Roxanne nodded. "And like my ladies told you, Death hovered over your suspect. He just decided to harvest her as well."

"You're right about that," Helen said. "There were bodies strewn all over the place every time that woman went somewhere."

Roxanne flicked water in my face. "Barty didn't pay enough attention to what my ladies had to say. Someday he might, though…"

I flicked water back at her.

Roxanne wiped water from her nose and took another sip of wine. "You really should come meet the ladies in my chapter of the Black Hat Society, Helen. We don't have anyone of Nubian extraction. Your presence would bring us special powers. Possibly ancient ones."

Helen perked up at the invitation, as though she had been hoping for it. She looked at me, then back at Roxanne. "Maybe…"

## A word about the author…

Born in Massachusetts, Edward Baker traveled widely as a child because his U.S. Marine father was transferred on a regular basis to new assignments across the U.S.A. By the time Ed was twelve, he had crossed the United States three times. And as a licensed driver at the ripe old age of sixteen, he drove a stick shift Ford across the nation, following his dad, who was pulling a camping trailer behind the family's station wagon.

An English major at Elon College, Ed earned a master's degree at Appalachian State University and a doctorate in Educational Leadership at the Sage Colleges' Esteves School of Education. After thirty-five years in higher education and after retiring as Interim President of a public community college, he turned his attention to his first love, writing, while continuing to teach undergraduate and graduate courses on an adjunct basis at a private college in upstate New York.

During the cold months, they "hole up" in their winter quarters in Saratoga Springs, New York. However, during the warm months, Ed and his wife reside in their cabin on Galway Lake, New York. When he's not writing or engaged in a woodworking project, Ed can be found on the lake or playing with his grandchildren or his four-legged canine companion Sudsy.

See his web site and read his blog at:
www.edwardsbaker.com

Thank you for purchasing
this publication of The Wild Rose Press, Inc.

For questions or more information
contact us at
info@thewildrosepress.com.

The Wild Rose Press, Inc.
www.thewildrosepress.com